Parlor Games

FORFEITS

AE LISTER

Forfeits
ISBN # 978-1-80250-766-9
©Copyright AE Lister 2024
Cover Art by Kelly Martin ©Copyright May 2024
Interior text design by Claire Siemaszkiewicz
Pride Publishing

Published in 2024 by Pride Publishing, United Kingdom.

Pride Publishing Publishing books by AE Lister

Persuasions
Various Persuasions
Various Distractions
Various Intentions

Northern Horizons
760 Miles
Repentance and Absolution
Return to Telegraph Creek
A Port Essington Christmas

Parlor Games
Are You There, Moriarty?
Forfeits

Collections
Dark and Deadly: Skeletal Equation
We Three Kings: A Spoonful of Sugar
His Harem: Alternative Medicine
Hot Bite: Bloodlines

FORFEITS

Dedication

To the many facets of grief.

A Note on the Title

Forfeits: To start, all players must forfeit an item of value to them and give the items to one player — maybe the winner of a previous game — who has been designated 'the auctioneer'. The auctioneer will sell off the items to other players, who must pay an amusing price — singing a song, doing a dance, making another player laugh, imitating an animal, etc. This game could be added to the end of other games or be played on its own.

~ *The Old Operating Theatre (oldoperatingtheatre.com): Victorian Parlour Fun and Games*

Prologue

Oh, he was cute as hell. Twinky and beautiful, sweet and sexy. The way he danced with his friends gave me a boner in two seconds. I watched him through whiskey-dimmed eyes for a long time, until he finally noticed.

He said something to one of his friends then came over.

"Hi."

"Hi," I replied, my gaze traveling over his lithe body, covered with glitter, a crop top and very tiny shorts. He was wearing bubble-gum-pink Doc Martens boots. So different from...

I took another drink of my whiskey sour, finished it and put the class down on the bar.

"You're watching me," the twink said.

"You're beautiful," I said.

"Wow, thank you. You're kinda hot yourself," he said, looking me over. "Wanna go in the back?" he waggled his eyebrows. "My name's —"

"I don't care."

"Oh. Wow. Okay, then." He stood there, but moved the whole time, shifting back and forth on his feet, tossing his head, blinking. He was probably on something.

"I'd love to suck you off," I said, focusing on the words so they wouldn't blend. So I didn't sound as drunk as I was.

"Hmm, okay. Sure." He extended his hand. "You've had a bit to drink."

"I am...a bit." I cleared my throat. "Drunk."

Because it's the only way I can do this. And I need to do this...desperately. Anything to get out of my head. Anything to touch someone else. Anything to escape for an hour or two.

I'd come to this place once with...but we'd only stayed for twenty minutes. We'd decided it wasn't for us and gone home. But this time, I'd stayed — because there was nothing at home but a black hole right now, particularly because my only reason for not jumping off a bridge was with her grandparents. My kid. *Our* kid...

I'd come to this establishment—a combination dance bar and gay kink club, just across the river from Ottawa—where men came to dance their troubles away, or to dominate or be dominated. I'd hoped to attract the attention of an older man, someone who could put me in my place for an hour. But when that didn't happen, I'd turned my attention to the pretty twink. He would do. I only needed to distract myself, after all.

As he led me out of the dance area and through the main room, I noticed a man by the bar, talking to a friend or his sub, or something. He was dressed in leather pants and a burgundy button-down, wearing motorcycle boots and standing with the air of someone who told other men to kneel.

The lights were brighter here, and I could see his nutmeg-colored skin and appreciate the way his brown hair curled tightly around his skull. He was sleek and sexy and in control, everything that I loved.

I stopped dead and stared. He was gorgeous, and I wished I'd seen him earlier.

The twink tugged at my hand. "Come on. I'm so fucking horny."

I resisted for a handful of seconds, wondering if I should continue or if I had a chance with *this* guy. While I waited, he turned, fixed me with his dark eyes and smiled.

But his friend said something, and he turned away, taking the man's wrist and bending it behind his back, as my cock throbbed and the twink pulled at me.

"Come *on*!" the glittery twink said, laughing.

I went. I didn't think I had the ability to seduce anyone else at this point. I'd had too much whiskey.

"Wait! Wait," I said, aware that we were heading to the dirty hallways in the back. "My car."

"What?" the twink said, frowning. Gosh, he was cute.

"We can do it in my car…if you want. It's cleaner." I smiled, hoping I didn't look sketchy.

He thought about that.

"I promise I'm not a creep. I just want to blow you. You don't have to do anything. If you change your mind at any time, we can stop. *Please*." I squeezed his hand with a gentleness that came from somewhere beyond the booze, beyond the black abyss of my grieving heart.

"Okay, fine. I guess I'll risk it. I have good instincts," he said. "Hold on."

He let go of my hand and went up to the bartender, pointing at me. I waved and smiled, so they'd know I was a good guy—tired and lost, maybe, but a decent man deep down, despite what I was doing with the twink.

The bartender nodded, and the twink pranced back and took my hand again.

"Come on, old man," he said, "Where's your car?"

He straddled me in the passenger seat and took my cock out, even though I'd said I wanted to blow *him*.

"Oh, yes, I needed to see this," he murmured, wiggling with glee as he stroked my erection up and down like a kid playing with a new toy.

"I just... I wanted to..."

"I know, I know. I'll let you. Trust me. But first I want to play with yours. Is that okay?" He blinked baby blue eyes at me, and how could I resist?

I couldn't.

"Oh God," I groaned as he touched me. It had been so long. I stopped him from going so fast. "Wait. You're gonna make me—"

"Already?" the twink said, with a cheeky grin, but he slowed his hand as I gripped the locked door and the console.

"I'm sorry," I whispered, my head starting to swim with alcohol and regret. "I'm so sorry."

"You want me to make you come? You can suck me if you want but...we'll have to move..."

I shook my head, feeling dizzy and old. "You don't have to..."

"It's okay. I can make you come, baby. I like giving handys."

I watched open-mouthed as the pretty twink lifted his palm and licked it like a cat preparing to groom itself, the blue polish on his nails glinting in the light from the streetlamps. He held my gaze as he took my cock again and began to stroke me in earnest.

My breaths stuttered in my chest as I gripped his bare knees, my gaze falling on the bulge in his little, cut-off shorts.

"Oh yeah, you are so hot, whoever you are. You are *so* fucking hard. You want me to get you off? You need that, baby?"

I moaned and nodded, desperate for it, blitzed by the whiskey and the need and the fucking desperation.

"Please," I said. "*Please.*"

Whimpers. Begging. Almost sobs.

"Oh yeah, baby. You really want it, don't you?"

I hoped he didn't notice the tears spilling down my cheeks when my cock erupted in his hand, as I choked on a moan.

It was as if I were watching myself. I felt disconnected, even as my cock and body throbbed with the vaguely familiar sensation of being jerked off by another man.

"Thank you," I whispered. "Thank you."

"S'okay. That was fun. You needed it."

I stared at the floor of the car. As the pleasure faded much too quickly, the whiskey took over and the guilt, and I couldn't look at him.

"Do you want to suck me? It's okay if you don't…"

He sounded unsure, wary all of a sudden.

"I—I—"

"Hey, it's okay. How about I just go?"

"I'm sorry. I'm sorry."

"No, no. Don't worry about it."

He shoved open the door, and he was gone in a flurry of stomping boots and glitter, and a muttered curse, as I sat there in the passenger seat with the car door open and my wet dick out.

I blinked back tears as I opened the glove box for a pack of tissues, fumbling with the lip of the opening. With shaky fingers I mopped at the wetness, then zipped my jeans and exited the car, throwing the soiled tissue to the ground. I went around the car and got into the driver's side.

I stared at the steering wheel. I shouldn't drive. I couldn't. I was so drunk and so tired and so...fucking broken.

Instead of starting the car, I folded my arms on the steering wheel and sobbed, the sounds loud and unhinged in the closed space, and I felt bad for the twink and guilty for my behavior and angry at the whole fucking world.

Chapter One

Proof of Life

Two years later

There were times in my life when I'd had to put my foot down.

"No, Lucy. We are *not* getting a baby goat."

"But, Dad! Come on! I heard they can live indoors, and you can train them to —"

"I said no. Not up for discussion."

"But, *Dad*!" Lucy tossed her strawberry-blonde, shoulder-length hair and huffed a long-suffering sigh. Her blue eyes, *his* eyes, sent me an accusatory glare.

"Are you ready to go? The bus will be here in a minute, and I've got to get to work."

Lucy side-eyed me as she grabbed her jacket and picked up her backpack. "You work from home."

I shook my head. "Not today. I'm going into the office."

"Fine. I'm leaving."

"Patrick will be here when you get off the bus," I said, ever grateful that my nephew didn't mind spending a couple of hours with his younger cousin a couple of times a week.

"Cool. Hey, Dad, think about the goat idea," she said as she opened the door and slipped out, shutting it behind her.

"Fuck," I said. "No fucking goats. Jesus."

I turned to look down at the dogs, who gazed at me with expectation in their eyes. "The two of you are enough."

I slipped on my fall boots and leather jacket, then hitched the dogs to their leashes and we left. I took a direction opposite to where Lucy would be waiting for the school bus, since she'd probably start talking to me about goats again. It was a good thing that she was so tenacious. It would serve her well in the future. But right now, with only me to win over, it was annoying and exhausting. For about the hundredth time, I wished that Daniel were still here helping me to raise this spitfire of a girl that had many of his physical characteristics and his outgoing personality.

I didn't regret being a dad. Lucy was my reason for getting up in the morning and for fighting against the grief that had threatened to pull me under those first couple of years. I loved her so much, and it would have been nice to have had someone to help me raise her.

But, yeah, sometimes the best laid plans go to shit. I pushed memories of Daniel and our life together out of my head and took the dogs over to the neighborhood park so they could do their business. This was my morning ritual, and it wasn't a bad one. I had Lucy and I had the dogs—Cocoa, an overweight chocolate Lab just shy of being a senior, and Eddy, a younger, more energetic corgi cross. I had a job I enjoyed and only had to go into the office two days a week—and my twenty-one-year-old nephew, Patrick, who looked after Lucy for me when he could.

It wasn't a terrible life.

I was an editor and copywriter at a Toronto-based publisher, and the Ottawa offices were located smack downtown in a sun-filled building on Slater Street. It wasn't a hardship to be there, but the fact that I could spend most of my week working from home was a godsend, especially as a single parent. Even the two-day-in-person per week requirement could be adjusted if there were events at home that required attention. It did me good to get out of the house. Most of my life revolved around Lucy and the animals, so to be in an adult environment with no distractions was a good break from it all.

My day went predictably well. I was working on a couple of different projects so could switch things up if I got bored. The deadlines were still a couple of weeks away, and I was making good progress, so I wasn't stressed about getting them done.

When I got back home at five-thirty, Patrick and Lucy were in the middle of a game of Monopoly.

"Who's winning?" I asked.

"Me!" Lucy stated.

I laughed and met Patrick's gaze. "You've got to stop letting her win."

"Hey!" my daughter said with indignation.

"I'm not. She's got good instincts and a way with money. You'd better watch out." Patrick stood. "Sorry, cuz, I've got to go," he said to Lucy. He looked at his watch.

"But we're in the middle of a game," Lucy whined, "that *I'm* winning!"

"Just leave it, and we'll continue it Thursday when I'm here again."

"Fine."

"I have to drive Patrick to work. See you in about thirty minutes?"

I was only beginning to feel comfortable leaving Lucy on her own for a half hour every now and then. It was possible that, if Daniel hadn't died, Lucy and I would be further along on our journey toward her independence, but his unexpected passing had affected every part of our lives.

"Yep."

"Don't answer the door to anyone, okay? You know the drill."

"I know the drill."

Come to think of it, Lucy didn't answer the door when I was here. She waited for me to do it.

"So how is Maverick Molly's these days?" I asked Patrick.

He was a server at a relatively new entertainment venue that had set up in a quieter part of Centertown about a year ago. It was called Maverick Molly's and heralded itself as a kink club and gaming parlor. I'd never been inside but Patrick raved about the place.

"It's fun. I get great tips," Patrick said, grinning.

Patrick had told me that the owners, Jacob and Sebastian Moriarty, had the young male servers dress in vintage Victorian undergarments. It sounded bizarre, and I couldn't imagine it. I didn't acquaint myself much with historical dress, so I didn't even know what that meant.

There had been a day when the appearance of a new kink club in town would have been of interest to me, but those times were gone—buried with Daniel and better off laid to rest.

As I drove out of the driveway and down the street, I realized that I should have used the bathroom before we'd left. I needed to piss, but Patrick's workplace was only a ten-minute drive away. I could hold it until I got back home.

Or could I?

By the time we pulled up to Maverick Molly's I realized the situation was more urgent than I'd thought.

"Um, Patrick?"

"Yeah?" he asked, his hand on the door handle.

"Do you think I could come in and use the washroom? I should have gone before we left my place..."

"Sure. Of course. There's one in the staff changing room."

"Oh, thank God," I muttered, embarrassed.

I parked in the spot right behind where we'd stopped and followed Patrick up the steps and through the front doors. The sounds of conversation, laughter and light jazz piano, trickled out of a nearby room and into the carpeted hallway. A rack of hangers with jackets and coats on them sat to the left, and I could see doors to another room at the end of the hall.

A tall man with blond hair in a ponytail, holding a bar cloth and wearing fancy clothes from another time that made him look like a Victorian gentleman, came toward us.

"Patrick, hey." He smiled. The lines on his face spoke of a good disposition and graceful aging.

"Hey, Sebastian! This is my Uncle Fletcher," Patrick said, gesturing to me.

"Lovely to meet you. Welcome to Maverick Molly's. Sebastian Moriarty."

He held out his graceful hand. I shook it and looked around.

"This is...a cool spot."

Even the entry hall gave off Victorian vibes. The interior design had been expertly done. There were crown moldings on the high plastered ceiling, what looked like hardwood underfoot and pieces of antique furniture against the walls. Replica oil lamps hung on the walls to give the place the soft glow of a decades-old salon.

"Thank you so much," Sebastian said. "Are you here for a drink or — ?"

"He needs the washroom," Patrick said.

"I'm so sorry. I should have gone at home," I said.

"I'll just take him into the changing room."

"Of course. All the servers are on the floor." Sebastian nodded to me, then said to Patrick. "I'll see you in a few minutes."

"Yep."

"Thanks so much," I said.

"No worries at all." Sebastian smiled and went into the other room, above which a sign said 'Gaming Parlor'.

I followed Patrick through a door marked 'Staff Only' into a large, sparsely decorated space with a couple of chairs and a beat-up settee.

"Washroom's just there," Patrick said, pointing to a door at the back.

"Thanks." I hastened into a room with two stalls and a urinal, did my business quickly and washed my hands.

When I came out, I was greeted to the sight of Patrick sitting on the settee in a pair of lacy panties and a garter belt, pulling a black stocking up his calf.

"Better?" he asked, as I stood there, staring.

"Oh my God, yes. Thank you." I stood there, gobsmacked. "They really get you to dress authentically, don't they?"

Patrick smiled and attached the top of his stocking to the belt.

"Uh-huh. It takes some getting used to."

The door to the changing area swung open. A young man wearing white bloomers and a corset over a white linen blouse came into the room. He had makeup on, black nail polish and spiky, shortish hair.

He stopped when he caught sight of me.

"Oh shit. I didn't know we could have guests in here." He looked back and forth between the two of us.

"Hi, Toby. This is my Uncle Fletcher."

"Oh, okay," Toby said. "That explains everything."

"He needed to use the washroom."

Toby put a hand on his hip. "A likely story. Or did he only want to see me in my bloomers?"

"So sorry, I'll get out of your way," I said, moving toward the exit.

"Not so fast Mr...." Toby crossed his arms over his corset and looked at Patrick with raised eyebrows.

"Marin. Fletcher Marin," Patrick said with an amused look at his saucy coworker.

"Mr. Marin. I need to memorize the way you look standing in the midst of a pile of Victorian undergarments in your"—he looked me over and sighed—"fancy business suit."

"Toby," Patrick warned, standing up and pulling on a pair of white bloomers that he buttoned at his waist.

"What?" Toby said, keeping his gaze on me.

I was starting to feel uncomfortable. Ironic that I was the one on display when the two of them were wearing vintage underclothes.

"I'm enjoying the aesthetic," Toby murmured, his eyes still on me.

"Did you need something?" Patrick asked.

"Oh shit. Yeah. I forgot my choker."

Why was I still standing there?

"Oh," I laughed awkwardly. "I'd better get home to Lucy."

Toby gave me a piercing look. "Your wife?"

"Oh no," I laughed in earnest this time. "Lucy's my daughter."

Toby whistled. "I knew there were daddy vibes." He looked me over wistfully.

If these were the kind of theatrics that went on at Maverick Molly's every day, no wonder it was doing so well.

Now Patrick was laughing. "Oh my God, Toby, stop. I don't want to think about my uncle that way."

I started for the door.

"Wait," Toby called.

I turned to see him standing by a row of cubbies, holding something black in his fingers.

"Would you help me with my necklace, Mr. Marin?" He batted his eyelashes at me with a saucy grin.

Patrick rolled his eyes. "How does Alastair even put up with you? I'm gonna tell him you asked a strange man in a suit to dress you."

Toby collapsed into irreverent laughter and put on the choker, attaching the clasp in the back and meeting my gaze with dancing eyes. "Ah, he's not that strange. Sorry. I'm a fucking brat. Can't seem to stop."

"Cute," I said. He was *very* cute. "I'd better go. Thanks, Patrick."

"You're welcome. See you."

I took one more look at saucy Toby and got the hell out of there. Those outfits were incredibly titillating — not so much on my nephew, although he did look adorable.

But on Toby? I didn't know who this Alastair guy was, but if Toby was his partner, he was a very lucky man.

When I got back home, Lucy was doing homework at the table and feeding Eddie bits of cheese off her plate.

"Lucy," I said, "you know I don't like you feeding him from the table."

"But he's hungry. And he loves cheese so much."

Pick your battles. Pick your battles.

I went upstairs to change out of my suit, thinking about Maverick Molly's and the pleasant atmosphere and good-humored employees. But there was no point, because I didn't have anyone to take there, and I'd be damned if I'd go by myself. And anyway, I didn't have time, with Lucy and the dogs and work.

I sat down on the bed in my boxer briefs and picked up the photo of Daniel that I kept on my bedside table.

"You would love that place," I said, talking as if he were in front of me and not six feet underground in the Capital Gardens Cemetery. "I wish it had been there before you…"

I blinked, thinking I had more tears to shed over the loss of my husband and partner and co-parent. But there was nothing. Only a memory that came to me of holding Lucy for the first time. Lucy, our daughter, who was now my number-one priority, and meant I didn't have time to go gallivanting around to kink clubs or even to find someone to share a pleasant meal with.

The loneliness of my current existence hit me all of a sudden, but I pushed it away and thought back to that incredible moment twelve years earlier.

"My God," I said, as Daniel placed our baby in my arms. "She's so beautiful!"

I blinked back tears as I stared at our daughter's – our daughter's! – perfect face.

"She does have my genes," Daniel said, touching his fingertip to her cheek. "Of course she's beautiful."

I nodded, at a loss for words. She was so tiny and miraculous! I thanked the universe for Daniel, for our surrogate, Tamara, and for a world that allowed us to experience parenthood the way we wanted. It hadn't been easy, but Daniel had wanted a child so badly and I loved him so much, and even though I was scared of the responsibility of guarding and guiding a new life, I'd been a hundred percent on board.

"So...what do you think? Do you still want to go with 'Riley'?"

"I don't know. She looks more like a 'Lucy'."

Daniel rolled his eyes. "So traditional."

"But everyone's naming their kids 'Riley' these days. 'Lucy' may be kind of traditional but it's not common."

"Lucy, huh," Daniel said, moving the cloth of the hospital blanket so he could see our daughter's face. "All right, then."

As it always did, my gut clenched at these heartwarming memories, and now the tears threatened. I sighed and stood, blinking them back, and got dressed.

Chapter Two

Him

I had to take Lucy to the dentist the next day, so I spent the morning editing on my laptop at home, taking the dogs for their lunchtime walk, then drove to the school to pick her up. The office was quiet except for the subdued tapping of Kate, the office administrator, on her keyboard, and the hum of the printer and photocopier. One glum-faced child of about six sat in a chair, crossing and uncrossing their ankles and shifting from side to side.

"Hello, Mr. Marin," Kate said, glancing up from her typing. "Do you need Lucy?"

"Hi, Kate. Yes, please. Dentist."

She picked up the phone beside her and pressed a few buttons, then waited.

"Aiden, can you please send Lucy to the office? Her dad is here. She has a dental appointment... Thank you."

Kate hung up and smiled at me. "She's on her way."

"Perfect."

I sat in one of the chairs and pulled out my phone, tapping on the CBC news app and girding myself for all of the unwelcome but needed information that I was about to access.

After several moments, Lucy opened the door to the office and came in with her backpack and umbrella.

"Hi, Dad."

"Hey, Lucy."

"Is it still raining?" she asked, trying to see out of the office window.

"No, I don't think so," I said, standing and shoving my phone in my back pocket. I took the umbrella from her.

"Do I have to go to the dentist?" Lucy asked.

"Yes, Lucy."

"We have the coolest supply teacher. Aiden is so —"

At that moment the door to the office opened and a man, presumably a teacher, came in. When he saw me he stopped and seemed surprised, but then smiled warmly and turned to Lucy.

"You forgot your notebook."

"Oh thanks! Dad, this is my supply teacher, Aiden. He's the best!"

Aiden looked at me and it was at that moment that I recognized his dark-eyed gaze, the color of his skin and the close curl of his hair.

There had been a twink and an embarrassing encounter in the passenger seat of my car, months and months ago, when I was still reeling from Daniel's unexpected passing. But before the twink and the car, I had seen *him*. I had a sudden recollection of him stepping toward his 'friend', gripping the other man's wrist and forcing it behind his back.

The man named Aiden stared at me, and I was tongue-tied.

Did he remember seeing *me*? A lost, grieving, drunk man being pulled by a gorgeous, barely dressed, glittering twink whose name I still didn't know.

For a long moment we seemed to be hypnotized, and I realized that whatever was holding us was mutual. Maybe he did remember me. And he might even be into me. *I* was definitely into Aiden.

He was the first to break free. He forced his gaze from mine and turned back to Lucy.

"Have fun at the dentist," he said.

"Yeah, thanks a lot," Lucy replied, grinning. "Bye."

"Bye, Lucy," Aiden said.

"Oh, there's Mia!" Lucy said, pushing through the door and into the hall where she hailed her friend and probably complained about having to go to the dentist.

Kate made a shushing sound then rolled her eyes and shrugged.

Aiden straightened and looked at me.

"Nice to meet you, Lucy's Dad," he said with a smile that just about knocked me off my feet.

"Fletcher," I said. "Fletcher Marin."

"It's nice to meet you, Fletcher. Lucy is hilarious — and so smart."

"Thanks," I said. "You're replacing Lucy's regular teacher today?"

"Yes. Actually, I'm on contract for a few weeks."

"Oh. Well, Lucy will be happy." I certainly was. That would give me the opportunity of running into Aiden again…somehow.

"Have a wonderful day, Mr. Marin," Kate said from her place behind the desk, giving me a smug smile.

"Thanks. You, too," I said, wondering if she'd noticed the attraction between Aiden and me.

"Well…I'd better get back to my class before all hell breaks loose," Aiden said.

"Yes, good idea," I agreed, following him out of the office and into the hall, where Lucy was standing, shifting her backpack and tapping her foot, now that Mia was gone.

"See you tomorrow, Lucy," Aiden said.

"Bye, Mr. Thompson."

I watched Lucy's supply teacher walk away from us, appreciating his slim, well-dressed form. Before he turned the corner, he glanced back and smiled. The blood pounded in my ears as my dick twitched.

"Dad," Lucy said, concern in her voice.

"Yes?" I said, turning to her.

"What's wrong?"

"What?" I asked. I didn't know what she meant.

She was gazing at me with concern. "You look like you're going to pass out."

Oh fuck, do I?

"Sorry," I said, clearing my throat and attempting to look normal, even though my entire world had changed in a moment. "Let's go."

"Are you sure you're okay to drive?" she said. "Maybe you're having a stroke."

"I'm *not* having a stroke," I said, following her out through the main doors, my heart fluttering in my chest like a trapped butterfly.

"Damn. Because I wouldn't have to go to the dentist if you were."

"Nice. Thanks a lot," I said. "And watch your language."

"Oh please," Lucy laughed. "I'm twelve."

Twelve going on eighteen sometimes. It scared me just how close Lucy was to being a full-fledged teenager.

The fluttering in my chest diminished as we walked to the car, but the shock of seeing the stranger from the kink club and that mess of an encounter stayed with me. What were the odds of that? One in a million…or even a billion?

As I sat in the waiting room, I tapped on my photo app. I had a picture of the twink somewhere. He'd snatched my phone and taken a selfie before we'd decided to hook up, and I'd never deleted it. My memories of him were fond, even if they were overlaid with the guilt of a drunken disaster. He'd been kind and he'd taken care of me, even though I had said it would be the other way around. And he'd left me when I'd needed to be by myself.

I found the photo. I'd saved it in my favorites. His happy eyes and smile stared back at me from that long-ago place where I'd gone to distract myself and tried to soothe the pain of Daniel's recent demise. Part of me wished I'd learned his name, but another part of me saw him as the universe extending a helping hand to me that evening.

It hadn't been pleasant, sobbing in my car after he'd given me a quick hand job. But afterward, the pain around my heart hadn't hurt so bad and, looking back, it was the beginning of a healing journey. I'd stopped looking for casual hookups at bars after that and focused on Lucy, going to my therapist and doing good work. The pain had gotten easier to bear, slowly, gradually, like the healing of a wound. For a while it was angry and raw, then it became a constant throb, until eventually, it somehow scabbed over. Every now and then I'd still feel it, and sometimes it itched and I had to attend to the memories and cry again, or do something to honor him, like my therapist had suggested.

But I'd come a long way.

"Got my goody bag," Lucy said, when she swaggered out ahead of the hygienist.

"Hi, Mr. Marin," the hygienist said. "Lucy's doing pretty well with her brushing, but I've told her she needs to floss."

Lucy made a face.

"Okay," I said. "Sure." I didn't tell her that sometimes it was all I could do to get Lucy to have regular showers these days.

"It's something she can do while she's watching TV or before bed. It's really important."

The hygienist smiled, as if she were sharing happy news and not setting up a battle between my daughter and me.

"Of course."

"See you next time, Lucy," the hygienist said in a bubbly voice.

"Yeah, yeah," Lucy said, giving her a vague wave as she moved past me. "Can we go now?"

"I have to pay, sweetheart. This isn't like going to the doctor."

She gave me a look. "Do I really need to come for a cleaning every six months?"

"Not up for discussion," I said, raising my hand to stop her from going on a tangent.

I settled up with the receptionist, paying the fee outright since I didn't have health insurance myself and we no longer had access to Daniel's comprehensive plan. Lucy's grandparents—Daniel's mom and dad— had offered to pay for Lucy's dental needs and encouraged me to stay up-to-date with whatever was recommended. I was very grateful for that and appreciated them giving me a financial hand. They seemed happy to do it, and it let them be involved in a way that fulfilled them.

Lucy spent a weekend every month with Daniel's parents, which was hugely helpful to me and extremely beneficial to Lucy. She loved her grandparents, and I was thrilled that she had such a close relationship with them.

"Come on," I said. "Let's go."

We got in the car, and I started the engine.

"So, Dad, what did you think of Mr. Thompson? He's hot, right?"

My ears burned. "I beg your pardon?"

"Aiden. I think he's gay. Do you think he's gay? I wonder if he has a boyfriend…"

"Lucy, this is not an appropriate discussion."

"I'm just saying, he seems like a pretty cool guy. You could do a lot worse."

"I—I can't date your supply teacher." Could I? No. Probably not.

"Why not?"

"Because it's…it's not appropriate," I said, hating that that was true.

"Why do adults say that so often?"

I sighed. "Because there are…rules to the way society…works. I don't know."

I gave up and did the only thing I could think of to change the subject.

"You want to get pizza for supper tonight? I'll let you pick the place."

"Awesome! I guess this makes up for the dentist appointment."

"Uh-huh." I mumbled, pulling out of the parking lot and into rush-hour traffic.

"Can I get a pizza to myself? So I can get pineapple on it?"

"I guess so."

"Yes!"

As I merged with the heavy traffic I asked about Mia and how she was doing.

Lucy started talking about her friend, and I was saved from more discussion about Mr. Aiden Thompson. If only I could turn my thoughts in another direction as easily as I'd switched Lucy's focus.

* * * *

I'm naked and on my knees. Daniel stands above me, clothed, fondling a braided crop.

"You want this or the paddle? You can choose, Fletcher...this time."

"The paddle." I don't even have to think about it.

Daniel smiles knowingly, his blue-eyed gaze on me with that singular intensity that tells me he is in the Dom zone that I love so much. He looks young and, even in this situation, I can see the love for me in his gaze.

He glances at the place where we keep our implements, then looks at me again.

The smile widens.

"Well...I said you could choose. I didn't say I'd go along with your choice."

My heart sinks, but my body sings with the knowledge that I am his, and I will suffer what he wants me to suffer. I don't hate the crop. But I love the paddle and I want it. Maybe if I suffer for him under the crop, which he enjoys very much, he'll give me what I want — or maybe not. But it doesn't matter. I'm thrilled to be here, under his control, and he knows it.

I close my eyes and nod. "Yes, Sir."

Suddenly, without time passing, I am on my belly on our bed in the home we share, my wrists and ankles bound, the snaking tease of the crop along my ass and down my thigh leaving excitement in its wake. Daniel likes to edge me before he gets down to the nitty gritty of my suffering, but this is its own form of torture.

"Please," I whisper.

I don't know what I'm asking for, but my heart lurches in my chest, and for some reason, I start crying. He's barely touched me. I don't usually get this upset. I love our kink sessions.

So why am I crying?

The sensation of the crop on my body becomes a whisper, gliding over my ass again, then along my hip and…then it's gone.

"Daniel?" I sob. "Daniel!" I scream, struggling against the leather cuffs as I turn my head.

There is no one in the room but me. And I can't move. I lurch and fight in my bindings, panicking and sobbing his name.

"Daniel! Daniel, come back! Please!"

There's nobody there — and I'm trapped.

"You have to let me up!" I say, fighting the bonds. "Let me go!"

I wake with a jerk as my dark bedroom comes into focus around me. It's not the same room as in my dream. It's not the same house. We moved when we knew we were going to have Lucy.

I blink rapidly, trying to focus through the tears that are still falling. I lift my hands to my face and sob as quietly as I can, so I don't wake her. Luckily, her room is on the other side of the house, and she likes to keep her door closed at night.

I turn in the bed and cry into the pillow — for Daniel, for the loss of him and for the loss of that feeling of being *his* and suffering *for* him.

I missed that so much, and I couldn't talk to anyone about it.

* * * *

"Daniel and I, we..." I met the non-judgmental gaze of my therapist, Jinta, and felt my cheeks heat. I knew she wouldn't judge me, but I'd not talked about this before. "We kind of had a..." *very kinky Dom-sub thing going on.*

Jinta waited for me to continue.

"We were kinky, Daniel and I."

"Oh?" she said, with a quirk to her smile. "Really."

"Yeah."

"You haven't mentioned that before. Why now?"

I blinked, suddenly overcome. "I...I don't... I didn't..."

My head swirled with memories and voices. I was breathing too quickly.

Jinta stood and walked over to where I sat on the couch by the window. She placed her hand on my back.

"It's all right, Fletcher. Breathe. Count with me."

I focused on her familiar and calming presence and counted my breaths in and out until I had a hold of myself.

"I'm so sorry."

"It's fine. You're in the best place for it."

A panic attack. I'd never had one before Daniel had died. Now I had them often enough to be inconvenient.

"I had a dream," I blurted.

"Oh?"

I described the dream to Jinta in fragments. I took breaks in between to count some deep breaths. I was embarrassed, but at least Jinta knew what I was struggling with.

"I'm sorry," I said, when I was finished.

"No, Fletcher. I'm sorry I didn't ask you sooner if there was anything you missed about Daniel that you hadn't told me."

"It's just—" I said, with halting breath. "I didn't think—"

"Grief can take a long time to get through, Fletcher. And it never completely goes away," she said. "Perhaps you weren't ready to deal with those particular memories until now."

We sat in silence. I tried not to fill it with awkward chatter.

"Can you think of anything that happened recently that might have reminded you about that part of your life with Daniel?"

Huh.

Dropping Patrick off at work and going into Maverick Molly's for the first time. Meeting Aiden and recognizing him from a *different* kink club. It wasn't so strange that I'd remember.

"Yes, now that I think about it."

She cocked her head.

"Have you...heard of Maverick Molly's?"

"No. What's that?"

"My nephew, Patrick, works there." I scratched at my neck, embarrassed, even though I trusted Jinta with this information. "It's a gay kink club—a relatively new one."'

Jinta looked surprised but not offended or embarrassed. "Really."

"Yeah. It's set up like a Victorian" —I'd almost said brothel but stopped myself— "gaming parlor."

"Interesting."

"And…" I felt the heat flooding my cheeks. I glanced at Jinta, reminded myself that I'd only ever found support here. "You remember I told you about the months after Daniel died? When I…" I swallowed, the guilt like a lump in my throat. "I was going to clubs and getting drunk and having…having…"

"I remember."

I nodded. "I saw this man one time, when I was…following another guy and…I knew he was a Dom by the way he was acting with his friend or lover or sub—or whoever was with him."

"Okay."

"Well, you're not going to believe this," I said, running a hand through my hair, "but I ran into him unexpectedly…at Lucy's school."

"Huh. Another parent?"

"No, he's a supply teacher."

"I see."

"I think…I think he remembered me. Maybe. I could be imagining that."

"How interesting."

I ran a hand over my forehead, glad that the heavy emotions that had come over me seemed to be dissipating.

"Yeah. I mean, we had a moment."

"What kind of a moment?"

"Well, we looked at each other. And…I mean, there were fireworks…at least on my end. I think…maybe on his, too."

She sat back in her chair, contemplating.

"I definitely think those events had an impact and probably led to the dream you had."

"Yeah."

She didn't say anything for a long moment. She simply watched me. Finally, she said, "It's good to remember things."

I felt the emotion start to rise again, but I pushed it down.

"Yeah," I said, focusing on the clock on the wall. "It feels...good to talk about it with someone."

"I understand that certain subjects can be scary. I want you to know that my practice is very kink positive. I should have told you before."

I nodded. "Thank God."

She smiled. "Thank whoever you want. I'm glad you trusted me enough to share that."

The relief of letting her know about my dream and about that part of my life with Daniel, was welcome.

"Okay, so...now what?" I said. "What do I do about it?"

Jinta raised her eyebrows and shrugged. "Well, I guess you'd better find someone to get kinky with. Maybe you already have."

I blushed and cleared my throat. "Do you think I'm ready for that?"

She shrugged again. "There's only one way to find out."

I stared at her, hope lifting for a second, then plummeting. "It's not that easy."

"You'll never know if you don't try."

Chapter Three

Flirting

"So that was what I was thinking, honestly. If I go through it a few times and I still can't figure it out, do you want to have an in-person meeting?" I asked my client, who was on the other end of my connection. I happened to glance at the clock on the kitchen wall and realized I had to pick up Lucy at school. Usually she took the school bus, but she had a project that she wanted to bring home and didn't want to risk it getting damaged.

"I'm so sorry, but I have to go, Louise. I'll send you an email with my thoughts on this tomorrow morning," I said.

"No worries, Fletcher. That's perfect."

I hit End and shoved my phone in my pocket, grabbing a ginger cookie from the plate on my way past the kitchen. I ate it in two bites, trying to remember if I'd had lunch. The dogs watched me with tails wagging as I waved to them and headed out, setting the touch-panel lock.

I didn't like going to the school at pick-up time. There was so much traffic, with students of all ages walking and running around. People brought their dogs. It was a shit show. So by the time I parked the car, I was frazzled but relieved to get out and find Lucy. I couldn't see her anywhere, so I thought maybe she was still inside.

There was a tug on my sleeve. I turned around, expecting a child and seeing tan pants and adult-sized classic Vans. My gaze drifted up and landed on Aiden's attractive face.

"Hey, there, Lucy's Dad," he said, his beautiful smile lighting up his features.

"Oh," I said, "Hi, Aiden."

His smile widened. "You remember my name."

I found myself returning his smile. "Did you forget mine?"

"Actually, no. I didn't. It's Fletcher."

"That's right. So why did you call me — ?"

He laughed, glancing down. "I thought it was cute to call you Lucy's Dad. Was it?"

"Adorable."

"Yes!" he said, making a triumphant gesture. "Look... I forgot to give Lucy her test back," Aiden said, holding it up. "A-minus. She's killing it."

My heart filled with pride.

"Thanks. She's bright."

Aiden nodded and handed me the test. "Does she get that from you?"

"Huh, maybe. More from...someone else."

"Yeah? Her...mother?" he asked, raising his eyebrows, hopeful for some clarification of my status.

"No. My late husband," I replied, feeling my heart break for about the thousandth time since I'd lost Daniel but glad to clear things up for him. I wanted him to know I was single.

But Aiden frowned and his cheeks reddened. "Oh, my God, I'm so sorry."

"It's fine. Do you know where Lucy is?"

"Yes, she's by the flagpole with Cassandra. I swear, those two girls are joined at the hip."

"Cassandra's been an amazing friend to Lucy."

"Yeah, I know," Aiden said, gazing at the girls then looking at me. "I was going to ask you…" he said, then looked away nervously. "Never mind."

We stood there in silence for a moment.

"I lost my husband three years ago," I said.

"That must have been rough…for you and for Lucy."

"Yes, it was. It still is. But…life goes on." I shrugged, as if that sentence could contain all the grief and pain we'd gone through since Daniel's passing. One thing you learned pretty quick with a loss like that—words were pretty fucking inadequate most of the time.

Aiden nodded. "I suppose that's true."

"What were you going to ask me?" I asked, glancing to see Lucy and Cassandra still laughing together. They looked so young and carefree, and part of me wished I was Lucy's age instead of forty-one. I turned back to Aiden.

I was struck again by his beauty—then by his next question.

"I'm…I'm Lucy's supply teacher for another two weeks, then I'm going to a different school. And I was…I was wondering if you might want to go out for dinner at that point?" He looked awkward and embarrassed, and he glanced at his shoes, then back up at me. The hopeful expression on his face was adorable. "I probably shouldn't even be ask—"

"Yes."

He looked so shocked it made me smile. "Really?"

40

"Yes."

And the sun came out from behind the clouds as Aiden smiled the widest smile I'd seen in a long, long time.

"Okay. Great!"

I dug in my back pocket for a business card and passed it to him. "I feel like we're doing a drug deal or something."

He took the card and quickly pocketed it. "Thanks. I'll be in touch," he said.

I nodded, holding his gaze for a moment, then went to get Lucy, my heart doing flips and my hands getting clammy.

Was I ready to date someone? I had two weeks to get used to the idea, and I could always back out.

But I wasn't sure I wanted to.

* * * *

Two weeks was a long time to wait when you wanted to find out more about someone. I tried to get information out of Lucy when we took the dogs for their after-dinner walk. We didn't always go together but, when the weather was good, like it was on this evening, it was a nice way to connect.

"So, your supply teacher, Aiden. He's a nice guy?"

"Yeah. He's strict, though. But that's good, because some of the kids in my class are assholes," Lucy said, waiting while Eddy squatted on the grass.

"Wow," I said, giving her a disappointed look and passing over a poop bag.

"It's true! Some of my other teachers have trouble keeping them under control. But not Mr. Thompson." Lucy gave the bag I was holding out to her a derogatory look. "Dad, can't you do it? It's so gross."

"Lucy, come on. At least Eddy's shits aren't as big as Cocoa's."

She smiled. "Okay, fine." She waited until Eddy was done, scooped the poop into the bag and tied it off, then handed it back to me. I guess I got to carry it.

"Huh. That's...kind of unusual for a supply teacher. Usually they're seen as easy targets, from what I remember."

"Yeah. But Aiden's been filling in for Ms. Kelly since April, so he's more of a replacement." She shrugged. "Also, he's got this—I don't know what to call it. But when he's pissed at you, you know it, and you want to be good. It's weird, but it works."

That right there was Dom energy. I knew it well.

"Huh. Is Ms. Kelly all right?"

"Yeah, she just had to get some minor surgery or something. I don't know. But she's coming back next week, I think."

"Oh," I said, as if I'd had no idea. "That's good."

Lucy frowned. "No, it's not. I'd rather have Aiden."

I waved to Mrs. Anderson, who was walking her poodle across the street. She kept her dog away from other dog walkers because it tended to bark.

She smiled and waved back.

"But you like Ms. Kelly," I said to Lucy, as Cocoa squatted to piss.

"Yeah. But Aiden's cool. He plays guitar, you know...in a band."

"Really?"

"Yeah. They aren't famous or anything. But he plays gigs here and sometimes in Montreal, he said."

"Oh wow. That is very cool."

We turned the corner and headed back home. The sun would be setting soon. In a few weeks, when the time changed, we'd be taking them out in the dark.

"Also, Ms. Kelly doesn't let us call her by her first name. What's up with that?"

I laughed. "Well, not all teachers are comfortable with it. I guess it's her choice, right?"

"Sure, sure."

We got home and Lucy went downstairs to play video games. I was pretty lax when it came to homework, letting her sort things out. She was twelve and seemed able to pinpoint what she needed to work on versus what was simply busy work that the teacher handed out to appease that subset of parents who assumed they weren't teaching properly if they didn't assign work to do at home. Her marks were consistently great, so I didn't come down on her about how she spent her free time. And, after Daniel had passed, video gaming was both an escape and a way to connect with his memory, since he was the one who had gotten her into it, much to my chagrin.

"Daniel, I think Lucy's too young for video games."

"What? It's LEGO Star Wars," Daniel said, showing me the front of the game. "I picked up LEGO Indiana Jones, too."

"Huh. You don't think they'll be too violent?"

He showed me the package, pointing at a large E in a box in the corner. "Rated E for Everyone. 10+."

"But she's seven."

He gave me a look.

I gave him a look.

"Okay, technically. But we both know she's a lot more advanced than other kids."

"Sure. But…"

"Relax. They'll help her with hand-eye coordination, and I bet she's going to love playing them."

I raised my eyebrows. "Just her? Something tells me you've been waiting for an excuse to try these out."

Daniel grinned. "Okay, fine. You know me too well. Trust me. It'll be great."

He'd been right. Lucy had been hooked from the start. Now she had moved on to more mature games, and we occasionally had battles over what was and wasn't appropriate for her. She'd been after me to buy The Last of Us, because some of her friends played it, but it was rated Mature 17+ and I was hesitant. I'd told her she'd have to wait until she was fourteen, which was still three years younger than the rating suggested.

She'd rolled her eyes and told me that she'd literally watched gamers play it on YouTube, so she knew all about it. I'd held fast, though.

So far.

* * * *

For two weeks I vacillated between anxiety and excitement. I worried that Aiden wouldn't call me. I worried that he would. I worried that he'd want to go somewhere that reminded me of my time with Daniel, and I'd have to explain why I didn't want to go there. I worried that we'd go to dinner, he'd turn out to be nothing like I hoped he was and I'd have to awkwardly find an excuse to leave. Or that he'd be more wonderful than I hoped, then...then we'd go for a second date, and a third, and at some point I'd want to have sex with this gorgeous creature and... Oh, who was I kidding? I already wanted to have sex with Aiden.

Those months after Daniel's death, when I'd get drunk and pick up a friendly young guy at a local club to enjoy on a purely physical level, had been exhausting and mind-numbingly shallow. And the guilt that hit me afterward was never worth it.

Now I'd give myself frantic hand jobs when I was horny, thinking about random porn videos, while I tried to be quiet. Even though Lucy's room was at the other end of the house, I was paranoid she'd hear me.

I hadn't had full-on sex with anyone but Daniel for the past fifteen years — and he'd been gone for three of those.

But I craved it. I couldn't lie to myself anymore and say I didn't.

And apparently, I craved the submission, too — the suffering for someone special that for some reason quieted my brain and body and fulfilled me.

I was pretty sure Aiden *was* a Dom, from the impression I'd got at the club so long ago, and also from what Lucy had said about his teaching style. But I had no idea if he still liked to engage with men that way. It could have been a passing fancy. And there was no guarantee he'd want to Dom *me*.

* * * *

Lucy was despondent when she came home from school the first week of Ms. Kelly's return.

"Why can't we have Aiden as our regular teacher!" she moaned on Wednesday, tossing her backpack on the chair and putting her arms around Eddy, who had come to welcome her home. Cocoa wagged her tail from her spot on the sofa.

"I'm sorry, sweetie. He does seem like a cool guy," I said, ruffling Cocoa's neck fur. She made a soft groan and laid her head back down.

I felt guilty to be keeping something from Lucy, but all I'd done was give the guy my business card. He might never even call me. He was probably way too cool for me, anyway.

Just before I went to bed that night, a text came in from an unknown number.

Hi, Lucy's Dad. It's Aiden. Is this a bad time?

I immediately smiled then felt sick to my stomach. I pondered what to say.

Did you forget my name again?

Lol. I was trying to be cute. Can't help it. Blushing face.

You don't have to try. Call me Fletcher. Please. I'd like to forget I'm Lucy's Dad when I'm talking to you.

Laughing face emoji. I'd like to forget you're Lucy's Dad, too. Even though she's spectacular.

Well, we agree on that. Look at you, using punctuation and capitals in your texts, just like I do! It's refreshing to text with a grown up!

I am a teacher. May I just say, you have...very nice sentence structure, Fletcher Marin.

I gave a soft laugh, my thumbs tapping.

You as well. Very...smooth and...good rhythm.

Lol, thanks. Are we...flirting?

God, I hope so. It's been a long time.

Can we get together? Soon?

Oh wow, okay. He was asking me out. And what's more, I was thrilled...and terrified. But it was good to feel strong emotions about something other than memories of my previous life with Daniel.

I'd like that.

Tomorrow? I'm free for dinner.

I think I can get that to work.

* * * *

Thank God Patrick was free. When he arrived, he gave me a look that demanded an explanation.

I shrugged. "What? I have a date."

He and Lucy exchanged a glance.

"That's awesome," Patrick said.

"A date!" Lucy exclaimed.

"Yeah. Just some guy I met...online." I really didn't want to tell Lucy who it was, because it might not go further than this and I didn't want her to be invested — or pissed off, or whatever her reaction would be.

"Online?" she said, gasping. "Are you sure that's safe?"

I stared at her. "Well, I'm over forty. I think I'll be okay. I'm meeting him at a restaurant." God, I hated lying. But I couldn't tell her it was Aiden. Not yet.

Her eyes went wide. "Wait! Are you going to have *casual sex,* Dad? Did you meet him on Grindr?"

Patrick started laughing while I turned beet red.

"I did not meet him on Grindr. How do you know about Grindr? Jesus Christ."

"Everyone knows about Grindr," Patrick said.

"Make sure you use protection," Lucy said, in a very sober voice.

"Lucy, cut it out. I know how to—and we're not having— Patrick, help."

Patrick raised his hand and shook his head. "She's your kid."

"Is he cute? Can I see a photo?"

"Lucy!"

Patrick doubled over, as I glared at him. "I could use some help here."

"I mean, she's right. You might want to."

I didn't know what to say.

"No, I'm not going to have casual sex, not on the first date." *Wow, nice hypocritical stance, there, Fletcher.*

"Okay," Lucy said, grinning with a wickedness that came right down the gene lines from Daniel.

"Don't you have homework to do?"

"Fine. If I hear you come home with someone, I'll put my noise-canceling headphones on."

"I'm not bringing him here!" I was definitely not bringing him here...for many reasons.

Patrick offered to stay overnight, if necessary.

"I don't need you to—" I said, tidying up the papers on the dining room table, my cheeks aflame. "For God's sake, it's the first time I've dated the guy. I don't work that fast."

Chapter Four

Hunger

Aiden had suggested we meet at Johnny Farina at seven o'clock.

I hadn't gone for dinner with a man since Daniel had passed, which was going on three years. And I hadn't gone on a first date with someone since long before that. No wonder I felt out of my depth. My curiosity about Aiden, my attraction to this man that I had seen in a moment of misguided recklessness, who might be kinky, helped me to gird my loins and push forward.

But I was in no way prepared for the sight of most likely kinky Aiden Thompson in black skinny jeans, Doc Martens and a black button-up that did wonderful things to his athletic physique. And that smile! He stood outside the heritage building that had housed a movie theater before being transformed into one of Ottawa's most renowned Italian eateries.

Some of the anxious knots in my stomach turn into lust as I moved forward to greet him. Except, what was the etiquette? Did we shake hands? Did we kiss on the cheek?

"Hi, Aiden," I said, hoping he would help me out.

"Fletcher, it's great to see you outside of school." Aiden grinned, then frowned. "Wait! That sounds wrong."

We laughed.

"Well, way to make me feel young again," I said, offering my hand.

Aiden took it, but instead of giving it a cursory shake, he held it for a few extra beats and let go, keeping his eyes on mine. I found myself adrift in them.

"How are you?" he asked, with genuine concern.

"I haven't gone on a date in a long time—like, a really long time."

"Well, thank you for agreeing to this. I'm honored."

He opened the door and beckoned me in after him.

"I'm starved! I hope you're hungry."

Famished, I thought, staring at his ass as he moved forward.

I shook my head, trying to keep it clear, when I was one huge horny mess, a second away from making a fool of myself.

"I wasn't expecting Lucy's supply teacher to be so..." I hesitated. "Never mind."

Aiden gave our name to the hostess and turned back to me.

"Incredibly sexy? Astoundingly attractive?"

I smiled, amused. "Wow."

"I know. My ego's as big as my—"

I almost choked as the hostess interrupted him with a wide smile.

"This way, gentlemen."

I met Aiden's gaze with a stern one, but that just made him laugh. He was delightful. I was already having a good time.

The hostess guided us to a table for two in a corner spot that was somewhat private.

"Thank you," Aiden said, gesturing for me to sit down.

I took the chair he referred to and picked up the menu. "I haven't been here in a while."

Daniel and I had come once, at some point near the beginning of our relationship, but he hadn't been a fan of fancy eateries. He preferred the pub-type environment, of which there were plenty in Ottawa.

"It's one of my favorite places. The pasta dishes are out of this world."

I didn't want to think about Daniel and what he had liked or not liked.

"Where are you supplying this week?"

Aiden glanced at the menu, his gaze scanning the offerings. "Fuck, all the way out in the west end. D. Roy Kennedy School. It's so *far*."

"That's a pain," I said. I tried to think about what I wanted to eat, but all I could see in my mind was Aiden's ass in those killer jeans.

"The kids are great, though," he said.

"Really? Being in a room with that many kids for even a couple of hours would probably drive me to drink," I admitted. "Lucy says you're…strict."

I hoped that didn't sound to him the way it sounded to me. I'd heard the sound of a riding crop slicing the air as I'd said it. I swallowed and hoped I wasn't blushing too much.

"Did she say that?" he asked, looking more amused than surprised. "As a supply teacher, you have to be if you want to survive and keep your sanity."

A very handsome male server approached our table.

"How are we doing tonight? My name is David, and I'll be your server this evening."

"Fantastic," Aiden said, greeting David with a smile.

"Have you had a look at our spirits and wine menu?"

Aiden and I glanced at each other.

"Not yet. What would you recommend in the way of wine?" I asked.

I could do this. And a glass of wine was exactly what I needed.

David listed off a number of Australian and Chilean wines, and Aiden deferred to me to choose. I picked a Chilean red that was pricey enough to guarantee its taste but not kill my bank account. When David brought it to our table, he had me sample it.

"Oh, that's wonderful."

He filled our glasses then took our food order. Aiden requested the mussels, and I chose the gnocchi in a rosé sauce.

As I took another sip of wine, I noticed movement out of the corner of my eye. When I focused on it, it became an orange and black spider that was making its way along the wall toward me.

"Fuck!" The metal feet of my chair scraped the concrete floor with a loud screech as I stood. Expensive red wine sloshed over the edge of my glass, but I put it down before there was a major disaster.

The look on Aiden's face was almost comical. If I'd been in the right mood, I would have laughed, but there was nothing funny about being this close to an arachnid on the loose.

I pointed at the offending insect.

"Sp — Spider."

Aiden was astonishingly calm. He glanced at the spider then looked at me, and his smile lit up his face.

"Oh, Fletcher. You're scared of spiders?"

"No," I said, shaking my head and trying to stand straighter. I glanced up to see more than a few people staring in our direction. "I'm not *scared* of them. They just gross me out."

Aiden pushed his chair back, slowly and carefully, so it wouldn't make noise, and came around to my side of the table. As he passed me, he gave my shoulder an affectionate squeeze.

"What are you doing?" I said, unable to look away from the small creature, which was still making its merry way toward my chair.

"I'm going to take care of it," he said.

"Thank you." I cleared my throat, and tried to look at ease, even though I wasn't. "Lucy usually…usually kills them for me."

"Oh, I'm not going to kill it."

"What?" I said, the breath leaving my chest as I took a step back. "Why not?"

"Because, Fletcher, as much as I want to please you on our first date, I'm not going to commit murder."

He wanted to please me?

"I have to set some boundaries," he asserted.

I watched in horror as Aiden herded the spider into the palm of his hand. Then he closed his fingers around it and took a step to get by me.

"Oh, holy fuck. No, no. Stay away from me," I said as I backed into the corner, invading the personal space of the man at the neighboring table.

"Easy, man. Relax," the stranger said, moving his chair back.

"I'm sorry. I'm *so* sorry," I said, watching Aiden with wide eyes as he carried the trapped — hopefully! — spider past me and took it around and presumably out of the front doors.

I was torn between relief that he'd taken care of the problem, and irritation that he hadn't dispatched it quietly and not humiliated me in front of everyone. But that wasn't fair, because I'd embarrassed myself before he'd said anything.

This date was off to a fantastic start.

While Aiden was gone, I surveyed the table and the wall and the window ledge for other spiders or bugs of any kind. I didn't see any. By the time Aiden returned, I had gingerly lowered myself back into my seat.

"I'm so sorry," I said, as Aiden sat down across from me.

"Don't apologize. I was worried you were perfect. I'm glad you have some quirks."

I blinked, heat rising in my cheeks. That was such a nice thing for him to say.

I picked up my wine and took a drink. "Thanks. But I'm still worried about you," I said, with a smile.

He laughed. "Oh, I have plenty of quirks. Don't worry."

I wondered if he was talking about his kinky side. It was the right moment to bring up the club.

"You know we've been in the same room before we met at Lucy's school, right?"

He stared at me, and there was so much in that look. But he didn't say anything right away. He picked up his glass, holding my gaze, and took a very long sip as my cock got hard and my pulse quickened.

"So, that *was* you."

I nodded. I didn't know what else to say. I hadn't thought this through. I'd been focused entirely on how he'd looked to me. I hadn't even considered how I might have looked.

"Did the glitterboy take good care of you, then?" he said, in extraordinarily quiet tones.

Now I regretted bringing it up.

"I…" I gazed at the table. "I was still in a bit of a state at the time. That was…about three months after Daniel died."

"Oh, God, I'm sorry. I didn't mean anything. I genuinely hoped that he made you very happy for a moment. That's all."

I nodded. "Thanks. He was great. He was very kind to me."

"That's *good*," Aiden said, his expression filled with concern.

"So…why were you there?" I asked the question that I'd had on my mind since we'd run into each other at Lucy's school.

He was the one blushing now and smiling a conspiratorial smile.

"Well, I…I was out with my partner at the time."

"Oh." I nodded. "You seemed…very much *in control* of the situation."

I hoped it was enough of a hint that I was searching for his position in that dynamic. I desperately needed to know if my instincts had been correct.

Aiden sat back and contemplated me. He smiled and crossed his arms over his chest. "I wasn't prepared to have this conversation."

"I'm sorry," I said. "It's none of my business."

"Well, it might be…your business. Depends how things turn out."

We gazed at each other, a force of energy charging the air between us.

I nodded. It was suddenly hard to breathe.

"That club," he said, "was a place where a certain subset of gay men felt welcome."

"Yes. I know."

"Huh. Can I ask you something?"

"Yeah."

"Was the twink actually what you were looking for that night, or did he just...fall into your lap? So to speak," Aiden said. He looked at the table then back up. "Were you really looking for something else?"

"I was looking for...for someone to..." I took a deep breath. God this was so hard. I hoped the people at the nearby table couldn't hear us. "Take me...in hand. You know..." I didn't want to spell it out.

Aiden smiled with such happiness, butterflies started battering the walls of my belly. A feeling I hadn't had in a very fucking long time.

"Oh, I *do* know, as a matter of fact."

We sat there, staring at each other in a daze of recognition and realization. It took the server coming with our plates to break the trance.

"I have the gnocchi?" he said, hovering by the table.

"Here," I said, with some relief.

He placed it in front of me, the scent of tomato cream sauce with a hint of basil, flooding my nostrils.

"And the mussels must be for you, sir," the server said, placing the bowl of swimming bivalves in front of Aiden.

"Thank you," he said.

We ate in silence but stole glances at each other. Watching Aiden delicately pry apart each shell and bring the tiny piece of meat to his pretty mouth was a treat, and I had to consciously refrain from staring. My cock had been hard since we'd talked about the club. This wasn't helping anything.

I tried to enjoy my gnocchi, which tasted fantastic. But I was so very distracted and antsy.

"Does Lucy really take care of any spiders around the house?" Aiden asked finally.

I swallowed the piece of pasta in my mouth and smiled. "Yes. She absolutely does."

Remembering the spider incident brought something else to mind. "Wait! Did you wash your hands?"

"Pardon?"

"After you took the spider outside. Sorry... I — It just occurred to me you might have spider germs still."

He laughed and his eyes sparked with amusement. "As a matter of fact, I did...with soap, even. They have very nice bathrooms in this place."

I smiled with relief. "Oh, thank God."

"You like to be clean." It was a statement of fact.

"I suppose I do. Yes. Isn't that...a good thing?"

"It can be. But it's also good to be able to tolerate a little filth."

The way he enunciated those last two words made my cock jerk in my pants.

Filth. I wanted him to make me tolerate some.

We looked at each other.

"Fuck," I said under my breath. I had to change the subject, or I was going to embarrass myself. "Daniel used to get the spiders, then Lucy took over. I think she feels closer to the memory of him that way — or she just can't stand my screaming."

Aiden's eyes went wide.

"It's a joke. I don't scream."

"Hmm. Never?"

I stared at him. He stared at me.

"Not from spiders," I said.

He grinned wider. "Huh."

I blushed and poured myself more wine.

Aiden fondled the stem of his wine glass and licked his lips. "Did you always want kids?"

Okay. We were diving right into this.

I swallowed. "It was Daniel who really wanted them. But as soon as he placed Lucy in my arms, it was a done deal. Emotionally, I mean."

Aiden nodded, his expression midway between sadness and understanding.

"She's pretty amazing," he said.

"Yeah. She's...she's Daniel's biological daughter."

"Is she? That's wonderful."

It was wonderful. I thought that every single day, even when it made me cry.

"Yeah."

Daniel was gone. I'd come to accept that very real fact. But part of him was still here, and that was in Lucy. I saw him in her all the time, and it was a goddamn miracle and a blessing.

"You're a good dad, Fletcher," Aiden said, with so much confidence in his assertion I huffed a laugh.

"How do you know?"

Aiden held my gaze. "Because of how Lucy is — how she thinks, how she talks, how she talks about *you*."

"She talks about me?"

"Yes. A lot. The fact that she talks about you at all shows me you're an important presence in her life. A lot of these kids...You know, they come from families that have split up for reasons other than someone having passed away. And it's hard being a single parent and staying engaged in their lives."

"So, what does she say about me?"

Aiden laughed. "She says you spoil the dogs."

"What? *I* spoil the dogs? Lucy's the one that's always giving them treats!"

"Oh, I've hit a nerve," Aiden murmured.

And the way he said it made it sound like he wanted to have his way with *all* my nerves.

I frowned. "Lucy spoils the dogs. But I let her because I'm just happy to see her functioning again. There was a dark, dark time, after Daniel died, where…" I swallowed. "… neither of us knew if we were going to be okay."

"Oh, Fletcher. I'm so sorry."

I gave him a shaky smile, trying not to remember how bereft those times had been.

"Yeah. We've come a long way…her more than me. I can't imagine what it's like as a child to lose a parent."

"I'm sure you had as much, or more, of a loss, Fletcher."

"Well. We're both much better now."

We finished our meals and even ordered some dessert. Aiden offered me a bite of his tartufo, smiling as if daring me to take it.

His gaze landed on my mouth as I leaned forward and sucked the ice cream off his spoon.

Delicious—as was the sight of him giving a barely audible little gasp as I did. I wasn't ready for our date to be over.

"Shit. Do you want to go for a walk and get a coffee somewhere? I need to sober up before I get behind the wheel," I said.

"Good idea," Aiden replied.

"On one bill?" the server asked when he cleared our dessert plates.

I was about to say no, when Aiden beat me to it.

"Yes. I'll take it."

"Oh, you don't have to pay for mine," I said, reaching for my back pocket.

"Fletcher," Aiden said, in a tone that brooked no argument. "I'll get it. You can pay next time."

Next time? My heart beat faster, and my dick twitched at the command in his tone.

"Thank you, Aiden."

"You're welcome."

We walked along Elgin, the streetlights and store lights making a pretty backdrop against the darkness. A winter chill hung in the air, even though it was still October. I buttoned up my jacket and hunched my shoulders against the wind.

"Cold?" Aiden asked.

I nodded.

He unwound the checkered scarf from around his neck.

"Come here."

I went there, my heart beating under my too-thin jacket, and waited while Aiden wound his scarf around my neck and tucked it into itself.

"There you go. I was a little warm anyway."

"Thank you...again."

"I love hearing those words from you, Fletcher. I'd like to get you to say them often."

I stared at him. I wanted to kiss him, so badly. But we were on the sidewalk, in plain view of a lot of people, and I was too aware of the possibility of inciting anger or disdain that I held back.

"Want to stop in and get a coffee?" Aiden asked, pointing at a Bridgehead across the street.

"Yes!" At least we'd get out of the cold.

He let me keep his scarf while we chatted. When my neck got too hot, I unwound it and held it out to him.

"Keep it. It looks good on you."

"Aiden, I can't take your scarf."

"Sure you can. I've got lots."

"Fine," I said, grinning.

Aiden was thirty, bisexual and besides teaching English and music, he played guitar in a band, like Lucy had told me.

"That's very cool."

He laughed. "Well, we haven't got a record deal or anything. It's just me and some other teachers."

"Still cool. Do you only play guitar?"

"I sing, too."

"Backup?"

"Lead."

"Really," I said, completely charmed.

"Here," he said, tapping on his phone and turning it to face me.

A video was playing. There was Aiden, standing at a microphone, playing his guitar and singing *Sweet Caroline*. I hadn't realized he could look hotter than he did already, but this clinched it.

"*The Tardy Boys?* Seriously?"

He shrugged. "We're all teachers."

"Wow. Do you have groupies? You're super-hot," I said.

He laughed, putting the phone down. "No groupies."

"Can I be one?"

He tilted his head, gazing at me like he was asking me to get naked right this minute. "Definitely."

"I wish I had talent like that."

"You said you're a writer?"

I nodded. "Technically. I only write copy. I write what I'm told to write."

He sat back. "Do you like doing what you're told?"

The look in his eyes said he wasn't talking about my writing.

"Most of the time. Yeah. It's…easier."

"I get that."

I'll bet you do.

"But did you ever write for yourself?"

Did I ever write for myself? I had. A long time ago, before Daniel, before Lucy.

"In high school I won a short story contest." I'd almost forgotten. It had felt like such an accomplishment, but my parents had shrugged it off. And I had done the same.

"That's amazing."

"Yeah, but I could never write a novel or anything like that."

"No? Have you tried? Do you even want to?"

"I mean, maybe someday? Aiden, I only just managed to get back to functioning as a human being. This is the first date I've had since…since I've been with…"

"Daniel," Aiden finished for me. "This is a big step."

"Huge."

"And…how's it going?"

I smiled. "Like a dream. A really good, really hot one."

Aiden let me pay for our coffees. We stepped out into the night.

"Do you want to come back to my place?" Aiden asked. "I've got a bottle of nice Scotch, or we could just hang out, chat some more. Or…"

I knew what that meant. And boy did I want to say yes. But it was already ten o'clock and I wasn't sure how late Patrick expected me to be.

"Can you give me a second to check in with my nephew, Patrick? He's with Lucy."

"Yeah, of course," Aiden said, his gaze running over me in a very appealing way. "I'm just going to step into the bakery. Do you like scones?"

"I do like scones."

Aiden smiled and walked away. I found a quiet spot and took out my phone, texting Patrick. Hopefully he'd answer.

Just checking in. Is it okay if I stay out a bit longer?

I waited, watching the people walking by, wondering if going back to Aiden's place was a good idea. It had been a long time since I'd been physical with anyone, and I really liked Aiden.

My phone chimed and I looked down.

Lucy's in bed. I'm watching America's Top Model. *Btw, that chili you made was so good!*

I grinned.

Thanks. Look, I don't know if I'm ready to come home…

Huzzah, huzzah. Eggplant emoji.

Lol. Can you stay another couple of hours?

YES.

I'll pay you overtime.

Not necessary. Go have fun.

I'll try to be back by midnight.

I can sleep on the couch. Stay out as long as you want. It's good for you.

I sent him a super happy face emoji.

I pocketed my phone just as Aiden came out of the bakery holding a paper bag that he shoved in his coat pocket.

"I hope that smile means you can accept my invitation?" he said.

"Wait! What have you got there?"

"Never mind. You'll see in a bit."

"Should we take two cars, or..."

"Actually, we can walk. I live across from the Museum of Nature."

"Oh!"

"Yeah, it's a great old building, but it's a walk-up and I'm on the fourth floor. Do you think you can make it?"

"Very funny. How out of shape do I look?"

Aiden gave me a hungry glance. "You look fucking fantastic. But let's see how hard you're breathing when we get to my apartment."

* * * *

The stairs to Aiden's apartment were a workout, but that wasn't the only reason I was breathing hard when we made it to the top floor.

"You're as out of breath as I am," I pointed out.

"It's not from the stairs," he said, keying the door and pushing it open. It made a creak that echoed off the plastered walls of the high-ceilinged hallway.

"Come in." He flipped the light switch. Old wood floors, polished to a shine, and a hall closet in front of me, opened up into a central hallway with two doors off the left and what looked like a living area at the far end.

The door swung shut with a loud bang that echoed in the old building. Aiden locked the deadbolt.

"What a cool—"

He grabbed my shirt and pulled me against him.

"Whoa." My breath caught in my throat as our bodies collided and my gaze landed on a pair of dark brown eyes.

"I need to kiss you...if that's okay," he whispered, his mouth inches from mine, the smell of coffee and vanilla wafting up my nose. "Please let it be okay..."

"God, *yes.*"

He cupped the back of my head as our mouths met in a searching, scorching kiss that made my toes curl.

Aiden gave a little groan as he parted his lips and accepted my searching tongue, our hands grasping at each other as he turned me around and guided me through a nearby doorway.

"This is my bedroom," Aiden gasped in between kisses.

"Convenient," I whispered. "Right beside the front door..."

He inhaled a shuddering breath. "Goddamn it, you're gorgeous."

"*You're* gorgeous," I countered, reaching for the buttons on Aiden's shirt. Then I paused and pulled back. "Are we doing this?" I asked, breathless with need and excitement. *Please say yes.*

"I really want to," Aiden murmured, pulling my shirttails out of my pants.

"Good. Good," I said, kissing him again, breathing in the scent of his clean body and oozing testosterone. "Fuck, I need this...*so* bad."

He kissed me harder, then pulled back and got to work on his own clothes, stripping off his shirt and pushing down his jeans as I stood there, open-mouthed and enthralled. It felt like I was in some kind of movie as I watched him reveal himself.

When he was stripped to a pair of navy boxer briefs that made his erection pretty obvious, he grabbed my shirt and pulled me into another kiss.

"Strip, Fletcher."

It didn't take me long to get down to my white boxer briefs.

"Okay. Now what?"

"Oh, fuck yes," Aiden said, as I threw my jeans aside and faced him, tossing my bangs out of the way.

"I need a haircut." I laughed as my hair fell back in front of my eyes.

Aiden shook his head. "No. You're perfect."

He moved forward and carded his fingers through my hair. "Have you always been blond?"

I quirked an amused eyebrow. "You mean is my hair dyed? It's natural."

"Mine, too," he said, pulling at the tight brown curls that framed his handsome face. "I can't be bothered fighting it."

"I love your hair," I said, pulling him into another kiss. "And the way your eyes go so dark when you're horny...like right now."

I slid my fingers along his side, over his hip and traced a knuckle over his erection.

He shuddered and pushed me backward.

"I really hope there's a bed in here. I haven't had a chance to look," I said.

"I'd do you on the floor at this point. But yes, there's a bed."

"By 'do me' do you mean…"

He rolled his eyes. "I mean, whatever feels good, yeah? And whatever makes you comfortable," he said, stepping forward.

I went to take a step back and found the bed right behind my knees. I fell backward. Aiden climbed over me.

"No more. No less."

"Easy," I gasped. "I'm so turned on I might go off."

"I don't fucking care if you do," Aiden said, examining my face and my neck and meeting my gaze. "And I don't want to go easy."

Chapter Five

Confessions

Now that we were here, naked and safe together in this private space where Aiden lived — hopefully alone — I was eager and so, so hungry. Maybe it helped that he looked nothing like Daniel, who had been red-haired and pale-skinned, with freckles everywhere.

Stop thinking about him, I told myself. I pushed his image from my mind. I couldn't fuck a ghost, and it was time to stop torturing myself. Daniel was dead, and I was still fucking alive.

Aiden pulled away and grinned. "I don't either."

He pulled me onto the bed.

"Do you want a lamp on?" he asked, between hungry kisses.

"No. Don't need it. Don't care."

God, I was so desperate, I didn't want anything to distract me from getting what I needed. The moonlight and glow from the streetlamps gave the room an ethereal illumination.

"Hey, Fletcher," Aiden said, pulling back and regarding me with concern. "Nobody's gonna take it from you. We don't have to rush."

"Okay. I know. Sorry," I said.

"Oh God, don't be sorry, baby," he murmured. "It's very flattering. Come on. Let's get these off."

He slipped his fingers under the waistband of my boxer briefs and dragged them down my thighs and all the way off. Then he did the same with his.

We came together now, completely naked and desperate, kneeling on the mattress, our breaths and soft moans the only sounds in the room.

"I want to suck you," Aiden said.

"Okay. Please."

He gave me a wicked grin and slid down the bed. My hips thrust up as he took me into his mouth.

"Oh my fucking God!" I gasped, my whole world becoming warmth and suction and Aiden's dark eyes gazing at me. "Fuck, fuck, *fuck.*"

It felt so good. So right. He ate me like I was his last meal, slobbered over my cock like he was starved for it, and used his hand to jerk me like a porn star.

Daniel had been all about slow teasing and long make-out sessions. Aiden was a whirlwind of hunger and lust, and I let him take me over. I splayed my arms out and closed my eyes, focusing on the way Aiden was going at me. He was fierce and desperate, and my body responded to his actions with unpredicted fervor.

"Oh fuck, oh fuck. I'm gonna come. Stop."

He stopped.

"I want to keep going," he said.

"I'll come."

"So?" he said, waggling his eyebrows. "Good."

I swallowed. "Isn't it too soon?"

He laughed. "Too soon for who? Not for me. I want to watch you."

I blinked. "But then it'll be over."

"Oh, no, Fletcher. It will have just begun," he said, as he wrapped his fingers around me and took me down his throat again.

I groaned and gaped at the ceiling as he brought me to the edge again.

"You probably don't want to—" I said, before the orgasm bolted through me and my cock overflowed, pleasure rolling in waves. "Oh...fuck..."

Aiden popped off my cock and spat out the jizz that had started to fill his mouth. But he kept jerking me as I rode the waves, making sounds of enjoyment.

"How are you so beautiful? Honestly."

I gazed at him, blinking, trying to get my breath back. "What?"

"When you come. You're radiant. It's so fucking hot." He glanced at the digital clock on the dresser. "How long have we got before you have to get home?"

"A couple of hours," I said, my head still spinning from the comment.

"I can work with that."

"Do you have a towel?"

"Hold on."

I lay there while Aiden got a cloth and wiped up the mess I'd made. As he leaned over me to put it on the side table, I reached for his cock.

"Oh, hello there," he murmured, covering my hand with his as he settled back down on the mattress. "You going to jerk me?"

"I'd like to. Lube?"

"Here," he said, passing me a jar.

"Coconut oil?"

"Nothing but the best. Smells good, too," Aiden said. "Don't use it with a condom. But it's great for manual activities."

I scooped some onto my fingers and found his dick again. He was longer and narrower than I was, and it leaned slightly to the right when he was erect, like now.

"You're really hard."

"Yeah," he panted.

"Like, rock solid."

"Feels like it."

"I'll say."

"Oh, fuck yes," he breathed, placing his hands on his thighs as he watched me. "That looks so hot, what you're doing."

"That coconut oil does smell good," I said, meeting his gaze.

He sat back on his heels as I jerked him. I watched as he got more and more turned on. He was a stunningly beautiful man, even more so now, with his cheeks darkening to a rosy color and his sweet mouth open, his eyes deep pits of longing.

I sped up as Aiden's breaths made a staccato rhythm and he thrusted into my hand.

"Oh fuck, I'm gonna come...gonna come," he groaned as hot spurts shot over my fist. "Oh...my... God...yes..."

I kept going until he put a hand down to stop me.

"Too much. Too much," he laughed. "Mmm."

He took a shaky breath as I reached for the towel. I wiped my fingers and passed it over. Aiden cleaned himself up.

"Oh, I feel much better," Aiden murmured, sliding down to the bed and gathering me close. "Where have you been, Fletcher Marin?"

I waited for panic to start, or tears to come, but there was nothing, nothing but a soothing calm that spread over me, everywhere. I could have fallen asleep.

"Don't let me fall asleep," I whispered, snuggling closer.

"Don't worry," Aiden said, as his fingers gripped my hips and he surged against me. His cock was soft but his lips and tongue on my neck told me he was still aroused and ready for round two. I hoped I could keep up.

Turned out I needn't have worried.

Aiden easily got me hard again, and soon we were as desperate as we'd been before. This time, we stretched out and frotted our cocks together.

"Look," I said, gazing between our bodies.

"So pretty. The dark and the light."

'I wrapped my hand around them and surged against him.

"Oh, yes, yes, yes," Aiden gasped as we thrust in a quickening rhythm until, with a groan, he came, and I followed.

As we lay there, recovering, we gazed into each other's eyes like long-time lovers.

"So hot. So lovely," Aiden said, gliding his fingers along my hip and over my ass. "So...are you a bottom or a top, my dear Fletcher?"

"Wow, so direct," I said, amused. "I've done both."

"Really? And which do you prefer?"

"How about you?"

Aiden laughed. "I asked you first."

I made a show of sighing, but I wasn't annoyed. "I prefer to bottom. But I'm open to anything."

Aiden stroked his tongue in a languid path over his bottom lip.

"Versatile. Excellent."

"You?"

"Well, I like to top, so I suppose this might work out after all."

He gazed at me, and I gazed at him—and I wondered if my days of being lonely in my grief were gone…at least for a little while.

* * * *

I punched my code into the door lock and went in as quietly as I could at around two in the morning. Cocoa came up to me wagging her tail, and Eddie followed, giving one small bark and whining, as if complaining about me being out so late.

When I rounded the corner into the living room, I saw Patrick snuggled under a soft throw on the sofa, sound asleep, with a magazine laying on his chest. I turned on a lamp, then went up to him and touched his shoulder.

"Hey…I'm home."

Patrick blinked in the sudden light. "Oh. Hey. What time is it?"

"It's two in the morning. I'm so sorry." I gave him a guilty look, but I couldn't help smiling.

"I guess you had a good date," he said, rubbing at his face.

"Yes, it was. Thank you for being here. I'll call you an Uber."

Once I had seen Patrick off, I wandered around the place, tidying up and thinking about my date. It had been an incredible evening, and I wondered when we might see each other again.

My phone dinged with a text message.

Gnight, Fletcher.

Gnight, Aiden. Ty.

For what?

For looking after me so well. I don't just mean the spider.

* * * *

"Why don't you bring Aiden to Maverick Molly's?" Patrick said, out of the blue, a few weeks later.
"Huh?"
Aiden and I had been dating and becoming more intimate. It had been going well, but we hadn't broached the subject of kink. I wasn't in a rush, although the idea of being dommed by Aiden was intriguing.
"The vibe in the gaming parlor is so cool. You feel like you've stepped back in time. And there's the kink room in the back, if you think you guys might want to give it a try?"
Patrick poured himself a glass of milk.
"You'd have to go when I'm not there, if you want me to watch the wombat, so you won't get to see me in action."
"Huh. Bummer," I said, with heavy sarcasm.
"Ha-ha. Anyway, it's a trip. You don't have to go hardcore or anything."
Ever since I'd had to go in and use the washroom, I'd been thinking about the place and wondering what it would be like to go there. But would Aiden be into it?
There was only one way to find out.

I asked him about it the next time I went to see his band, The Tardy Boys, play. I'd been a few times, and it was always a good time. Aiden had a great voice, and the way he interacted with the other band members was fun to watch. He became this other guy, this ultra-cool musician, that upped his attractiveness factor by at least twenty points. And I'd thought he was amazing already.

The band was taking a break, and Aiden was sitting at a table with me, chatting briefly with anyone who came up to the table and wanted to say hi to the lead singer. I tried to take it in stride, but it felt like I was dating a celebrity. I supposed the fact that he was very attractive, a compelling vocalist, excellent guitar player and gay had something to do with his general appeal.

"Patrick thinks we should check out Maverick Molly's."

Aiden took a sip of his IPA. "*He* thought we should check it out?"

"He's a server there. I've never been," I admitted. "Well, I went in to use the bathroom once."

"I've heard good things about the place. Don't the servers dress as Victorian tarts?"

"As a matter of fact, yes."

Aiden laughed. "I love that your nephew works there. That's fantastic."

"Yeah, it's pretty funny."

"There's a kink room for rent there, too, isn't there?" Aiden said, affecting disinterest, as he met my gaze.

"Patrick said it's called The Bordello. I think you have to reserve it in advance..."

My voice trailed off as I took in Aiden's expression. His face had lit up, as if I'd proposed a trip to Paris. And now he seemed to be trying to temper his enthusiasm.

"Wait. Did you want to go to the kink room?" I asked.

He lifted his tankard to his lips and took a long sip, holding my gaze as he did.

"Fuck," I said, my dick getting hard in my pants. Seemed to always happen around him. I didn't say anything for a long moment then I said, "If we did go to the Bordello, what would you be interested in doing there?"

"In general?" he asked. "Or...more specifically?"

I kept my gaze on his and shrugged. "You can be specific."

Aiden rubbed his hands together. "Oooh boy. I wondered when we might have this conversation. Didn't expect it to be so soon."

"I guess we can thank Patrick for that."

He laughed. "Yeah."

"Are we having this conversation?"

"I think we are."

"All right." I sipped my beer. "I should tell you that...Daniel and I...we had a sort of arrangement..."

I didn't know what to call it. It hadn't been a twenty-four seven deal at any point. But before Lucy had come along, it had been a frequent thing.

"What do you mean by 'arrangement'?" Aiden asked, his eyes widening.

"I mean," I said, blushing and worrying the place where my wedding band had been.

I'd kept it on for a year after Daniel had passed. But on the first anniversary of his death, I'd put it in the little wood box that held his cufflinks, his watch and his matching wedding band. It seemed like it kept us together somehow, more than me wearing mine on my own would.

It was important to be honest.

"I mean, an arrangement where..." I swallowed, gazing at the table. "Where I...I served him...in all kinds of ways."

There. I'd said it.

He blew out a long breath. I didn't dare look up.

Then his hand was on my back, soothing me.

"Served him...how? Like domestic stuff?"

"Sometimes."

Aiden's hand stopped. He cleared his throat. "Sex stuff?"

The breath whooshed from my lungs and the relief I felt was incredible.

"Yeah."

"Is that why you remembered me from so long ago? Because you knew what I was, and it drew you to me?"

"Maybe that was part of it. But also, you're you," I said, waving my hand at him.

He smiled a languorous, confident smile.

* * * *

We made plans to go to Maverick Molly's that Thursday, when Patrick was off and could look after Lucy.

I hadn't known what to wear, but I ended up in a dressy pair of black pants and a light gray sweater over a T-shirt, with a black blazer over top. Patrick had said that most of the men who came to Molly's dressed a little formal, since it harkened back to times when people got fancy to go out.

Aiden had texted me that he was running late, so I'd said I'd go in and get us a table or at least scope the place out, and he could find me inside. Maybe that had been a mistake, because I felt decidedly out of my depth as I entered the lamplit interior of the club.

I stood in the hallway after hanging up my coat, feeling uneasy and anxious, when a young black man wearing bloomers and the rest of the molly-boy outfit under a red kimono came out of the main room.

He stopped and cocked his head. "Well, hello there, handsome. I've never seen you before!"

His smile was cheeky and cheerful, and made me feel welcomed.

"Nope. This is my first time." I didn't want to reference the bathroom incident. "But, my nephew works here."

He gasped. "A virgin!" He looked me over. "And who is your nephew, if you don't mind me asking?"

"Patrick Lafferty."

"Oh! My, my, my. He didn't tell me he had such an attractive uncle!"

I didn't know what to say to that. He was obviously putting me on. I smiled.

"I'm Robin. And welcome to Maverick Molly's. Can I help you get settled in the gaming parlor?"

"That would be great. I'm expecting someone."

"Wonderful! And you are?"

"Oh, I'm sorry. I'm Fletcher Marin."

"Excellent. If you'll just follow me, Mr. Marin, I can show you around and introduce you to a few people." Robin turned and beckoned me to follow. The red kimono had a large dragon embroidered in gold on the back of it.

Introduce me to some people? This was already more than I'd bargained for. Why hadn't I arranged to meet Aiden out front?

Chapter Six

Pretty Boys and Kinky Spaces

I took a deep breath, fixed the collar of my blazer and followed Robin into the gaming parlor.

The spacious, lamplit room contained several round tables, around two of which groups of men were seated. Polished, dark wood floors peeked from under a vintage burgundy rug. An expansive hearth loomed against the far wall, containing a blazing fire that crackled and popped. The weather had gotten significantly colder over the past couple of weeks, so it was welcome.

"Now, Mr. Marin. Would you like to join a table or would you like me to seat you at one of the empty ones?"

"Hmm." I gazed at the two busy tables. A game of backgammon was in play at one of them, and cards at another. "I'd love to sit by the fire, at the empty table."

"Lovely. Come this way, please."

I glanced at the bar to my left, where a black man in fancy historical clothing was mixing a cocktail. He flashed me a smile and gave me a nod. I returned the smile, then followed Robin to the table I'd indicated. There was a small stage with a piano beside it. If anyone performed, we'd have front row seats.

"Thank you," I said.

"Of course. You'll be able to see your friend when he arrives. May I have his name, please?"

"Aiden Thompson," I replied. "He should be here soon."

"I'm sure," Robin said, eyeing me with interest. "Can I get you a drink?"

"Of course. Yes. Hmm."

"I'll get you a cocktail menu," Robin said, flitting to the bar before I could say anything else. He leaned over the bar top and whispered something to the bartender, who glanced at me and shrugged, then passed Robin a laminated sheet.

Robin came back to the table and placed it in front of me. "Have a look, and I'll be back in a moment."

"Thank you."

He went off to another table, and I was able to relax and scan the list of cocktails on offer. The atmosphere of the place, with soft jazz playing in the background — which might not have been historically accurate but added to the relaxed ambience — and the sounds of men chatting and egging each other on, gave me a glimpse into another time. I received some curious glances from a few of the customers, but otherwise was left to myself. I wondered how it would have felt to have found a place like this, where a gay man could be himself, in a society that was openly hostile and that criminalized same-sex behavior. Would I have had the courage to go there? Or would I have lived a life of misery trying to be something I wasn't? I didn't even want to contemplate the answer.

There were two other servers in pretty Victorian undergarments moving about, and I had to say that the concept was brilliant. Titillating and unique, it was a glimpse into a subset of kink and gender fluidity that might have existed in secret locations back in the day. The men at work here at Molly's were lovely young things, who seemed perfectly at home and happy to serve drinks and small snacks to the men who observed them. I noticed lots of flirting between the molly boys and the clients but no bad behavior. The men seemed to know what would be tolerated.

Then Robin came back into the room leading Aiden, who seemed absolutely delighted with the attention and also happy to find me waiting for him.

"And here you are then, Mr. Thompson, Mr. Marin. Have a look at the drinks list and I'll be back in a moment—or flag down one of the other mollies to assist you."

"Thank you so much," Aiden said, taking the chair next to mine and subtly eyeing Robin's cinched waist. "Fletcher, you look amazing."

"Aiden," I said, looking him over. "You always look nice but…wow."

"Oh, you like?" he asked, sitting back so I could have a better look.

He was wearing artfully faded slim-cut jeans with a crushed velvet navy blazer over a matching vest, with a pinstriped navy and white collared shirt and a navy tie.

"Oh, yes," I said, grinning.

I felt much more at ease now that Aiden was here.

"So," he said, looking around, "this is where your nephew works."

I laughed, raising my eyebrows. "I wonder if my sister-in-law knows?"

"Have you asked her?"

"I keep forgetting. I doubt she'd care. I think she's just glad he's out on his own and doing well."

"That's good."

One of the other molly boys approached our table.

"Hello, gentlemen. I can't help but notice that neither of you have drinks. Can I get you something?"

"Oh, shit, I keep forgetting to look at the list. Is there a drink you'd recommend?" I asked the petite peroxide blond, who was wearing a little bit of rouge on his cheeks and vibrant red lipstick.

He cocked his head. "Well, that depends. Are you looking to get hammered or simply to chill out?"

I glanced at Aiden.

"Oh, I think chill out," he said.

"Definitely," I agreed.

"All right, then. My name's Cory, by the way. Robin got busy and asked me to stop by your table."

"Well, thank you very much, Cory."

"So, if you want something traditional, you could get a whiskey sour. Or if you want to be adventurous, you should try the Sazerac."

"Oh, what's in that?" Aiden asked, leaning forward.

Cory grinned. "It's very nice—rye whiskey, bitters and a dash of absinthe."

"Sold," Aiden said, then turned to me. "Fletcher? What's your poison?"

"I'll stick with the whiskey sour."

"Great," Cory said. "I'll be back in a moment."

Cory took our requests to the gentleman at the bar as another man in period clothing—Sebastian, I think, whom I'd met previously—came into the room and proceeded to the piano. His naturally blond hair fell to his shoulders in soft waves, and he was wearing a cute boater hat on the top of his head. He picked up a microphone from where it rested on the piano and tapped it to get everyone's attention.

"Hello, everyone! Welcome to Maverick Molly's on this chilly November evening. Is everyone feeling toasty and warm now that they're here?"

The men at the nearby tables uttered various affirmatives.

"Excellent." He turned to one of the tables. "Mr. Anderson, I hope you're winning for once."

"He's not!" a man at the same table yelled out.

"Oh, that's a shame," Sebastian said "Well, to soothe your spirits, I'll have one of our entertainers up here to perform for you."

The room filled with hoots and hollers.

"Robin, are you free?" Sebastian asked the young man who had returned.

"Oh no, sir. I fetch a very high fee, don't you know," Robin said with a comical lilt.

Sebastian clicked his tongue. The men laughed.

"You're worth it!" one yelled.

"Awe, shucks," Robin said. "What would you boys like me to do tonight?" he asked, then held up his hand. "No rude remarks. I mean, a dance, a song or some racy poems."

"Striptease!" someone yelled.

"No," Sebastian stated. "Not an option."

"Dammit," the man said. "How about a dance?"

Robin heaved a dramatic sigh. "Fine. Even though my feet are killing me."

I turned to say something to Aiden but his gaze was fixed on Robin.

"Hey," I said in a sharp tone to get his attention. "You're here with *me*, remember?"

Aiden glanced over and gave me a look full to the brim with unadulterated lust. "And very proud of that fact. But this little minx is entertaining as fuck."

I laughed out loud.

Sebastian started playing the piano, and Robin turned his back to the audience, reached up with both hands then bent over at the waist in one fluid motion.

"One, two, one, two," he said, touching one toe in its little brown shoe, then the other.

Aiden grinned at my expression of disbelief and amusement. "Oh my God. I love this place!" he said.

"Wow," I commented, picking up my drink and taking a sip. But his enjoyment made me happy. For the first time in a very long time, I felt almost carefree. Everyone in this place was having a good time, even the servers, and *especially* Robin, who contorted himself into all kinds of scintillating positions.

"Ah fuck it. Now I'm too tired to dance," he said with an impish grin and a red face from all the yoga. "How about some jokes?"

"More stretching!" someone yelled out.

"You need your own YouTube channel!" another shouted.

"Gay Victorian Yoga for Horny Bastards?" Robin suggested.

There were hoots and hollers.

"Oh my God," I said, but I couldn't help smiling.

Robin struck a pose and cleared his throat.

"Why can't Miss Piggy count to seventy?"

Nobody knew.

"Because every time she gets to sixty-nine, she gets a little frog in her throat."

Now there was laughter all around.

"Nice one."

"I miss *The Muppet Show*!"

"That Miss Piggy," Robin said, nodding. "She was an icon."

I rolled my eyes because how the fuck would he know? He, like the other entertainers-slash-servers at Maverick Molly's, seemed to have barely entered adulthood. Probably the start of the Gen Z wave that would take hold of society in a handful of years. God help us all.

"You're two fucking young to know about that!" someone yelled, thinking the same thing as me.

Robin batted his luscious eyelashes and put his hands on his hips, evincing confusion. "What? About sixty-nining?"

Laughter.

"No, *The Muppet Show*! You weren't even alive when it was on television."

"Well, I'd like to introduce you aging gents to something called *the internet*," Robin stated. "It's where I get *all* my info." He tossed his head in an insouciant manner.

"All your porn, you mean," a man said.

"Well, of course. That, too." Robin said, winking. "All right, quiet down. Why is Santa's sack so big?"

"I can't even guess!"

Robin struck a pose with a saucy smile. "Because he only comes once a year."

All during this, Sebastian played little riffs on the piano to accompany Robin's performance. It was very entertaining to watch a vivacious, curvy twink dressed in Victorian undergarments prance about on the stage.

Robin's British accent and plump figure made him all the more adorable.

"All right, you lot, one more," he said. "What gets longer when pulled, inserts in a hole and works best when jerked?"

"Your cock!"

"Penis!"

"A dick!" Aiden shouted, much to my surprise. I broke into laughter, covering my mouth.

Robin gave Aiden an incredulous look and put a hand to his choker. "Well, I never! Mr. Thompson, you have a *very* dirty mind!"

Aiden shrugged and laughed, sitting back in his chair with his arms crossed over his chest.

"The answer is...a *seatbelt*," Robin said, shaking his head and descending from the stage as if he was very disappointed in the bunch of us. "Dirty buggers, all of you."

"Oh, hell yes, we are," a man agreed.

"You know it, lovely boy!" someone else said.

"Well," I said, throwing back the last of my whiskey sour and grinning at Aiden. "That was interesting."

"I haven't felt this entertained in ages."

"How is your Sazerac?"

"You know, it's pretty good." He lifted his glass, and we brought our drinks together with a clink, just as Robin came up to us.

"So, did you enjoy the show?" he asked, eying Aiden as if he wanted to climb into his lap, then turning a similar gaze on me. "And you, Mr. Marin? Was it everything you'd dreamed of?"

"Oh, yes," I said.

"Loved every moment of it," Aiden agreed. "Especially when you did the yoga."

Robin gasped. "Oh, you scoundrel! Next thing, you'll be wanting a peek in my chemise," Robin said, leaning forward and gaping the material above the corset to flash his nipples.

My cock swelled, and I cleared my throat, trying not to look, while Aiden leaned forward.

"Oh hello," Aiden said, giving himself an eyeful. "May I just say, Robin, that this entire establishment is absolutely delightful."

"Why thank you!" He straightened up and fixed his chemise. "But you should see what we have in the back."

Aiden and I exchanged a glance.

"You mean the kink room," Aiden said.

"Oh, you've heard of the Bordello! I can ask the bartender Jacob if anyone's using it if you'd like to give it a go."

Aiden's eyes widened, and he gave me a look of hope and excitement.

"Aiden...tonight?"

"Well, if...if it's available? It probably isn't," Aiden floundered.

"I'll check," said Robin, heading to Jacob at the bar, who was now discussing something with Sebastian.

"Why not tonight?" Aiden said, leaning toward me. "Patrick's watching Lucy. We don't have to do anything. We can just have a look at what's there and discuss what we might want to do at some unspecified date in the future."

I gave him a skeptical look. "We should find out how much it costs per hour."

Aiden shrugged. "I'll cover it, whatever it is."

"Are they paying supply teachers more these days? So much money to throw around..."

Aiden laughed. "It's an investment."

I gave him a shocked look.

"In what?" I asked.

"In getting to know more about you, in letting you know more about me, in finding out if we want to take this thing between us in a kinky direction."

Robin returned with a shiny silver key attached to a vintage Victorian one. He dangled it in front of Aiden.

"Looks like it's yours if you want it."

"How much?" Aiden asked with a smile and a devilish glance my way.

Robin leaned forward, so that his nipples were again visible through the gap of his chemise. "Well, you see, I got you a discount, seeing as it's your first time."

"How much?" I asked, trying not to stare at the dark brown buds peeking from the gap in Robin's chemise.

"A hundred. It's normally two."

"For an *hour*?" I asked.

"Not just an hour. An hour to have the use of a wide variety of implements and furniture." He looked me up and down. "Historical clothing, even. Trust me. It's worth it."

Robin looked as if he wanted to join us in the Bordello for an hour...or longer.

"Also, if you decide to become a member of our lovely little club after you try the space, we'll deduct that amount from the annual fee. Membership gets you discounted prices on drinks and priority when making a future reservation of the Bordello." Robin let the word drag out in a sultry way as he gazed at us.

Aiden leaned toward me. "Come on, Fletcher. I promise, we don't need to actually do anything. Let's just see what it's like. It's worth a hundred for the novelty alone—and the privacy to have an interesting conversation."

"Fine. Whatever."

Aiden sat back. "You romantic, you."

"I'm sorry. Yes, I'd love to."

Robin beamed. "Excellent."

He gave Jacob a thumbs up and turned back to Aiden and me.

"There are some electronic forms to sign and safety protocols to go over. Then you're in!" He glanced my way and waggled his eyebrows. "Get it? *In*?"

"We'll see. I've only agreed to talk about it," I said.

Robin put a hand on Aiden's shoulder, regarding me with a tolerant expression. "Playing hard to get, is he?" Robin said. "Come on, then."

I stood, wondering if this was a good idea or a huge mistake. But Aiden was right. It might be fun to have a look at this kink room and discuss where we might want to take this fledgling relationship. Being in an actual room with those sorts of items at our disposal would certainly give us something to talk about. I was buzzy and happy from my whiskey sour, and maybe that helped.

Jacob was very professional, if not as entertaining as Robin, and gave us the lowdown on the rules. We signed the electronic consent forms and transferred the reduced fee, then Robin offered to escort us.

"Now, Robin," Sebastian murmured to the cheeky server, "you're to come right back. You're not allowed to go into that room with Mr. Thompson and Mr. Marin."

Robin frowned. "Fine. But you're no fun." Robin lifted his chin. "This way, gentlemen."

We followed Robin out of the door of the gaming parlor and along the hallway that contained the coat rack. We went past a small kitchen and into the back where a large wood door with the word 'Bordello' on it stared at us from a broad wall.

"This is it. I'll give you the key now, and please bring it back to whomever is at the bar when you're done. You have the room until ten, which is slightly longer than an hour, so you've gotten quite the introductory deal."

Aiden gave him a salute and gestured to the door.

"Shall we?" he asked as Robin left us.

"I suppose we shall," I said, wondering what glories awaited us inside this room.

As the large door pushed open, pot lights in the ceiling gave a dim illumination to the space. It was much bigger than I'd expected.

Aiden closed the door behind me, locked it and turned on a lamp. "I think we can turn up the main lights as well. Hold on."

I waited as Aiden made the room brighter so we could see our way through this kinky wonderland. Looming furniture and period details came into focus as I looked about.

"Okay. Well, there's a lot of stuff in here," Aiden commented.

To our left was a cozy area with a rug, a settee and a mirrored vanity. There was a rack of vintage clothing hanging between that space and the rest of the space — sort of a divider. Then an antique school desk and a bigger wood desk were in front of a blackboard. Someone had chalked some math problems on the board, for realism.

But my gaze was drawn to the bed and the St. Andrew's cross, then to a line of implements hanging on a rack affixed to the wall beside it.

"Jesus Christ."

Daniel and I had enjoyed a relatively gear-free BDSM relationship. We'd discussed going to a place like this once or twice, but it hadn't seemed necessary. The power play in our relationship didn't require accouterments. It was something that had come about naturally as we'd become more intimate. But I'd always wanted to see a place like this.

I felt a flash of guilt because I was here with Aiden and not Daniel. But I couldn't be here with Daniel, because Daniel was dead. And I'd be damned if I was going to live a celibate or kink-free life to pay some kind of misguided homage to our love. It wasn't anyone's fault that he'd died, but he had, and I was still here.

I was still alive, and I was beginning to feel that way at last.

Getting close to Aiden, physically and emotionally, had been a way through that door, and I wasn't about to turn around. No matter how strange it seemed, and not the life I'd expected, I needed to embrace my circumstances and make the most of them.

"Are you okay?" Aiden asked, coming near to me and gazing at me with kindness.

"Yes. I'm good. More than good. Look at this place."

"Oh, I'm looking." He took my hand. "Come on."

He led me to the space that was farthest away from us, which seemed to be the most intense section of the room, designed for serious bondage and impact play, with kink furniture I'd never seen up close and personal — only online.

Aiden led me to a wooden pillory standing innocently in the center of the space and dropped my hand.

"Wow. Will you look at this!"

He lifted the wood bar on its hinge to make space for someone to put their head and wrists inside. The creak of the hinge echoed as he raised it.

"Well?" he turned to me with a devilish grin. "What are you waiting for?"

I gave him a skeptical look. "Seems extreme for our first time."

The hinge squeaked again as he lowered the bar.

I moved a few feet to a different piece of kink furniture.

"This looks like an intriguing contraption," I said.

It seemed like it was built for a person to be strapped in on their front, with cut-outs that exposed their face and genitals, then maneuvered into whatever position was desired.

"That's a Berkley Horse!" Aidan squealed, with such delight that I gave a start.

"A what now?"

"This is incredible. I've never seen one in real life."

"Huh," I said.

"Your face goes here," Aiden said, giving me a wink, "and your other bits can be got to, and someone can paddle your ass while you're played with. It's ingenious."

I immediately pictured myself in the contraption with Aiden in control of my bits and my backside.

"Ingenious," I whispered, staring at the device as my pants got tighter. The submissive side of my personality was still here.

Aiden watched me, the sound of my breathing loud in the space.

"You like that idea," he said finally. "I can tell."

I forced myself to meet his gaze, but I couldn't speak. My body was an inferno all of a sudden, as if a dragon had been sleeping and now it had awakened.

"Yes," I admitted. "But..."

"You don't want to do it right now."

I didn't answer, because the truth was I wasn't sure. Part of me did want to do it now—and we *could*. We had the room for an hour. But it was diving into the deep end when we'd only planned to check the place out and discuss it.

"Or do you?" Aiden asked, coming close to me and lifting the hair by my ear. He kissed my neck and placed his hand around my throat, forcing my chin up as I gasped a breath of air.

"Yes," I said.

We breathed in tandem, his excitement as tangible as my own.

"How many men have you dommed?" I asked, curiosity overpowering my mouth filter.

He stared at me for a long moment. "Is this an interview question?"

I huffed. It was supposed to be a laugh but sounded more like a gasp.

"No. I'm curious."

He shrugged. "I don't know. Quite a few, but that was years ago. I haven't dommed anyone in a long time."

"How come?"

He smiled, shrugged. "I got bored of doing it just for kicks."

"Oh. But...do you want to dominate me?"

"Maybe. Do you want me to dominate you?"
I let out a long, quavering sigh. "Yes."

Chapter Seven

Taking Liberties

"Fletcher, we can do that, if you want."

"So…you don't do it for fun anymore?"

"Well…not just for fun. I don't meet strangers for the express purpose of getting kinky with them, if that's what you mean."

I focused on breathing and on my hard, standing cock that wanted nothing but to be controlled and managed.

"Can we?"

"Yes," he said, turning my head toward him and making his grip on my neck more confining — enough that it took effort to get another breath.

We gazed at each other, and my heart pounded, roaring between my ears.

"Okay," I said.

Aiden closed his eyes and took a shuddering breath as he relaxed his hold on my throat. I almost cried. That was what I'd needed — a firm hand to hold me still, a will to guide me toward my own desires. I missed that so much.

"We're supposed to talk about limits and all that sort of thing."

"I know," I said. "But I don't care about that right now. I just want to...to try it."

I looked at the Berkley Horse.

"Okay. I'll be careful to get your consent for everything I do."

"God, yes," I hissed, aflame with desire.

All I wanted was right here in front of me. I just needed Aiden to make me take it.

"All right, then," he said, removing his velvet jacket and rolling up his sleeves. He loosened his tie. I was transfixed by his hands and forearms as he came near to me.

"I'm going to undress you. I want you naked, but you're going to let me do it."

"Yes...Sir?"

"That's right. That word sounds so good in your mouth."

Aiden stepped close and took the edges of my jacket in his hands, pushing it back and off of my shoulders as I tried to keep breathing.

I was incredibly attracted to Aiden. We'd become progressively intimate over the past few weeks. We'd started fucking. But this...this was something else.

This Aiden was *someone* else...a someone I was reacting to as if being near him for the first time. So far, I'd met the self-effacing supply teacher, the easygoing band member and the charming man-about-town.

This was something else. There were so many layers to him. As he peeled the clothes off of my pliant form, I saw past those other things and to the heart of him.

He took my jacket and draped it over the closed pillory, as if we were in Aiden's home and not a kink room in the back of a club. He came back and took hold of the bottom of my sweater, meeting my gaze.

"You need a safeword."

"Do I?"

"Yes."

"Fine. I'll use..." A safeword came unbidden to me—the one I'd used before—but I pushed it away as soon as it came. I was going to choose a new one. My gaze flitted about the room and latched onto the vintage lamp by the bed. "Lamp," I said, my voice husky. I was literally being tortured by Aiden's nearness, the promise of this room and the things in it— and the way it had changed Aiden into someone who seemed to know and see the real me.

"Arms up," he said.

I lifted my arms over my head, the movement causing my pants to tug at my erection, which made me moan.

"Oh, honey," Aiden murmured, "I know."

He drew the sweater over my head and off my arms, then did the same with my white T-shirt, piling all my clothes on the pillory.

"Glad it has other uses," I joked with a half-hearted smile. I was too caught up and aroused to smile fully. I could barely keep my composure.

I wanted to kneel. The urge was so strong I had to fight it with everything I had, at least until he commanded it. And probably I should wait until I was naked.

I didn't know if I could.

When I was bare above the waist, Aiden drew his fingers along my shoulder and down my arm, taking my hand.

"You want this."

"Yes."

"All right. For God's sake, use the word 'lamp' if you want me to stop at any point...for *any* reason."

"Mmm."

"Fletcher? Promise me?"

"Yes, Sir. I promise."

"Good. I'm going to take your pants off now."

I nodded, going tingly all over as Aiden's fingers went to my belt. The buckle rattled as he undid it and drew it through the loops, then tossed it onto the floor with a clang.

"Sorry."

"Don't be sorry," I said. "This is... This is...everything."

"Good."

He worked my fly open and yanked my trousers and boxer briefs down to my thighs in one quick motion. My cock bobbed free and eager in the air, moist with longing at the circumcised tip. I cursed.

Aiden grinned. "What's the matter?"

"Nothing, Sir. I just... I'm so horny."

"I can see that...easily."

He pulled my pants down the rest of the way, and I stepped out of them. Then he took my socks off one by one, which might have seemed silly if I wasn't already deep into subspace—a place I hadn't been for a long time and which welcomed me with open arms.

"Are you okay with this, Fletcher?"

As an answer and because I couldn't resist it anymore, I sank to my knees on the rug before him, bowing my head and placing my hands on my thighs.

Aiden took a deep breath.

"Okay. I take it you're fine with it." he asked, cupping my chin in his hand and tilting my face up.

And suddenly I was in a different room, in a different time, with a different man.

Daniel's hand was rough with callouses from his work in the garden as he cradled my chin and gazed down at me.

"You are so fucking beautiful. I can't even stand it," he said.

My heart pulsed with love for this man…and submission.

I didn't say anything. I wasn't allowed to speak unless I need to safeword. I closed my eyes.

When I opened them, a different face stared down at me.

I gasped at the concerned look in Aiden's dark brown eyes, so different from Daniel's blue ones.

"Are you okay?" he asked.

I blinked rapidly and swallowed. "Yes. Only, it's been a long time."

Understanding dawned in Aiden's eyes, and he took his hand away, then nodded.

"You look good on your knees."

I smiled.

"That's what…" I cleared my throat. "That's what Daniel always said."

Aiden regarded me with such affection. "Probably because it's true."

"Probably."

"Tell me if anything I'm doing is upsetting you — or use your safeword. Either is fine. All right?"

"All right. Is it…?" I wanted to ask something, but I wasn't sure what his answer would be. "Would it be…acceptable…if I started to cry…at some point, Sir? Because I can't promise I won't."

Aiden frowned but then smiled. "Fletcher, you can react however you need to. You're safe with me. I promise."

I sighed, and it felt like years of tension leaving my body.

"Thank you," I whispered.

My arousal had not flagged at all through this, and I was reassured that I wanted *Aiden*, that I wanted *this*, and that I could think of Daniel—remember Daniel— and that was all right. It wasn't his ghost, but it was a part of him that would always be with me…and that was a good thing.

"All right. Come with me," Aiden said, beckoning me to stand and follow.

The gesture was something different. Daniel would have simply told me to follow. But Aiden used a familiar motion to show me what he wanted. I needed to stop comparing them, but it was difficult not to, when Aiden was only the second man to have taken me in hand like this.

He walked me over to the Berkley Horse.

"Stand there. Keep still."

I felt Aiden's hand drift down from my shoulder blade, over my back and the curve of my ass.

"Fuck, you are so perfect."

He gave me a swat—hardly anything, really—but the way he delivered it, with casual intention, then moved on, made me shiver. It sent me to a place that was familiar and welcome. I was drifting on endorphins and need already, and hardly required anything else.

Oh, but I wanted to be strapped to the Berkley Horse.

"Here we are," Aiden said, and in a moment he'd wrapped leather cuffs around my ankles and wrists. Soon I was strung up on the historical piece of equipment with my genitals and chest and face accessible from one side, and the entirety of my back available from the other, for whatever he desired. The polished surface of the wood was cold on my bare skin but it would warm up soon.

I tested the strength of the cuffs while I stared at the floor through the face hole and tried to remember how to breathe.

"Okay?" Aiden asked, stroking my ass again. I loved that he couldn't keep his hands off me, especially how focused he was on my ass.

"Yes, Sir."

"Good," he said, then brought his hand down on my ass three times, hard, in succession. The sound rang out in the large room.

I moaned, and Aiden laughed. Then he roughly parted my ass cheeks and swiped a finger over my clenching hole as I stuttered a gasp.

"Now I have you right where I want you."

"Yes, Sir."

My voice sounded strange, as if I were miles underwater. I saw myself strapped to this bizarre contraption for Aiden's pleasure and felt like I was home.

He swatted me with his palm for several moments, until I squirmed and yelped.

Then he laughed. "I've barely started."

He came around in front of me.

"Having fun, slut?" he asked with an absolutely joyful smile, right before he wrapped my cock in his hand and gave it a few strokes.

"Oh, fuck...fuck!" I cursed, feeling overwhelmed in the best of ways. I was teetering on the edge, and we'd only just begun.

"Answer me."

Aiden swiped his fingers over the leaking tip of my cock and spread the fluid around as he teased me, jerking me and tickling the underside and my taint and balls. I panted and groaned and struggled.

God, it felt good to be managed! All the stress of being a single father with a deceased partner disappeared, and all I could think about was how Aiden was making me feel.

"Yes! Yes, please don't stop."

"Why would I stop?" Aidan asked. "I'm having fun, too," he said, going behind me again and delving between my cheeks with wet fingers. "Oooh, yes, so soft and pretty here. Whoever could have known that I'd be fingering you in the Bordello at Maverick Molly's on our first visit?"

As he spoke, he rubbed at my hole and teased it open, sinking a finger in deep as I choked on air.

"Oh, yeah. What an ass."

He pumped me with his finger, then added another as I struggled, as my cock dripped and my submissive heart pounded in triumph.

"Yes," I whispered.

He withdrew his fingers and slapped my ass, hard. "All right, now. Let's get serious."

Then he was right in front of me. But he didn't grab my dick. He looked at me instead.

"Want the paddle or the whip? This might be the only time I ever give you a choice, so choose wisely."

My brain swirled with memories and desires, and it took some concentration to form the word.

"Leather paddle. Please. Please, Aiden."

"Hmm. How did you know that was my favorite?" he said, pinching my chin and smiling as if I'd just told him my preferred kind of cookie. "Hold still. Let me see what we have to work with."

Aiden disappeared again, and I closed my eyes, listening to his soft muttering as he searched for his tool.

"This'll do. You want to see it?"

"Yes, Sir."

When he held up the narrow brown leather and showed me how flexible it was and even brought it down with a swack against his palm, I almost cried.

"Yes. *Yes.*"

"All right. Count for me, because that way I'll know you want it. Count if you accept what I'm dishing out. Safeword if you want me to stop. Okay?"

"Yes, Sir."

"Such a good slut," he crooned, and it was everything. My breathing was loud, and my heart pounded in my ears as he moved behind me.

"These are just practice. Don't count yet," he said, using it very lightly to give me a sense of its shape and potential impact. He didn't realize how desperate I was. Perhaps my eager whimpers gave it away.

"All right," he said. "We start now."

He landed a powerful strike against my bottom that made fire bloom and liquid surge from my dick.

"One!" I said, in a helpless voice that expressed everything I loved about this.

"Damn," Aiden said, before landing another.

"Two! Oh fuck, yes, yes, yes." I whimpered, thrilled to be used and abused when I'd gone without it for so long.

"Three. Four. Five," I counted as Aiden warmed my ass with skill and precision.

"Five more. Safeword if it's too much."

"It's not. Six. Seven. Eight. Nine! *Ten!*"

I came on ten, with a yell as my body spasmed in its restraints, and all my pent-up need spilled onto the floor as I babbled incoherently. When I finally started coming down, I became aware of Aiden's hands on me, soothing me and stroking me, his lips on my shoulder and his surprised curses.

"Oh, fuck yes," Aiden murmured. "That was...*fuck*. I didn't expect you to get off like that."

Really? He was surprised that I'd come hands free from a good round with a leather paddle? If he thought that was amazing, I had a lot to show him. I was a trigger release kind of guy, and impact play was one of those triggers. But I had more...lots more.

Some Doms didn't like a sub being so reactive, but others saw it as a challenge and a minor fault that would take lots of delicious sessions to correct. I had a feeling that Aiden was one of the latter ones, like Daniel had been.

Daniel had taught me control. Daniel had taken great pains to teach me to save my release for the moment he permitted it. But it had been a long time since I'd been in any kind of kinky situation, and it looked like Aiden would have to start from square one.

I didn't think he minded.

He unbuckled me from the contraption and made me kneel again. He still had his clothes on, except for the jacket. His sleeves were rolled up, tie loosened, and he looked like a professor who had gotten pissed off at a student, which totally worked for me—especially when he folded his arms over his chest and gazed at me with a stern expression.

"Why are you looking at me like that?" Aiden asked, bemused.

"I..." It was still hard to talk. "I like the way you look, Sir."

"Yeah? The clothes or...?" He raised his eyebrows.

"Partly. But also, you look stern and...*professorial*."

Aiden smiled. "Well, now. That's a hell of a promotion."

I smiled, remembering his job.

"Well, you look the part."

"Thank you." He stroked my head as I floated in a heady, relaxed state. "But I'm going to work on that hair-trigger reflex of yours."

I nodded, because I knew that working on my sexual control was everything I needed right now — to take my mind off of my grief, to return to something that made me feel safe, and to find another person who could manage me when I needed it.

It was early days, and I didn't know yet if Aiden could be that person. But even if it didn't last, I knew in my heart and soul and through my whole body that Aiden could give me what I desperately needed right *now*.

He seemed to be thinking about what to do with me. I didn't say anything, because in this room, Aiden was my Dom, and he needed to figure things out. I was sure that soon we would sit down and have a discussion about what had gone on here, about the needs that I had, about the things I wanted to do and about the things that Aiden wanted out of this. But right now, he was in charge and navigating this entire experience. So far, he was exceeding my expectations.

"I want you to suck my cock, Fletcher. Will you do that?" he asked, his hands going to the buckle of his belt.

I sighed. "Yes, Sir. Of course, Sir. Whatever you want, Sir," I said, flashing my gaze to his.

His eyes widened and he smiled, and the unspoken understanding that passed between us made me feel more at peace and *actually seen*, than I had for a very long time. I felt like a balloon that had been aimlessly floating about, and now Aiden had taken hold of my string and was keeping me from disappearing into oblivion.

The clang of metal and the rub of leather on denim echoed in the large room as Aiden undid his belt then his fly, digging his cock out of his drawers as my mouth filled with saliva. I could smell him. I could smell my earlier release that hadn't been dealt with. Daniel had sometimes made me clean up my own mess, but I didn't think Aiden would do that—at least, not yet.

We'd talked about the level of risk we were comfortable with in our physical relationship and were awaiting test results so we could bareback without worry, but we'd decided that swallowing was worth the negligible risk.

"Come here," Aiden said, beckoning me with a curl of his long fingers. He liked that gesture and so did I, maybe because Daniel *hadn't* done that. Daniel's commands had been short and terse, and if I hadn't obeyed them right away, he would have been displeased. And I hadn't minded. I had loved how demanding and rough he'd been. But Aiden had a softer way about him. It was possible that I was getting the Dom-lite experience, since we were so new to playing the game together, but I liked his kindness and patience in this sphere. I needed that as much as I needed a firm hand. Maybe, once we got to know each other better, he would be sterner and rougher with me. But right now, I felt like a skittish colt and his manner was perfect.

I shuffled closer to him and again laid my head against his thigh, to let him know that I was happy, and he was doing everything I wanted.

He stroked my hair then wrapped some around his fingers and guided my face to his cock.

"Suck, Fletcher. Do a good job. Make me come."

I opened my mouth and took him in, gazing up with an adoration I felt deep inside. He hadn't known how desperately I'd needed this. I hadn't known, either.

He dropped his chin and puffed air out of his mouth as I got to work with all of my substantial skills.

"Oh, yeah. Oh, hell."

Aiden's cock was obviously different, too. Uncircumcised and bigger than Daniel's had been, I had to stretch my mouth to accommodate him. A strange image came to mind, of Daniel standing behind me in the Bordello, and watching, making sure that I pleased my new Dom the way I'd pleased him.

The thought thrilled me. We'd never shared our sexual or personal lives with another person, but I felt him here, in this room, with Aiden and me, and it was astonishingly comforting. I sucked and licked and deep-throated Aiden as he poured words of appreciation and praise upon me.

Finally, I could tell he was getting close. His hold on my hair tightened, and he held me still as he pumped my throat once, twice then came with a sigh and a curse as I held my breath and swallowed.

"Oh fuck, fuck, *fuck*..." he groaned, his gaze on me even more adoring and approving. "Oh, my fucking God."

He made soft sounds as he rode his climax, and I kept swallowing and sucking until he pulled carefully out and took a step back, tucking himself away.

"Here," he said, offering me his hand.

I ignored it and pushed myself into a standing position, using my thighs. My bones protested but I managed it. I was older now, with knees that sometimes complained, but I was far from being unable to comport myself well.

"Fletcher, you should accept help if it's offered," Aiden said.

"Yes, Sir," I said. But I was jubilant, and nothing could take away this triumphant feeling of renewal that tugged at my heart and filled me with warmth and light.

Chapter Eight

Trauma

"You can get dressed," Aiden said.

"Yes, Sir."

I put on my clothes slowly and methodically, because I was reluctant to get out of the headspace and worried I'd have a big drop from such an impactful experience.

Aiden grabbed his jacket and beckoned me to come to him. God, that gesture. I loved it so much. When I got there, he put his hands on my shoulders and stared into my eyes.

"Thank you for that," he said. "I enjoyed every minute of it."

"You're welcome," I said, suddenly self-conscious. But that feeling went away as soon as he leaned in and kissed me with care and concern.

"Let's go have another drink, now that our scene is over."

"All right. But...won't everyone know what we've been up to?"

Aiden laughed. "Hopefully."

He took my hand and led me out of the room, locking the door behind us. He kept holding it as he took me back to the gaming parlor.

I was a grown man. Believe me, I knew how to be an adult. I had a twelve-year-old child and a deceased husband. I paid bills and made appointments and dealt with clients.

But for an hour, I had been able to forget about all of it. I felt lighter and more relaxed than I had in years, and it was all thanks to this man. He dropped my hand as we entered the parlor but I followed him to a table like a well-behaved puppy.

"Sit," he said, using a gesture to indicate where he wanted me.

I sat. He must have sensed that I still needed his guidance as I slowly resumed the trappings of my regular existence. He took the key to the bar where Jacob was serving a customer.

Cheeky Robin appeared out of nowhere, batting his eyelashes and grinning.

"Well, well, well. Back for a little something after a little...something?"

"Hi, Robin. We're not ready to leave yet," I said.

"Wonderful. I'm glad you're enjoying everything Maverick Molly's has to offer." He looked me up and down and put a finger to his chin, tilting his head. "Are you escaping a stressful corporate job? Or do you" — he looked around to make sure no one was in listening distance — "work for the government?"

"No, I'm an editor."

"Oh!" He seemed surprised. "A wordsmith!"

I laughed. He was so damn cute, and I was feeling so relaxed. No sub drop so far, just a feeling of peace and familiarity. Maybe a drop would come later? I decided to roll with it and stop trying to predict everything.

"More of a bricks and mortar kind of thing," I explained.

"Do you write?"

Robin's questions charmed me. He seemed genuinely interested in my life.

"I have. Not recently."

"Oh." He frowned. "How come?"

I blinked, not expecting such a personal question.

"I'm…well…I have a kid."

"Oh!"

"And my husband died a few years ago. So, I'm a single dad."

He put a hand to his mouth in an almost comical level of pity for me. "Oh, you poor thing!"

The response was so genuine and so unexpected that I burst out a laugh just as Aiden returned with two whiskey sours. He placed one on the table in front of me and smiled at Robin.

"What's the joke?"

Robin frowned. "This poor, poor man."

Aiden looked confused.

"Fletcher?"

"Does *he* know?" Robin asked, gesturing at Aiden.

"Yes, he knows."

"About the husband that died. And the twelve-year-old. How awful!"

It seemed as if Robin felt equally horrified at the death of my husband and the fact that I had to care for a twelve-year-old. For once, the acknowledgment of Daniel's death didn't hit me like a dump truck. Robin was such a genuine and adorable presence, and I was still floating from my experience with Aiden in the Bordello.

I glanced at Aiden. "I'm adjusting."

Robin smiled. "That's good. I always say, grab life with two hands and jump. You know, make the most of it."

"I agree," Aiden said. He sat back and smiled at me contemplatively, looking older than he was.

"What?" I asked.

He shrugged as Robin left to attend to the other customers.

"You look like a burden has been lifted. I can't help but hope it's because of..."

"It is. I'm sure tomorrow the weight of it all will come crushing down again. But right now, I feel...good. Like, really good."

"Well, that makes me happy."

"Thank you for taking such good care of me."

"Anytime, babe. I mean that. I'm up for a visit to Molly's whenever you have time or whenever Patrick can watch Lucy," he said. "I may have just become a paying member of this very special place."

He held up a laminated card with the club's name embossed in gold on the front.

"Wow. You're easy," I said with a grin.

"When it comes to accessing all that equipment? I sure am," he said. "And, besides, we get discounts on drinks."

* * * *

When I put in my code on the front door lock a little after eleven, both dogs came up to me, whining.

"Shhh. Don't wake Lucy," I whispered, giving them pats and toeing off my shoes.

I rounded the corner into the living room and saw Patrick sitting up, awake, beside a tearful Lucy.

He glanced over and smiled. "She had a nightmare."

"Oh, Dad!" Lucy said and jumped up to throw her arms around me.

Patrick gave me a sympathetic look as the guilt of not being here when Lucy needed me hit hard.

I hugged her close. "Are you okay?"

Lucy shook her head and started crying. "No."

Patrick got up off the sofa and went into the kitchen, giving us some space.

"Was it about Papa?" Lucy had called Daniel 'Papa' and me 'Daddy'. Now she called me Dad, because she *'wasn't a baby anymore'*.

She nodded. "Yeah."

"Oh, honey," I said, squeezing her. "That's hard."

"I thought it was real. Then I woke up."

I'd had those dreams, too. The nightmare was waking up.

Patrick stood by the door, looking at his phone.

"I called an Uber. It should be here soon," he said.

"Patrick."

He turned to me.

"Thank you."

"Hey, no worries. Did you have a good time?"

"I…I can't even think about that right now."

"Yeah, sorry. She's okay, though. She's a tough kid."

I didn't reply. Patrick was wonderful, but how would he know how tough or not tough Lucy was? He hadn't seen her almost catatonic in the first couple of weeks after Daniel's accident, when I'd been barely functional. He hadn't heard her angry words when she went through that stage of her grief or seen her wracked with sobs a few days later. He hadn't been the one to try to tempt her to eat when she couldn't see past her sense of loss enough to have a snack, let alone a full meal.

As we sat together on the sofa after Patrick had left, I held her close and wished I'd been here instead of at Maverick Molly's with Aiden. I should have been. What gave me the right to have fun when Lucy was still suffering the effects of Daniel's death?

The carefree feeling I'd experienced was an illusion. This was real life.

I held her close, with the dogs sleeping at our feet, for an hour before I carried her to bed. She was getting big, but I could still lift her. In another year or two I probably wouldn't be able to manage it.

I remembered arguing with Daniel about who got to take Lucy to bed when she was small and up in the night. If I'd known what was coming, I'd have let him do it every single time.

I made sure she was still sleeping before I went to my own room, stripped to my boxers and got under the covers. I laid there for a long time, trying to get back to that feeling of peace and ease that I'd experienced at the club, but it was no use.

Maybe this was finally my sub drop. Moisture gathered in my eyes, and I did the only thing I could think of.

Aiden picked up the phone after a couple of rings.

"Hey. What's going on?" Aiden asked in a sleep-filled voice.

I'd woken him.

"Aiden, I—" was all I could get out before the tears came in earnest.

"Fletcher? Are you dropping?" he asked, with what sounded like a yawn.

"I don't know. I don't know."

"You're probably dropping. It doesn't always happen right after. I'm glad you called," he said, his voice filled with kindness.

"Yeah."

"Has Patrick gone home?"

"Yeah. I'm sorry."

"No, I'm glad you called me."

I played with the edge of my comforter. "Lucy had a nightmare while I was gone."

"Yeah? Is she okay?"

I sighed. "She's asleep now."

There was a long silence when all I could hear was Aiden's soft breaths.

"Fletcher?"

"I should have been here," I blurted.

"But…Patrick was there."

"*I* should have been here."

Silence again.

"Aiden, I had so much fun with you…at Molly's. It was wonderful, and I definitely needed that, but…I think I need to take some time."

More silence.

"All right. If that's what you need, you can have it."

He wasn't angry — and for that I was grateful.

"You're not mad?" I asked, my voice barely there.

"Why would I be mad?"

"I don't know."

"I'm sad. I'll miss seeing you. Please call me if you change your mind."

"Okay," I said, knowing I wouldn't. "Thanks."

Lucy was my priority. She was the only thing I had left of Daniel, and I needed to keep her safe. If that meant sacrificing my own personal fulfillment, that was the way it had to be.

I took a deep breath. This was so hard. "Thank you for everything, Aiden."

"You're welcome, Fletcher. I—"

"Goodbye, Aiden."

"Goodbye, then."

After I ended the call, a wave of relief hit me. This was the right thing to do. This was what you had to do when you were a parent, especially a single parent. You had to make your child the number-one priority.

* * * *

"Lucy, you need to get ready faster. We're going to be late!" I said, throwing some treats to the dogs. I'd let her have the day off school to attend a therapy appointment, and we were going to spend the afternoon together doing something fun.

"Almost ready!"

When Lucy came downstairs, she was wearing the strangest outfit I'd ever seen and the words were out of my mouth before I could stop them.

"Absolutely not. Go get changed."

She leveled me a glare. "You can't tell me what to do. It's my body."

Oh, here we go.

"Lucy. Go put on some unripped jeans."

"Dad!"

"Where did you get those?"

"At the thrift store."

"I think you got gypped. Half of them are missing."

They were ripped in several places, one of those spots being on the upper thigh, a little too close to areas that should not be exposed.

"Dad, all my friends wear jeans like these!"

"I don't give a fuck if half the city is wearing them. You're not."

She crossed her arms over her chest. "You know, for a gay dad, you really disappoint me sometimes," she said. "You can't actually see my ass. And anyway, why do *you* get to decide?"

I blew out a breath, sorry I'd even started this. I was usually big on bodily autonomy, but I was also big on appropriate social expectations in some situations.

"It looks…you know" — *Don't say it. Don't say it* — "slutty," I said it, digging myself in deeper.

"Really, Dad? You're going to slut shame me? Why is my female body automatically considered sexual?"

We stared at each other for a long moment, and I decided I didn't actually care and wasn't going to die on this hill. And, she had a point.

"Fine. I don't give a fuck. Let's go."

"Oh, wow. Great parenting there."

"Just get in the car."

Lucy and I had been on each other's cases for days, and it wasn't like us. We'd had our moments in the past, but for some reason, the last few weeks had been harder. Maybe it was because Lucy had tests and midterms and I had a couple of time-sensitive projects. Or maybe it was the brisk and depressing November weather. Whatever it was, we'd both been short-tempered and irritable.

Lucy listened to music all the way to the therapist's office, so I didn't have to make conversation, then felt guilty for that thought. I felt a burst of rage toward

Daniel for dying right before Lucy became a preteen and leaving me with the stress of parenting a teenager all by myself, then felt guilty for that. Too bad mine wasn't the therapy appointment today.

When I picked Lucy up after her session, her mood had improved.

"Good appointment?" I asked with a smile, determined to make an effort.

"Yep. She complimented my outfit." Lucy gave me a look that only a triumphant twelve-year-old could produce.

"Huh. I guess I'm just an old fogey with outdated attitudes," I said.

"You've got to stop policing my body, Dad."

"I...didn't know that's what I was doing."

"Where are we going for lunch?"

"I don't know. Where do you want to go?"

"How about Milestones?"

"Sure."

We had a wonderful lunch, then found ourselves at the Museum of Nature on McLeod street, right across from Aiden's apartment. I tried to forget about that. It was our favorite of all the museums in Ottawa, and I was glad that Lucy still wanted to go. In a couple of years, she'd probably only want to hang out with her friends at the mall.

"Look at this, Dad!" Lucy said, beckoning me over to a display of pretend dinosaur eggs. "It says that Gallimimus laid eggs in grassy spots near the bottom of cliffs but they were often found and eaten by T-Rexes and Carnataurs."

I loved that Lucy still got giddy over dinosaur facts. I walked over to see the exhibit a bit closer.

A familiar voice sounded from the back corner of the room.

"Connor, one more curse and I'm sending you back to the bus. Come on."

Lucy and I swiveled our heads to see Aiden Thompson in the middle of a gaggle of school-aged kids by the Triceratops display.

"Aiden!" Lucy said, running over before my brain had even caught up to what was happening.

She stopped in front of him, waving her hand enthusiastically.

"Hi!"

"Lucy! How are you?" Aiden said with a huge smile, before turning to his troupe of about six kids. "Guys, stay in this area please. We'll move to the next room in about ten minutes. Don't forget to write down at least three interesting facts about your favorite dinosaur in your notebooks."

Aiden looked even more attractive than I remembered. My dick twitched its recognition of that Dominant tone as well.

Fuck, what was I supposed to do now?

Aiden scanned the area. He found me before I had a chance to hide. He gave me his winning smile, and my will crumpled.

"Mr. Marin. How are you?" he asked, and I almost cried at the formal address. But Lucy hadn't known we'd been dating.

"Good. Lucy had an appointment, and I took her out of school for the day."

"Nice!" He turned back to Lucy. "Playing hooky?"

"Yep. Don't report me."

Aiden lifted his hands. "I would never. It's important to spend time with your dad."

He glanced my way again, and I thought I saw regret and melancholy in his expression.

Fuck.

Now I felt awful. It was so nice to see him. I'd missed him more than I'd expected. My life was busy, and I didn't have much time to mope. But, lying in bed at night, I'd recalled our time together with more and more regret that I'd broken up with him.

When I'd thought back to the night of Lucy's nightmare, I'd soon realized that I'd overreacted. I couldn't possibly be home every time something happened, and Patrick had been there because I'd made sure someone was looking after her. Soon, she'd be old enough to stay home in the evening by herself. I couldn't bubble wrap her. And I couldn't sacrifice my happiness for the sake of some misguided idea that I should always be beside her.

In a moment of guilt and possibly sub drop, I'd broken up with someone who had only ever treated me with respect and appreciation, even in the midst of a kinky interlude that had blown my world apart in an entirely positive way.

"What are you doing here?" I asked with a smile, to let him know I was happy to see him.

"I got a frantic call this morning to sub for a teacher that had a trip planned. I was free, so I took the job." He looked around and did a quick head count, then turned back to me. "Luckily, there are two other teachers at the museum, and we've each got six kids to keep track of. It's not too bad."

"You are a fucking saint, Aiden," I murmured, then remembered he'd gotten stern with one of his students for cursing. "Oh shit, sorry," I said, putting a hand over my mouth.

"Nice, Dad," Lucy said, grinning.

"Mr. Marin," Aiden said, in such a teacher-like way it made me blush. "Stop setting a bad example."

There was a twinkle in his eye and a sternness to his tone that went straight to my dick. Our gazes held for several beats.

"Hey, Aiden, you should date my dad."

We turned to see Lucy standing by the Gallimimus exhibit with her hand on her hip and a contemplative look on her face.

"Lucy!" I said. "You don't even know if Aiden is gay."

"Yes, she does," Aiden said.

"Yes, I do," Lucy confirmed.

I look back and forth between them.

"I told the class," Aiden said, and I felt even more affection for him.

"Yeah, and it was epic," Lucy said, "because some of the dudebros in my class are so homophobic. But then the coolest teacher in the school says he's gay, and they don't even know how to deal with it."

Aiden's cheeks went darker. "I'm sure your dad doesn't want to date a guy like me."

"Sure he does. Dad, you'd date Mr. Thompson, right?"

I gave them a nervous smile, determined to get myself out of this mess. Then I realized that I didn't even want to.

"Why not?" I said. "Mr. Thompson is very attractive."

Lucy giggled.

What the fuck am I doing?

Aiden's smile slowly disappeared as he stared at me with his eyebrows raised and a question in his gaze. I couldn't blame him.

Lucy grinned. "Come on, Aiden! My dad's a great guy."

Aiden blinked. "I'm…I'm sure he is."

Lucy looked back and forth between us. "I think it'd be good for my dad to go on a date. He's been really lonely since my papa died."

Lucy looked at me and I looked at her, as heavy emotions rose inside me that I really didn't want to display in the middle of the Nature museum.

"Well, I…"

Aiden dug his phone out of his pocket and handed it to me. "Here. Send yourself a text. Then I'll have your number."

I blinked at him and took his phone. I tapped in my number and a contact came up that read, *Fletcher Marin Do not call!* And my heart squeezed in my chest. I glanced at Aiden and hit edit. I changed the part after my name to *Please call me. I'm so sorry!* and handed the phone back.

The smile that lit up Aiden's face was magical when he looked at it. We stared at each other for a long moment. Then Aiden said, "Great."

"Mr. Thompson, I think one of your kids just left," Lucy said, pointing in the direction of the exit.

"Oh fuck," Aiden cursed. He clamped a hand over his mouth, staring wide-eyed at us, then waved and headed off toward the other room.

"How cool was that?" Lucy said. "You're welcome, by the way."

"Thanks. You're a good matchmaker."

"I know, right?" she said, waltzing off toward another display while I stared wistfully in the direction Aiden had gone.

Chapter Nine

Offside

I waited impatiently for Aiden to contact me. I almost called him, but what right did I have when I'd broken things off?

My phone finally rang with his name three days later while Lucy was hanging out with a friend, and I was just closing my laptop for the evening after submitting an editing job.

I almost dropped my phone, I was so excited. I hit the green circle.

"Aiden, hi!"

"Hello, Fletcher Marin. How are you doing?"

"Hardy har. Cut the pleasantries and please forgive me."

He laughed, and it was the most beautiful sound I'd heard in a while.

"Hey. You needed some time, and I gave it to you. We're good."

"Really? We can just pick up...right where we left off?"

"I take it you missed me?" he said.

"Yes. More than I— More than I thought I would."

He laughed again. "I'm trying to decide if that's an insult."

"It probably is. I'm so sorry."

"Would you stop apologizing? You didn't do anything wrong. I'm glad you took a step back if you needed it. And I'm thrilled to be talking to you again." There was a long silence and the sounds of Aiden's breath. "But I missed you every day...as much as I knew I would."

"Aiden," I said, full of emotion.

"Well, at least we don't have to hide our relationship from Lucy," he said. "But what do we do now? Go on a couple of dates then suddenly we're serious?"

"Well, I'm serious. You should know that. I...I wouldn't be talking to you if I wasn't."

"Fletcher, I feel that way, too. I just hope..."

"What?"

"I hope you don't have to put me through that again. But, honestly, I want to give you what you need, whatever that is."

"I think..." I said. "I think we go on a couple of dates then I start having you over here."

There was silence. "You know, Lucy may feel differently about this if I start coming to the house."

"Hmm. I wonder."

"Don't you think?"

"I suppose there's only one way to find out. She definitely likes you."

He laughed. "So, dinner?"

"Sure. I'd love that."

"I'll kill the spider this time."

"Aiden, I'll never ask you to commit murder for me."

* * * *

After Aiden and I had gone on a dinner date and a movie date with Lucy's knowledge, she grilled me.

"So, Dad, do you like him?"

We were putting the Christmas lights up around the front porch on a warmish day, before the temperature plummeted and the snow fell, which usually happened in December. Daniel had usually done this, and now Lucy and I took pleasure in taking care of it, knowing he'd appreciate that we kept the tradition.

"Yes, I do. Thanks for setting us up."

One day I would tell her that we'd already been dating and that she helped get us back together. Whatever happened, I knew Aiden and I would always be friends — and maybe this thing had longevity. It was too soon to tell.

"You should invite him over here. I could have McDonald's early and you could make Aiden supper," she said, passing me another string of lights.

"How did I know you'd figure out a way to get McDonald's?"

She shrugged. "I'll make the sacrifice."

We hadn't been back to the Bordello, but it was only a matter of time. And my mood was much improved. I realized that, as much as I sometimes felt I should sacrifice my own fulfillment for Lucy's sake, keeping myself happy and having my needs met benefited her, as well as it benefited me. My therapist had pointed that out when I'd told her what had happened.

"Fletcher, it's that analogy of the plane going down and making sure you put your own oxygen mask on first. If you're not functional and happy, nobody else will be."

"Yeah. I'm starting to realize that."

"You can't possibly be there for every little thing Lucy goes through, nor should you be. She's growing up, and she's going to have to figure some things out for herself. Even if Daniel were alive, he wouldn't be there for everything either."

All of that was true. But it was hard to keep that perspective when I felt that Lucy had been so cheated by fate.

My phone chimed mid-morning and I grinned, thinking it was Aiden.

But it was my father-in-law, Brian.

Fletcher, Annie and I would like to have lunch with you tomorrow, if you're free. We have some things we'd like to discuss.

Something felt off about this text.

Of course. Where would you like to meet? And with or without Lucy?

Won't she be in school?

Yes, but I can pull her out for the afternoon.

No. That's fine. It's better we discuss without her.

Okay. Now I was getting warning bells. A deep sense of foreboding formed in my belly.

Daniel's parents were wonderful people and had been a lifesaver after his death. They'd helped a lot with Lucy, even looking after her for a few months while I recovered from the shock of Daniel's death and completed all of the practical requirements of burying my spouse. They'd contributed to the cost of his casket and the funeral, which I hadn't realized would be such a huge expense.

Brian and Annie Marin were a big part of Lucy's life, and I was grateful for the monthly weekends they had her to their bungalow in the west end and for the two weeks that they had her to their cottage in the summer. It gave me a much-needed break from the strains of being a single parent.

But now I was wondering what this meant. Maybe they wanted to set up another tax-free savings account for Lucy's education and needed my consent for the form. It could be anything, but they'd never actually requested a formal meeting with me like this.

My phone chimed again. This time it was Aiden and my mood immediately improved. I decided that I was overreacting to my father-in-law's unexpected request.

Hey there. How's my favorite editor slash single parent?

Gm. I'm good. How are you?

Horny. I'm so horny. Eggplant emoji. Fire emoji. Sad face emoji.

Laughing face emoji. Get a hold of yourself.

Heart eyes emoji. Okay. If I must. Eggplant emoji. Hands together emoji.

Is that a prayer or masturbation?

A little bit of both?

Lol. Good luck.

I want to go back to the Bordello. Even though that's what scared you off, I feel like we really connected.

Me too. FYI Lucy is away this weekend, so if you wanted to come for a sleepover…

Hell, yes. Can we do both?

I don't see why not.

Celebration emoji.

Super happy face emoji

* * * *

I was meeting Brian and Annie at a Denny's near Baseline Road. I swallowed my pride and drove to the restaurant situated in the parking lot of a strip mall.

My father-in-law was waiting for me outside the restaurant. He looked a lot like Daniel, and every time I saw him I was a little bit taken aback by it. His red hair had gotten lighter and coarser, and there were almost as many age spots as freckles now. Some strong emotion hovered right under the surface, but I pushed it down and smiled.

"Hi, Brian. How are you?"

"Fletcher!" Brian said, smiling wide and reaching out to take my hand. He clutched my elbow with his other hand and squeezed. "How are you doing?"

I avoided the question. "Where's Annie?"

"She's sitting inside, saving our table."

Brian led the way to the table where Daniel's mother, Annie, sat tapping on her phone screen. She looked up and smiled when Brian and I approached.

"Fletcher! How nice to see you. Sit down."

"Thanks. I'm starved."

Annie was petite but had a confident way about her. Her graying hair was expertly coiffed, and she wore her makeup in a way that made her look younger than her actual age.

She laughed. "Oh good. So am I and I don't want to look like a pig. They serve breakfast all day, and I'm dying for French toast."

I grabbed a menu and had a look while Brian sat beside Annie.

"The omelets are pretty good," he said. "But I think I'm going to have the chicken sandwich."

"How's Lucy?" Annie asked.

"She's great," I said.

Suddenly, Annie became serious. "How's she fairing at school? Grade seven can be a challenge for kids like Lucy."

I stared at my mother-in-law. "What do you mean?"

"Oh, I just mean for kids who are dealing with other issues."

"Lucy's fine. She's happy."

My mother-in-law smiled, like she didn't quite believe me. "Is she still having nightmares?"

"Annie," Brian cautioned.

"Well, I'm curious. They make her so upset, and I'd like to know if that's still going on."

"Not as often as she used to get them," I said, wary at this line of questioning. "But occasionally, yes, Lucy does have upsetting dreams. But her therapist and mine have both said that's normal in our...situation."

"Of course," Annie said, with a glance at Brian.

At that moment the bubbly server came to take our order.

After she'd left, Anne picked up her napkin and placed it on her lap. She cleared her throat and smiled. "How are the animals?"

"Fine," I said, looking back and forth between her and Brian. Brian was red-faced and seemed like he wanted to be somewhere else. "They're all fine. Look… You said you wanted to talk to me about something. Does it have to do with Lucy?"

"Yes," Annie said. "It does."

"Okay. Can you tell me, please, before I guess something completely wrong…"

"Brian and I," Annie said slowly, "think that Lucy might be better off living in a…a two-parent household."

"A two-parent household," I repeated, a dull ringing starting between my ears.

"Fletcher, we were thrilled when you and our son announced that you were going to have a child, especially when we found out that Lucy was Daniel's biological child. It was a dream come true for us."

"It was a…a dream come true for us, as well," I said, my voice flat.

"Of course. But, Fletcher, we can't help thinking that Daniel — may he rest in peace — would want what's best for Lucy." She glanced at Brian, who nodded in agreement. "Brian and I think she'd be better off living with us."

I stared at Annie, who looked exactly like the Annie I knew who would do anything for Lucy and me. But now she was talking about taking Lucy away from me. I couldn't process it.

"You mean, for a few more weeks in the summer? I'm sure she'd like that. I'll —"

"No, Fletcher, honey. We think Lucy should live with us, full-time. We're going to request full custody."

No, no, no. Not happening.

"You can't do that," I said.

"Well, actually, since Daniel was Lucy's biological—"

I took a deep breath, a sudden, irrational urge to call Aiden for assistance hitting me, which I dismissed, because it wouldn't help and would probably make things worse. Brian and Annie didn't know I was seeing someone.

"No. Sorry, but *no*."

Brian steepled his hands'. "Be reasonable. For a single man — a *gay* man — to raise a child on his own. We don't think it's the best thing for Lucy."

"*I'm* Lucy's father," I said like a man in a dream. "I am what's best for Lucy."

"*Daniel* was Lucy's father, Fletcher," Annie said in a soft, gentle tone. "You were Daniel's *partner.*"

I felt queasy, and like I might have to vomit.

"*Husband.* I was Daniel's *husband.* I am as much Lucy's father as Daniel was. Just because she doesn't have my DNA…it doesn't mean I'm not her father."

"Well, in a court of law…" Brian began to say, and I turned on him.

"Mr. Marin, if your son heard you just now, do you know what he'd tell you?"

Brian shook his head back and forth, but it was more in frustration that I wasn't understanding what they were trying to say.

"He'd tell you that I am as much Lucy's father as he is. We'd never have had Lucy if he wasn't in a committed relationship with me. It was only our love for each other and his dream of having a child that brought Lucy into this world."

"And some help from the miracle of science," Annie muttered under her breath.

I stared at her, my heart breaking. I'd begun to think of her as a parental figure. She'd been so helpful since Daniel's death, and now that was tainted. Now I knew she had only been watching, listening and biding her time until she could use it all to her advantage. I didn't doubt that this was coming from a good place, but who knew what was best for Lucy but *me and Lucy*?

"I need to go," I said, running a hand through my hair.

"But, your French toast!" Annie said, as the server brought our food to the table.

"I don't need any fucking French toast!" I said, getting up and making my way hastily to the doors, gasping for breath and ready to heave the contents of my earlier breakfast onto the potted plants by the entrance.

"Fletcher!" Brian called after me, but I was gone, the door of the restaurant swinging and slamming behind me. My heart pounded in my ears as I tried to remember where I'd parked the car. Clammy sweat pooled in my armpits and behind my knees as I searched for it. I lurched over to the grass and puked, my stomach emptying itself as I gasped and coughed. When I was finished, I started walking aimlessly around the parking lot, before I remembered that I'd parked on the other side.

When I found my car, I unlocked the driver's side door and yanked it open, then got in, slammed it shut, then locked it. I folded my arms on the steering wheel and sobbed.

It reminded me of the moment I'd learned about Daniel's death and the way it had seemed like the Earth was turning too rapidly. I'd felt dizzy and nauseous, like I did now.

They couldn't take Lucy from me. She was all I had left. She was the only thing that got me out of bed some days. And maybe that was selfish, but I knew Lucy wouldn't want to live with Daniel's parents. My home was her home—always had been. She loved those animals as much as she loved me—well, maybe more. Sure, she was still having disturbing dreams about Daniel and his death, but her therapist was working with her on that. And who was to say she wouldn't keep having them if she did move in with Annie and Brian.

Goddamn it, I couldn't even contemplate it. I was Lucy's father, and I was *still here*. There had been a moment, in the aftermath of the accident, after Daniel had been buried and when I was only beginning to understand that I'd have to live the rest of my life without him, when I'd contemplated ending it all. But the next second showed me Lucy's face, and I knew I'd never be able to take the easy way out. She was my anchor, and I had a feeling I was hers.

I was the best person to look after her, and Lucy knew it. They weren't going to rip us apart.

When I was able to pull myself together, I drove home. The dogs could tell I was upset, and they swarmed me and bothered me as I charged upstairs to the bedroom. I noticed how cluttered and in disarray the place was. Maybe Lucy and I were messy, and I didn't tidy up as much as I should. But Lucy helped me with some of the chores, and I made sure to do the basic cleaning every week. Sure, there was dog hair everywhere, and sometimes the dishes weren't washed every day. But I'm sure I wasn't the most slovenly parent out there.

Lucy wouldn't be home from school for a few hours, so I had some time to think about what I was going to do. I had no idea if they could legally request full custody of my child. My name was on Lucy's birth certificate, along with Daniel's and the name of our surrogate, Tamara, which was legally required to be there, even though she had signed over all legal rights to parenting Lucy. Daniel had assured me that in Ontario, I didn't have to go through the process of formally adopting my own child, but now I kind of wished I had. If Annie and Brian could prove I was unfit to be Lucy's parent, maybe they could take her.

The thought made me want to vomit again.

I picked up my phone and found Annie's contact info. I texted her.

Annie, if you say anything about this to Lucy, I will never forgive you. I'm not going to tell her we had this discussion. And know that if you do take me to court over this, I will fight you with everything I have. And you'll be doing more to hurt Lucy, when she's already been hurt so much.

I waited on tenterhooks for her reply. It came about fifteen minutes later.

We didn't mean to upset you, Fletcher. But we will be looking into this. And we may have to ask Lucy what she thinks about it.

I hit the Call button. Annie picked up after a couple of rings.

"Don't you think she's gone through enough?" I said, choking on emotion. "She's so much better than she was, Annie. We're doing really good. I'm so much better now. We're both in therapy."

"Fletcher, I really am sorry, but Brian and I think—"

"Annie, please. I'm begging you not to make Lucy choose. You may not like the outcome, and it's going to cause her so much pain—"

There was a pause. "She's twelve years old, Fletcher. Don't you think a young woman needs a...a female influence?"

I wanted to scream, but I held on to my anger by a thread. "I can't have this conversation with you."

"*You* called *me*, Fletcher. What happens when Lucy starts menstruating? Will you be buying her supplies? Will you be talking to her about sex and all of that?"

The shock and disbelief at those words pushed some of my anger away. I took the phone away from my ear and stared at it in my hand. I tried to stay calm as I lifted it to my ear again.

"Lucy got her first period over a year ago, Annie. I'm surprised she didn't tell you about it." Yeah, that was a dig. "We talk about all kinds of things, including various topics in sexuality, gender and feminism." I put a hand to my forehead. "Just because I wasn't born with a vulva and a uterus doesn't mean I'm incapable of understanding the female perspective."

There was a tiny snort, but then an apology. "I'm sorry. You're probably right."

Probably?

"I'm sorry, Fletcher, but I can't help thinking that it would be better for Lucy to live with us. I have to go, but we need to continue this discussion. Please be open minded and consider our viewpoint. We've lost our son, and we'd like to raise his daughter. Goodbye."

She disconnected, and I was left staring at my phone with increasing rage and a sense of helplessness. I wanted to throw it across the room, like a frustrated adolescent. But I needed to be mature, and handle this like a grown man.

And I needed to tell someone.

I texted Aiden.

Hi, can I call you?

Chapter Ten

Keeping Secrets

In a second my phone was ringing. I hit Answer.

"What's up? Is this a booty call?"

If only.

"I'm so sorry to bother you. I just... I need to talk to someone." I made a noise halfway between a laugh and a sob.

"Fletcher, are you okay?"

"No. I'm not. Can you come over?"

"Sure. Tell me what's going on. You're not hurt, are you?"

"Not physically."

"Fletcher..."

"Daniel's parents... They want to take Lucy away from me."

There was a pause. "What?"

I took a deep breath to keep from screaming. "They want custody of our daughter."

"Oh my God. Is that what they wanted to tell you at lunch?"

"Yes. I'm just back. I didn't eat. I left right after they told me."

"I'll be there as soon as I can. When does Lucy get home?"

I checked the time. "In about two hours."

"All right. See you soon."

"Bye."

In retrospect, as I sat there on the living room sofa with the dogs around me, I wondered why my first instinct had been to call Aiden. I had friends that I'd known longer than I'd known him. But...I didn't want to tell them something so personal. Aiden knew me by now, mostly, and he knew Lucy. I guess I trusted him and respected him enough to value his opinion and input.

Aiden made me feel safe. And that was what I needed most right now, after the rug had been pulled out from under me.

While I waited for Aiden, instead of curling into a ball on my bed and sobbing, which was what I wanted to do, I took the dogs for a walk. The sun was shining, although it was a bit cold, and I needed to see that the Earth was still turning and the trees were still standing, even when I felt that my entire world was at its end.

Owning dogs might be messy and inconvenient, but the overall benefit to Lucy's and to my health was worth it. I didn't want to think about Lucy living with Annie and Brian full-time, without any animals to whisper her secrets to in the dark of night. It wasn't going to happen. I wouldn't let it happen. It was bullshit that they'd even proposed the idea, and they didn't have any legal claim on Lucy. She was my daughter, full stop.

By the time I got home, I felt much more in control of the situation. I needed to call a lawyer for advice, but I wanted to talk to Aiden first.

He showed up with a box of donuts and two coffees.

"I didn't know what you needed more, caffeine or treats, so I got both."

"Thanks. Come on in."

Aiden toed off his boots, and I put the coffee tray and bag of goodies on the coffee table.

"Fuck, Fletcher. What the hell? They can't take Lucy away from you."

"My name's on her birth certificate. She's my daughter."

"Do they have any parental rights because of being...blood related to Lucy?"

"I looked up the rules in Ontario, and as long as I'm her legal parent by birth, which is evidenced by the birth certificate, I don't think they can overrule my rights as a parent."

"Good!"

"Unless..."

"Unless *what*?"

"Unless they can prove I'm unfit."

"But you're not! You're a wonderful father to Lucy!"

I reached for Aiden's hand. "Thank you. I mean, I try."

I looked around at the house. Even with some of the clutter put away it was far from ideal. "The place could be a little cleaner and tidier."

"Fletcher."

"It's hard to keep up, you know? With the dogs and the two of us..."

Aiden took my face between his hands. "Fletcher, look at me. This house is fine. There aren't vermin and feces everywhere, I take it? I don't see any."

"No. But..."

"But what?"

"Is this really the best place...for Lucy?" I asked. It was the thing that scared me deep down, the feeling that maybe, just maybe, Annie and Brian were right.

Aiden kissed me, then gave me a little shake of the shoulders. He gazed into my eyes like he did in the Bordello when he was getting me to focus.

"The best place for Lucy is with the only dad she has left. The best place for Lucy is with *you*."

I nodded. "Thank you."

"You're welcome." He shrugged. "I'm only telling you what you already know."

I rubbed my face. "Goddamn it. I was starting to feel better. It's been rough since Daniel died. I miss him so much, Aiden."

He squeezed my hand. "I can't even imagine how hard it must have been, how hard it *still is* to parent Lucy on your own. But as far as I can see, you're doing a bang-up job. And I'm furious at them for making you doubt that."

We sat in silence for a little bit. Aiden passed me a coffee and put the donuts on plates, passing one to me.

"She's going to their place for the weekend," I said, after I'd had a sip of coffee and a bite of donut. At least the urge to be sick had left me. "I kind of wish she wasn't, except I was honestly looking forward to a bit of a break. Now I feel guilty about that."

"That doesn't mean you don't want to be her parent. In what universe would it mean that?"

"It makes me nervous to have her stay with them now. I feel like they might put things into her head, you know? To convince her that she's better off with them."

"Can you cancel?"

I shook my head. "Lucy would be devastated. She loves spending time with them, which is fantastic. I don't think she wants to live there, though." I lifted my hands as if I had no idea about anything anymore. "But who knows?"

We sat in silence for a bit longer, sipping our coffees. Then Aiden turned to me.

"Okay, look. This is how I see it, but feel free to disagree. Letting Lucy's grandparents have access is a non-issue, right? It's important for them, and it's important for Lucy."

"Right. I'd never in my wildest dreams deny them that. It's another connection to Daniel, and they all need it."

"Okay. So she goes to their place for the weekend, and you and me have a good time, and we take your mind off the things Daniel's parents said to you and any future challenges in that area. Because the alternative is that you brood and worry, and I'm not having it."

Aiden sounded so firm in his resolve to look after me. I couldn't say no.

"I want to call a lawyer," I said.

"Absolutely." He looked at his watch and showed me the time. "You'd better do that now, because in a few hours they'll all be going home to start their weekend."

"Yeah."

He leaned in and gave me a kiss on the cheek.

142

"Look… I'm gonna go. Call the lawyer, and get some advice. Take Lucy to her grandparents' place then call me. I'll pick up some takeout on my way back here, and we can have a sleepover."

"Okay," I said, relieved that he didn't want to go anywhere.

"I've, uh, booked the Bordello for tomorrow night. I was going to surprise you…"

This news, instead of making me feel guilty, gave me a huge sense of relief. "Really?"

"Do you want to go? I can probably get my money back if I cancel before tomorrow."

"Aiden, I think I need to go. If anything can get my mind off of this whole mess, it's being with you in that place."

Aiden smiled. "I was hoping you'd say that."

* * * *

When Lucy got home, I pretended everything was normal.

"Hey, Dad, maybe you can have Aiden for a sleepover," Lucy said, as I drove her to Brian and Annie's, wondering how I was going to act natural when I dropped her off.

She waggled her eyes and gave me a cheeky grin.

"But my Batman pajamas are in the laundry," I said.

She snorted. "I don't think Aiden would mind if you didn't wear pajamas."

"Oh my God, Lucy!"

"Oh my God, Dad!" she said. "I know what happens when two guys who are into each other have a 'sleepover'," she said, using air quotes.

"No, you don't. Come on."

"Yeah, I do."

I gave her a skeptical glance. "And how do you know that?"

"It's called the internet," she said, with the smugness of a generation. "You can look up all sorts of things."

"You...what...? I mean, Lucy! Really?" I was shocked and didn't entirely believe her, because I was aware that she liked getting a reaction, but I also didn't want to shame her for being curious. It was a difficult line to walk.

"Dad, relax. I think it's gross, but no grosser than what straight couples do. *Ick*. I might never have sex. With anyone."

"Jesus Christ," I said, with a sigh. I was glad she wasn't in a hurry to be sexually active, no lie, but this conversation was getting to be really uncomfortable.

"But you should totally take advantage of the fact that I'll be at Granny and Grandpa's."

My heart ached from the knowledge that Annie and Brian wanted Lucy and her commitment to shock value full-time. I didn't know if they were ready for that, and it amused me to think that they were in no way prepared for it.

"Listen," I said. "I want you to know that, even though being a parent can be hard sometimes, I love being your dad."

She gave me a weird look. "O-kaaay. Thanks?"

"Just know that I would do anything for you, Lucy."

She narrowed her eyes. "Dad, what's wrong?"

I forced myself to laugh. It sounded so hollow and fake, but I went with it.

"Nothing. Nothing's wrong. I just love you so much."

"I know. I...love you, too." She was looking at me strangely, and I realized I might have revealed too much.

"What? I wanted to say it. I don't say it enough." I said, backpedaling.

"Dad, don't go all Hallmark on me. It's embarrassing."

I raised my hands. "Sorry. I'm sorry."

I got out of the car, and Lucy exited on her side. She was still looking at me a bit strangely, like she knew something was up but couldn't quite figure it out. She took her backpack and slung it over her shoulder, while I went to get her duffel bag from the trunk.

Brian answered the door. "Hello!"

"Hi, Brian," I said.

"Hi, Grandpa. Dad's acting weird."

Brian frowned. blinked. He looked at me, and when he saw my big, fake smile, he matched it.

"Oh, Dads act weird all the time. Totally normal."

"Hardy har," Lucy said, throwing me a glance as she went inside. "Bye, Dad. See you on Sunday."

"See you on Sunday," I said, lifting my hand to wave, but she was already inside and I could hear Annie greeting her with much affection.

I looked at Brian.

"I'll pick her up around three o'clock," I said.

"Of course. Thank you."

I started to turn, but Brian cleared his throat. "We won't mention anything to Lucy."

"Thank you."

"But Annie is serious about this, Fletcher."

"Yeah, I could tell. What about you?"

Brian sighed. "We miss our son. And Lucy is all we have left of him."

"She's all I have left of him, too," I said. "I spoke to a lawyer."

"I see." He sighed. "I was hoping we wouldn't have to go that far."

"What? Did you think I'd just hand her over? Are you fucking kidding me?"

Brian lifted his hands. He continued, keeping his voice low. "You seem overwhelmed, Fletcher. Maybe it would be better for you if we looked after Lucy full-time. You'd have total access, of course, and she could stay with you on some weekends, just like she's been doing with us."

I didn't even know how to respond to that. "I'll see you on Sunday."

He gave me a nod and closed the door.

My stress had just gone up another three levels, even though the lawyer had reassured me that I'd win if they took the matter to the courts. The problem was, I didn't want to put Lucy through that. Lucy loved her grandparents, and she loved me. I couldn't even comprehend the damage that a full-on legal battle between us would have on her mental health.

I called Aiden from the car on the Bluetooth connection.

"I'm going to have a fucking coronary, and they'll get custody because Lucy will lose her only other parent. I'm on my way home."

"Try to calm down. We're going to have a fantastic weekend."

"Jesus, I hope so."

* * * *

When I got home, I felt better. The little bit of frantic tidying I'd done had made a difference, and I felt like the house looked like a typical family home now. Maybe even better than typical? I couldn't be the only single parent who let things slide now and then.

In spite of everything, I was glad Lucy was with Brian and Annie for the weekend. I was prepared to bury my worry for the time being, so I could let Aiden distract me in the ways he knew best.

Aiden showed up about an hour later with an extra-large Vegetarian pizza, which he'd already cleared with me.

I took the pizza from him and put it on the stove, then crashed against him in a desperate attempt to distract myself from everything. A conflagration of need and desire flowed between us, and I lost myself in its urgency.

"Is this ever going to get old?" I gasped against his mouth.

"God, I hope not. And if it does, we'll just have to get kinkier."

"I'm on board with that," I said, cupping his chin and grabbing at his pretty lips with mine. "How are you so fucking gorgeous?"

"Good jeans," he breathed, grabbing my belt loops and pulling me in. "Get it?" He smiled against my mouth.

I groaned, feeling the insistent probing of his tongue in every part of my body.

"Fuck, I need you — right the fuck *now*," I panted.

"Well, you can have me — right the fuck *now*," Aiden said, pulling back and whipping off his T-shirt. His nipples — a dusky rose color — were pebbled and hard.

I reached out to touch one, and he gave me an incendiary look and led me toward the stairs.

"I assume your bedroom is this way?"

"You assume correctly," I said. "Turn right at the top, and it's the last door."

"Aren't you coming with me?" he asked with a playful lilt.

"Of course. Lead the way."

Aiden turned and walked up the stairs, showing off his tight as hell ass in a pair of snug track pants. I was glad he'd gone casual tonight. It was a nice change for us. I still had my jeans and work shirt on, but I was ready to either get naked or change into pajama pants.

Aiden gave me a salacious glance. "Hey, do you want to fuck me?"

I stumbled at the thought of it. "I'm glad you didn't ask me that on the stairs."

"Do you, Fletcher? Because I'm into it if you are."

"Oh my fucking God. Are you kidding? Yes!"

He laughed.

"I thought you were an out and out top," I said.

"So did I. But for some reason, I want you to. I'm trying not to question it."

"Good. Don't."

"Plus, you can go bare, if you're comfortable with that."

"Oh, God. Now I want to do you even more."

We'd gotten our test results back and had only recently gotten used to going bareback, but it was usually Aiden doing the fucking. Now, I'd get to try it.

I'd given him directions to the guest bedroom, because I didn't think I could handle getting dirty with Aiden in the room I'd shared with Daniel. Not yet. I closed the door, even though nobody else was in the house and I'd locked the front door behind Aiden.

Aiden glanced around him.

"This is...not your room."

He was pretty perceptive.

"Correct. But there *is* a bed."

"I see that." He looked at me carefully. "You gonna be okay?"

"If we do it here, yeah. I can't do it in —"

"Hey, you don't have to. I'm happy to have you anywhere I can get you."

"I love that you're so versatile," I said, the double meaning intentional.

"You have no idea," Aiden said, stepping forward and bringing me in for a passionate kiss. "You make me want to do all kinds of things." Aiden grinned against my mouth. "And I'm good at topping from the bottom."

"I'll bet you are, you sexy fuck."

We laughed as we fell onto the bed.

"Why on earth aren't you undressed yet?" Aiden said, pushing his pants and shorts down.

"Working on it," I muttered, unbuttoning my shirt as fast as I could, and regretting that I'd not gone with a T-shirt.

"Here, let me help," Aiden said, going at my belt and fly as I finished with the buttons and wrestled the shirt off. Aiden dragged my jeans and boxers down my thighs then my cock was in his mouth and he was gazing up at me with those dark eyes as I gasped and said his name.

He didn't reply. He simply kept sucking and licking and doing all kinds of wonderful things with his tongue, until I warned him that if he wanted to get fucked, he'd better back off and get himself ready.

He pulled off me with a pop and sat back, his cock hard and leaking. "Fletcher, we have got to work on your self-control."

"Okay," I panted. "But not tonight."

He laughed. "Fine."

"How are we doing this?" I asked. "Do you want to ride me?"

A smile formed on his face. "Now *that* is a great idea."

"Then you wouldn't really be topping from the bottom. Because you'd be on top...technically."

He waved his hand in the air. "All these formalities. Fuck 'em. Let's just do this."

"So romantic."

"You want to fuck this ass or not, Fletcher?"

"Stop talking. Here." I opened a drawer where I had stashed supplies and tossed him a tube of lube.

He caught it. "I'm impressed. You seem to have everything at the ready. Do you really want to rush this?"

"Not usually, but honestly? Yes. I need to get my head out of my own ass and into yours, Aiden. Like, right the fuck *now*."

He laughed and lifted his hands, giving no argument. "Okay, okay." He offered me the lube. "Slick up that beautiful cock, then, and prepare to be boarded."

I squirted lube into my palms and rubbed my hands together. "Is that a *Star Trek* reference?"

He narrowed his eyes at me. "Absolutely not. It's *Our Flag Means Death*."

"Oh fuck, of course it is. How could I have thought otherwise?"

"Exactly." Aiden watched me lube up my cock and crawled toward me with a feline's grace.

"Who's supposed to be Blackbeard?"

"Me, of course. You're the Gentleman Pirate," Aiden said, looking devilish as he crawled over to perch on my thighs, his tawny cock bobbing in front of him.

I groaned as I moved my hand faster. "I hardly feel like a gentleman right now."

"Well," Aiden murmured, as he took the tube of lube from me and squirted some into his hand, "I'm ready to channel Blackbeard, so get with the program."

I made my eyes go comically wide and said, in a *terrible* New Zealand accent. "Ed, you don't mean you want me to put my…penis…in your…arse? Is that how it's done?"

Aiden's cock jerked as he readied himself for a fucking. I laid down on my back on the coverlet.

"On *my* ship," he said, his voice husky and commanding, "that's how it's done."

"Oh, Ed!" I said, my lashes fluttering as I held my cock at the base, and he positioned himself over it. "I do like it when you take control."

"That's a terrible accent," Aiden said, as he took my cock in his fingers and guided it to the right spot, just before sinking down on me with a gasp and a curse, as he closed his eyes and grimaced.

"Oh shit. Are you all right?" I said, the heat of his body causing waves of pleasure to go through me.

His expression relaxed. When he opened his eyes, they looked bestial and just like I imagined Blackbeard's would.

"Oh fuck," he whispered. Then he sank down farther with a groan, and I matched it as I clutched the bedclothes with one hand and gripped his thigh with the other. Then, with the most beatific expression on his pretty face, he started to move.

And I just about came right away because it had been such a long time since I'd fucked instead of *been* fucked, because Aiden was gorgeous and sexy, and because I had *feelings. So many* feelings, that for some reason hit me like a Mack truck at the sensation of warmth around my dick.

"Hold on," I stuttered, grabbing his other thigh and forcing him to be still. "Stop. I can't... You don't want me to come yet."

"No, Fletcher. I don't. Please don't come."

"I'll try not to, I promise."

Aiden gave me a stern look, as if we were in the Bordello already.

"Don't. Come," he said. "I'm going to enjoy myself, and you're going to hold off coming...or else."

"Or else, what?" I whispered, captivated by him.

"Shhh," Aiden said, leaning forward and gripping my shoulders as he moved fluidly on my cock. His unblemished skin shone in the lamplight, the color of burnished gold. His face went through multiple expressions, betraying every emotion and sensation.

I was beyond coherent speech, all my focus on not attaining the climax I could feel just within reach. Aiden moved like an animal, sinuous and stealthy, as he fucked me. He was in total control.

"Just stay still. Let me fuck myself on you. You're so hard. It's like fucking a stone." Aiden made a sound like a whine as he moved himself in a corkscrew motion over my stiff cock.

"Oh God," I gasped in a high-pitched, vulnerable voice, trying to keep from coming. But it was so difficult when Aiden moved like that! "Oh, please. Oh God. Fuck…"

"I'm so fucking full. I *love* this," Aiden said between grunts and groans. "Now," he said, as he grabbed his own dick and started jerking it in time with his movements. "I'm going to come. And you're going to hold off until I'm done. And you're going to watch me.

He sat on my cock, rocking gently, and jerked himself slowly, with the most indulgent expression on his pretty face, his mouth open and his eyes dark with need.

"Oh my God. Oh my God."

It was all I could say, my face scrunched up in concentration as I tried to keep from emptying my balls. I wanted to. I wanted to so badly. But more than that, I wanted to please Aiden. "Hurry. Please."

"Don't worry, baby. I've got you," Aiden gasped, giving his cock two more jerks then groaning as he spent in quick spurts, his spunk landing on my clenched abdomen and pounding chest.

"Okay. Now you can come," he said finally, and I exploded like a rogue firecracker.

The sound I made was almost inhuman as I let myself fall over the edge, and my balls and cock pulsed with pleasure. I stared at him, my fingers digging into his thighs as the waves of ecstasy rode me. The strength of my cries petered out as Aiden swiped his fingers through his own jizz and pressed them to my lips.

I lapped at them like a hungry kitten, cleaning them while sparks of remnant pleasure arced through me.

Chapter Eleven

Deep Clean

"So, how are you feeling now?" Aiden asked, once we'd showered and gotten into pajama pants and T-shirts.

"Oh my God."

"You keep saying that."

"Aiden, I feel fantastic. Thank you. That was fucking incredible."

He raised his wine glass, and I clinked it with mine. A couple of crusts with burnt edges were all that was left of the pizza in the open box on the coffee table.

"That was *incredible* fucking," Aiden said. "I'm still feeling it."

"You don't know how much I needed that," I said.

Aiden gave me a soft look of sympathy. "I think I have some idea, Fletcher. And I'm glad to help, in any way I can."

Aiden was sitting on the softest part of the sofa because he was a little sore. I couldn't imagine why, although it seemed my cock had something to do with it, since he kept calling it names like 'battering ram' and 'torpedo'.

"You're going to give me a complex," I said.

"Because I'm complimenting the size and power of your cock?"

"Is that what you're doing?"

"It's what I'm trying to do."

I gazed at him with concern. "I didn't hurt you, did I?"

"Just the right amount. And I'm glad I'm sore, so I can remember this while I'm making you crawl for me in the Bordello tomorrow."

At those words my mouth went dry, even though I'd just swallowed more wine. "Oh damn."

"Curse all you want, because tomorrow, your ass is mine — and all the other parts of you."

He waggled his eyebrows.

"Well, I can't fucking wait," I said, and we clinked our glasses again.

* * * *

We slept together in the guestroom, after I changed out the comforter for a clean one. Aiden seemed to get why I didn't want to use the main bedroom with him yet, and I appreciated his understanding. The dogs were a bit confused, but Cocoa was always with me at night, so she fought Aiden for space in the bed, and Eddie slept on Lucy's bed, which was his favorite spot when she was away. By 'fought' I mean she pretended to cuddle and pushed him over.

"Sorry. She's been a huge comfort to me, especially at night."

"It's fine, Fletcher. I'm happy to share you with her." He narrowed his eyes in the darkness. "Only her, though."

"Noted…and, same."

"Noted." He grinned.

In the morning, he insisted on making pancakes, and I enjoyed watching him move around my kitchen in his boxer briefs, more than words could express. The ghost of Daniel was there, but his appearances in my memory were less disruptive and more hopeful now...as if he was making sure I was okay. And I wanted to remember. Because our life had been wonderful.

After we'd walked the dogs, Aiden wanted to pop back home, so we went for a stroll by the canal and popped into the Lansdowne Farmer's Market, then stopped for a light lunch at Joey's. TD Place was always interesting and afterward we went through Old Ottawa South and stopped for gelato at Stella Luna. Then I thought I'd better restrict my food intake if we were planning an athletic visit to the Bordello later.

I hooked a finger with Aiden's as we walked.

"Do you want me to do a whole preparation thing before we go tonight?"

Aiden glanced at me with a twinkle in his eye. Then leaned in to whisper in my ear.

"Are you asking if I want you to douche?"

"Yes," I said, a light blush hitting my cheeks. It had been a long time since I'd prepared this way.

"Hmm. Good idea," he said. "Or even a proper enema."

He glanced at me, and I stopped walking. Daniel and I had never gone that far.

"Um..." I said.

"I can help you."

I looked at him.

He continued. "I have all the gear at my place."

"Wow. You are full of surprises."

Aiden shrugged. "I did two years of nursing school before deciding it wasn't the career I wanted."

"Really?"

"Yeah. I decided if I was going to be paid very little for a lot of effort I'd at least get two months off over the summer."

* * * *

We went back to my place around four to walk the dogs. They'd be fine until we got home after Maverick Molly's.

I'd already seen the rest of Aiden's apartment. The kitchen was tiny and the bathroom barely adequate, but the living area was a decent size, and the view onto the grounds of the medieval-looking museum was even better from there. The ancient architecture of the place charmed me.

"How did you swing a top-floor apartment?" I asked. There were four apartments per floor, and the top level was great, because you didn't have anyone living above and the views were the best.

"I answered an ad in the Centretown News for a guy subletting it. Then when his lease was up, I renewed it myself. It's a sweet deal."

I stood in the doorway of the kitchen while Aiden moved about in the small space, preparing a meal of fish, rice and green beans that tasted like it was from a gourmet restaurant. We ate at the small wood table by the wall in the living room. Twinkle lights surrounded the huge windows, which were draped with sheers, and the Turkish rug and humble furniture gave the place a casual, bohemian vibe.

When we were done, he told me to stay there while he disappeared into his bedroom. I gripped the edges of my chair, wondering how embarrassing this procedure was going to be. I'd never had an enema. But

I had looked up some very kinky videos on the internet, so I kind of knew what was involved, and how such an act of tender caretaking could be sexy. But I was nervous. It was such an intimate thing to share with someone.

Aiden took something into the bathroom, and I heard water running. He came out again after a few minutes and went back to the bedroom, holding what I assumed was the enema bag.

"All right. I'm ready for you. Come on."

I got up and made my way to the bedroom.

There were towels laid down on the bed and an IV pole standing beside it. Aiden hung the enema bag on a hook and glanced over.

"I need your bottom half to be bare. It's up to you if you want to be completely naked or to keep your shirt on..."

"Huh," I said, "My upper half is not what I'm worrying about right now."

I stared at the steel IV pole with the enema bag full of water hanging there, the tube held closed with a clamp and the nozzle looking particularly foreboding. I'd had a lot of things in my ass but never something so utilitarian. The little applicator on the douches barely counted, although that was closest.

"Nice setup. Very professional."

"There's even a plastic sheet under the towels...just in case."

My face reddened. "Oh my God."

Aiden reached for the enema tube and showed me the nozzle attachment. "This is actually an inflatable plug."

My eyes went wide. "Oh."

"It will help you retain the water. And it's only warm water. I haven't added anything else to the mixture."

"Do…do people add other stuff?"

"Well, a nurse might have to add medication, right? Some idiots put coffee in it. Whatever floats your boat, I guess." He shrugged. "I like to keep things simple."

"Well, you're a prince," I said with sarcasm.

"Take off your pants, Fletcher."

"Fine. Yep. Sure," I said, my breathing ramping up. My fingers trembled as I pushed down my trousers and boxer briefs.

"Oh, I like that look. Keep your socks and your T-shirt on."

"Really? You think this is sexy?"

"I think *you're* sexy. And, yeah, you look vulnerable, and that's sexy for a dirty Dom like me. More so, I think, than if you were completely naked."

"Yeah, okay," I said. "Can I call you Nurse Aiden?"

It was a joke, but the way his eyes lit up…

"I'd love it if you would."

"Wow. I mean, I guess I could."

"Maybe it will be easier for you," he said with a playful smile. "Now, I want you on all fours on the towels."

I stared at the bed. I looked at Aiden.

"Um."

"There's no reason to be nervous."

"Easy for you to say."

"Trust me. I know what I'm doing."

"That isn't really the issue."

"Well…you can safeword."

We stood there looking at each other.

Aiden shrugged. "I'm not going to force you."

He walked over to the IV pole, wrapping his fingers around the steel and rolling it closer to the bed.

"Unless you'd prefer it if I did."

My gaze flashed to his.

"Unless I — what?"

"I just think that, maybe, if I make you believe it's something you have to do for me, it will be easier." He smiled. "I want to make this as comfortable for you as I can."

I gave him a skeptical look, and he laughed.

"Fletcher, get on the bed. I told you how I want you."

I choked on a gasp, because that was exactly what I needed — Aiden telling me what to do in his stern, Dom voice. I could pretend that I didn't want to submit to this humiliating ordeal, when in actuality, my heart was beating fast, my cock was hard and my brain was short circuiting.

I got on the bed, the plastic sheet making a strange noise as I arranged myself on all fours and stared at the white towels beneath me. They looked clinical and practical, and I thought that maybe I could do this.

I felt hot all over. Why was I so fucking turned on? Even though I'd watched the videos of other men experiencing this, until now I hadn't understood the appeal.

As if he knew what I was thinking, Aiden piped up.

"Just so you know, lots of people have an enema kink, though few would admit it."

"Huh," was all I could say. I closed my eyes and focused on breathing.

Aiden's gloved hand rested on my ass cheek. "Just wait until this lovely warm water starts going in."

"Oh my God," I whispered.

"Spread your legs, Fletcher."

I swallowed thickly and moved my legs apart. Cool lube dripped onto my back and drizzled down the crack of my ass. I shivered. Then Aiden's gloved fingers were there, spreading the liquid around and teasing me, making me gasp with illicit pleasure.

"Fuck, I love doing this to you," Aiden murmured.

"You have some weird hobbies."

Aiden laughed. "You have no idea."

He sank a finger into me, and I groaned at the invasion—and at the feeling of being an object that needed to be cleaned...emptied.

"Really? No idea?" I said, my voice quavering.

"All right. Maybe some ideas."

He used his gloved finger to prepare me, turning it this way and that, moving it in and out.

I tried not to groan as pleasure sparked.

He withdrew it and patted my behind.

"Good. You're ready for the inflatable nozzle."

I don't know why the word 'nozzle' sent a burst of desire through me. I'd always had a thing for sticking objects up there—or having other people do it. But the word was so clinical, and my horny reaction so forbidden and perverse, it made it ten times more enjoyable.

"I've used this before—don't worry, it's been fully sanitized—and it's a little tricky to get in. But that's the fun of it. Once it's in, it's a dream."

"Some dream," I said.

Aiden laughed.

The floppy nozzle, wet with lube, poked at my hole. Aiden's fingers fumbled around, pushing and sliding on it.

"It's too flexible to go in easily."

"It's okay, Nurse Aiden. I trust you," I said, wondering if he might not be able to do it and we'd have to rethink this whole routine.

"Okay, here we go," Aiden said, as the slim rubber tube pushed in. He slid a finger in beside it in order to get it to work, then kept pressure on it and slipped his finger out.

"There we go," he said. "Hold it there."

I clenched my sphincter, so it didn't slide out.

"Great." Aiden's gloved fingers held the tube steady, and he used his other hand to pump the bulb that inflated the rubber.

"Oh...fuck," I muttered as I felt the plug nozzle expand.

"Feel good?"

"Oh...yeah. Jesus."

It did feel good. I shuddered a breath.

"Oh, yes, you like that," Aiden said, tickling my balls and scooping his gloved, lubed hand under my cock. He played with me while the plug nozzle expanded more.

"Oh fuck," I whimpered, then moaned as Aiden twisted the inflated rubber tube.

"Yeah, that's working now. I'm going to start the warm water."

I made a small sound.

"You okay?"

"F-fine."

In a moment, I felt the warm water inside my body.

"Still okay?"

"Yes, Nurse Aiden."

He stroked my cock with his gloved fingers again, up and down, down and up, then fingered the tip, where fluid was leaking.

"You really like this."

"Shut up."

He chuckled. "But how can I contain my excitement?"

"Nurse Aiden..."

"How fucking dirty are you, Fletcher, that you need me to clean you out like this?"

I gasped at the words he used and felt my cock swell even more.

"So dirty. Filthy. Fucking f-filthy," I stuttered.

Aiden stroked his fingers along my perineum, making me groan and shift position.

"Such a dirty slut, letting me clean you out like this," Aiden murmured, the cheerful tone of voice belying his perverse words.

"Oh my God. Stop," I whined.

"Stop what?"

"Talking about it like that. It's...so hot. Why is it so hot?"

He sat down beside me, one hand still on the enema tubing. "Because you know you're a dirty slut, and you know what's going to happen later. You know *why* I'm doing this."

"Yeah."

"And also, you like having your ass filled. It's as simple as that."

"Huh."

"This is going to take ten or fifteen minutes, so I'm going to ask you some questions."

I swiveled my head, giving him a look that said 'Really?'

He'd made me feel so vulnerable, and now he wanted me to talk? While he was filling my rectum with warm water?

"So. I know you like bondage and being played with...and impact play."

"Mmm. All of that."

"I want to use toys on you tonight. Plugs and big beads and things. Anal play."

"Yes, Nurse Aiden."

"Like, some serious anal play."

"Not...not huge toys."

"All right. Not huge. But...big?"

"Yeah. I mean, yes, Nurse Aiden."

"I had Sebastian send me the catalog of the things they have available in the Bordello, so I could do some planning."

Wow. That was...unexpected.

"You did?"

"Yes. Is that all right?"

"Sure. Good thinking."

"How are you feeling? The water's almost gone."

"Full. Fine."

"You look so good, with a tube running into your perfect ass."

"Thank you, Nurse Aiden."

"Can you roll over?"

"Um, I think so..."

"The plug will make sure there's no leakage."

Moving was interesting. The water sloshed around in my guts, and I felt a cramp here and there, but nothing terrible...yet.

I found myself lying on the bed with my legs close together, my cock a divining rod of desire. I was so fucking hard.

"Oh fuck, yes," Aiden said, climbing onto the bed. "My sweet Fletcher, full of water and hard as a fucking rock. Look at you!"

I gave him a glare. "You're enjoying this way too much, Nurse Aiden."

"Guilty," he said, with a grin.

He smiled with the utmost wickedness as he circled my cock with his gloved hand and leaned forward.

"Oh no. No..." I protested but once his mouth was around my cock, I could only gasp and make a frightened sound as pleasure coursed through me. The inflated plug felt huge, and a gut full of warm water gave the sensations of getting head a huge boost.

Aiden hummed, and the vibrations traveled along my spine, sending tingles and reverberations through my liquid insides.

"Oh fuck, fuck, *fuck*," I panted, trying to stay on top of everything. The sensation of being blown with a gut full of warm water was like nothing I'd experienced before.

Aiden gripped the base of my cock and sucked hard, making me crazy. This wasn't going to take long, which was probably a good thing. I hoped the inflated plug worked well, because if not, my orgasm, when it came, would result in a horrible and humiliating event — and multiple cleaning bills.

"Nurse Aiden, please…please…"

He popped off my dick. "What?"

"Are you sure this plug…will keep…everything in?"

"Pretty sure," he said.

I gaped. "*Pretty* sure?"

"That's why I've got the towels and the plastic sheet," he said, before bending to suck my cock again.

I yelled out, my gut starting to ache and the plug feeling as big as a municipal dam.

"Oh my God…"

Aiden seemed oblivious to my distress or uncaring of the consequences — or he had faith in the inflated plug. Sure, he'd put towels down, both on the bed and the floor, but there was a lot of water inside me. And a lot of…other stuff…

"Aiden, fuck. I'm gonna…I'm gonna…"

"Come?"

"Yeah…but I might…I might…"

"If it happens it happens. We'll deal with it."

I started to protest, but Aiden jerked my cock in time with his sucking, and my eyes rolled back in my head. Any worries about soiling the bed and embarrassing myself left me. I came so hard, filling Aiden's mouth with my jizz, my ass clamping down on the plug with so much force I couldn't believe it stayed in.

Once the pleasure began to wane and my body went all wobbly, I felt the intense pressure of a full bowel needing to be expelled.

"Nurse Aiden! Nurse Aiden!" I said with urgency, sounding ridiculous and like a bad actor in a porno.

"I know."

Aiden detached the other end of the nozzle tube from the IV stand and handed it to me. "You can walk with the plug in so you don't expel until you get to the toilet."

I grabbed it and held on to it for dear life. This plug was the only thing standing between me and the ultimate humiliation. I wasn't even sure I could walk — and not just because of the gut full of water from the enema. The orgasm had been intense and unexpected, and my knees wobbled as I made a desperate dash for the bathroom.

Luckily, removing the inflated plug was easy and everything happened as it should, in the safety of the bathroom. It wasn't until I'd finished and was basking in the ultimate sense of relief that I opened my eyes and realized 'Nurse' Aiden had followed me down the hall.

"Close the fucking door! Jesus Christ! This isn't a fucking floor show!"

His laughter echoed in the space before he carefully shut the door to give me some privacy, but only after I'd caught the look of unadulterated glee on his handsome face.

For fuck's sake. What had I gotten myself into?

When I'd finished on the toilet, I took a shower to make sure I was clean everywhere and also to delay appearing before Aiden. I felt embarrassed and massively humiliated about the entire procedure, but I couldn't say that I regretted it.

There was a knock on the bathroom door while I was toweling off and trying to figure out how to announce my reappearance.

"Are you okay?"

"Yes. I think so."

"All clean?"

I leaned my forehead on the door. I'd hung up the towel instead of putting it around my waist. What was the point of covering up when he'd seen everything already and we'd just had such an intimate experience together?

"Aiden, I'm so embarrassed," I said through the door.

"But, why?"

I couldn't help but smile. Aiden was so matter-of-fact about sex and kink and nudity and...medical procedures.

"You saw me... You saw me...on the toilet. *You* know." I couldn't say *shitting myself*. I just couldn't. But that was what I meant. Nobody had ever watched me do that, not even Daniel.

"Ah, I see." I heard a thump and figured he was leaning with his back against the door now. "Would it help if I said I don't care? Bodily functions are not something that gross me out. I probably *would* have made a good nurse."

"You would have, absolutely. Why did you switch?"

"Honestly? Mostly just the job, the hours. You know, not being respected by doctors. Having to work those twelve-hour shifts. Having to do all of these intimate procedures for people who'd take it for granted, for hospitals that didn't pay enough. I don't know."

There was a pause.

"Are you coming out?" he asked.

"I haven't decided."

"Do you want to cancel our booking?"

"No. Absolutely not."

"All right. Then get out here and get dressed, so we can drive to Molly's and I can strip you again and do all kinds of wonderful, dirty things to your beautiful, clean body."

I laughed, feeling better.

"Fine. You promise not to think any less of me?"

"Fletcher, I actually think more of you for letting me take care of you in that way. There's nothing better. I loved everything about that."

"Huh," I said. I girded myself and turned the door handle, hearing a noise indicating that Aiden had moved from his leaning position.

Aiden stepped back as I pulled open the door, and he smiled, beckoning me into his open arms.

"Come here, you."

I went there, and he enfolded me in his embrace, nuzzling my neck and nosing at my ear. "You're beautiful, you know—even bent over with a tube up your ass."

I laughed, feeling my cheeks get hot.

"It's actually really fun embarrassing you," he admitted.

"I knew it! You totally get off on that, *Nurse Aiden*."

"Yeah, well, so do you."

Chapter Twelve

Diving In

We arrived at Maverick Molly's a little before our booking time.

When we went into the gaming parlor, I was distracted by the bloomered bottom of a molly boy who had bent over to gather some glasses from a table. When he straightened and turned into my nephew, I was taken aback.

"Fletcher!" Patrick said with a friendly smile. He balanced his tray against his hip and came over to us. He looked fucking adorable in his molly boy gear.

"Hey! How are you?"

"Great."

He looked at Aiden then back at me with a wowed expression. I realized this was the first time he'd seen him.

"Patrick, this is Aiden. Aiden, this is my nephew, Patrick."

"Patrick," Aiden said, extending his hand. "Pleased to meet you. I think I have you to thank for all those times I've taken Fletcher out."

"I don't mind hanging out with Lucy." He turned back to me. "I guess she's with Grandma and Grandpa for the weekend?"

I glanced at Aiden, who smiled.

"Yep."

"You probably don't want to waste your time talking to me. Can I get you something?"

"Actually, we need the key to the..." I cleared my throat, only because it occurred to me that Patrick would know that we were getting kinky at his workplace. I hadn't really thought about how bizarre that was.

"The Bordello," Aiden specified. He didn't seem to find it strange. Then again, Patrick wasn't his nephew.

I turned to Aiden. "He could have figured that out."

Aiden shrugged with a nonchalant smile.

"I'll get you the key," Patrick said.

"Thank you," Aiden said.

Patrick glanced at me and gave me a look that said, *'Holy shit, that guy is hot.'* I gave him a smug little nod and he went off to speak to Jacob, who was manning the bar.

I looked around for Robin, who had seemed such an integral part of Maverick Molly's it was hard to believe he didn't work all the time. There were two other molly boys flitting about whom I didn't recognize but could absolutely appreciate in their bloomers and corsets. Jacob and Sebastian definitely knew what they were doing, getting these young men to act as pretty scenery and amusing entertainment for their customers.

Patrick came back after a moment.

"Jacob said that Sebastian's just doing a check to make sure the previous clients cleaned up properly, and that it'll be ready at ten."

I checked my watch. "Oh shit. We're early."

"Happens all the time," Patrick commented with a cheeky smile.

One of the other molly boys came up to us. He looked familiar, and I realized he was the young man I'd seen in the changing room when I'd had to use the facilities.

"Oh hey, I know you," the server said with a flirtatious smile, batting his pretty eyelashes at me.

"Honestly, Toby. You flirt with anything that moves," Patrick murmured.

Toby, right.

Toby gave Patrick a disdainful glance. "So?" He looked Aiden up and down. "My, my, my, so handsome."

A well-dressed, tall man with dark curly hair approached Toby and wrapped an arm around him from behind, then offered me his outstretched hand.

"Hi. I'm Toby's boyfriend, Alastair. Welcome to Maverick Molly's."

Toby gave the man a kiss on the cheek, then said in a loud whisper, "Alastair, you're ruining my vibe. Go away."

Alastair rolled his eyes. "What vibe is that? Cheeky young man who likes to flirt with everyone, even though he's entirely taken and living with his hot boyfriend?"

"Yeah. That one." Toby's sweet-as-fuck smile was incendiary.

Aiden grinned at Alastair and shook his offered hand.

"Hi. I'm Aiden." He gestured to me. "This is *my* hot boyfriend, so you have nothing to worry about."

Alastair gave me a skeptical look. "I always worry. Look at him." He gestured to Toby, who was indeed a sexy little minx.

"Ah. True."

"Oh, don't be ridiculous," Toby scoffed. "I'd never actually do anything. But I can't help being admired, can I?"

"Yes, that seems to be the general consensus around here," Alastair murmured.

Toby gently moved the other man's arm from around his middle. He gave his boyfriend a tolerant look. "Sweetheart, the clients aren't supposed to touch us. You're just going to confuse everyone." He let Alastair's arm drop to his side and gave the man a lecherous once-over. "But when we get home, you can touch me *anywhere* you want."

He blew a kiss to his boyfriend and walked away.

"Here," Patrick said, passing me the special key. I hadn't even noticed he'd gone back to Jacob.

"Thanks," I said. "Aiden."

I waved the key at him when he finally drew his gaze from Toby's cute little behind.

"Finally," he said. "This place is like a fucking aphrodisiac."

I laughed and followed him with a wave to Patrick.

Patrick had the most adorably happy expression on his face, which I took to mean he was glad to see me enjoying myself above and beyond being Lucy's dad. I appreciated his goodwill. But now I needed to stop thinking about Lucy or Patrick or anyone but Aiden.

We keyed our way into the Bordello and locked the door behind us. The place smelled of lemon disinfectant, which was comforting and reassured me that everything was kept free of germs and contaminants.

"Do you think they use one of those blue light detectors to see what needs to be cleaned in here?" I said.

Aiden smiled. "Hmm. I don't know. I'll have to ask."

"But not right now."

"No, not right now. Right now, I have other things on my mind." Aiden looked at me with an expression of unadulterated lust that became contemplation as he put his finger to his chin. "Hold on."

"Do you want me to…take my clothes off?"

"Yes, yes. Do that," Aiden said, giving me a cheery look.

I laughed, feeling giddy with expectation. I didn't pay attention to what Aiden was doing, but by the time I'd taken off my clothes, he was back and holding out a pretty red silk kimono with what looked like a giant purple koi fish embroidered on the back. "Here."

I smiled in response to the unexpected gesture. Aiden helped me get my arms into it then pulled it closed and tied the sash with a different kind of knot.

"It's quick release," he said with a wink.

"Ah. Goody."

"Fletcher, how do you address me in this room?"

"I'm sorry, Sir."

"I'm going to blindfold you."

"Yes, Sir."

He approached me with the black cloth and covered my eyes, then tied it behind my head.

"Give me your hands."

I crossed my hands at my lower back, and Aiden wrapped them with soft rope and bound them. I found myself drifting, even now, into that space of submission and acquiescence that seemed so much a part of me—a space where I could forget everything else and concentrate on simply being alive and serving someone in this particular way.

"Remember your safeword?"

"Yes, Sir."

"What is it?"

"Lamp."

"Good. That's for later. I want to gag you. Do you consent?"

"Yes, Sir," I said. "But how do I...?"

"If you need to safe-out, turn your head from side to side in a 'no' motion. Fast, so I can distinguish it from head rolling."

"Yes, Sir."

I heard him moving around, then something hard pressed against my lips.

"Open."

I parted them and Aiden placed something cylindrical between my teeth. It was made of leather — solid on the inside but soft on the surface. He fastened the straps behind my head. There was a tug on the rope that bound my hands together.

I walked carefully backward until he stopped me, securing my bound hands to something wooden.

"I'm tying you to the pillory. It's bolted to the floor, so you won't be able to move."

I tried to say 'Yes, Sir,' but the words were garbled, due to the gag.

"Don't talk. I just want you to relax and exist in your body."

I nodded my head, then tested the rope to see how secure it was. I definitely couldn't break free unless Aiden undid it.

Perfect.

"There are safety scissors hanging in several spots in this room and a first-aid kit by the door, just in case."

It was comforting to know that Jacob and Sebastian Moriarty had safety in mind, and that Aiden did as well. I wouldn't expect any less from someone who worked in a school on the regular.

I listened as Aiden's footsteps retreated then returned.

"Try to stay still. That's all I want from you right now, Fletcher."

Okay. I can handle that. It was such a simple thing compared to the rest of my life.

Something tickled the top of my foot. I almost moved it, but forced myself to keep it planted on the wood floor. Soft leather traced over my arch and down along my big toe. It tickled, and I had to concentrate on keeping still.

Aiden chuckled. "It'll get harder."

That wasn't the only thing getting harder.

The folded leather tip of a riding crop traced over my other foot, then snaked over my ankle and up the inside of my calf — then did the same to my other calf, then along my inner thigh, then the other inner thigh. The crop lifted the edge of my robe as it searched higher.

I struggled not to move.

As Aiden stroked the tip over various parts of my body, I became increasingly aroused. My breathing was rough against the gag, and I had to concentrate on keeping still.

"Oh, babe, you're doing so good."

His praise was everything I needed. As an adult, you didn't hear very often that you were doing the right thing. Sometimes you didn't even know what the right thing *was*. But here, in this room, all I had to do was what Aiden told me.

It might not be easy, but its difficulty lay in another direction from the struggles I dealt with on a daily basis. And it was such a *fucking* relief.

Tiny movements in the air told me he was in front of me. I could feel him there, hear his breaths and smell his scent. A tug on my silk robe and it fell open, the air hitting my standing cock like a caress as I gasped and raised my chin.

"Oh, yeah," he murmured. He pressed his lips against the corner of my mouth, where spit had gathered. He swiped it away with his tongue, then did the same to the other side.

He stepped back, and there was nothing except the hum of the HVAC and the tick of the analog clock. The tip of the riding crop snaked up my inner thigh again, higher and higher.

Swap!

The bite of it came like fire on my skin. I yelped. Then it happened again, on my opposite thigh, also on the inside. I made a sound of pain.

Before I had time to recover, the it made its way to the underside of my cock and up, up, up, to drift lazily over the head. I clenched all over, in case he would strike that sensitive spot, but the leather moved on me like a tongue, teasing and smooth, until I jerked and pulled against the rope.

Aiden laughed softly. "It doesn't take much, does it? Just a bit of rope, a gag, a blindfold and a leather crop, and you're mine."

I whimpered because he was right. But I didn't give myself to just anyone.

He shoved the tip of the crop roughly under my balls, jiggling and poking at them as I complained with grunts and whimpers. It didn't hurt but made me aware of my vulnerabilities.

He came close again and pushed the silk robe off my shoulders, so that it slipped and bunched, draping behind my legs, at the ropes that tied my wrists together.

"Oh hell. You look so good, Fletcher, like a Roman slave. A problematic comparison, but I've never claimed to be a saint."

He drew the tip of the crop over my hip and around to my backside, flicking it against my skin and poking at the top of my crack.

"I'm going to do so many things to this ass."

I loved that Aiden could be the responsible elementary school teacher in one environment and the depraved and stern Dom in another. I was so here for it.

Aiden teased me with the crop, giving me the occasional sting and slap, playing with my cock and balls and nipples, until the drool was dripping from the gag, and I gasped continuously.

"All right," he said. "I think you're ready for the next part."

Aiden went behind me and unbuckled the straps of the bit gag, removing it from my mouth. The corners of my lips were sore, and I licked the drool away and wiped my chin on my bare shoulder. Aiden took the blindfold off me, then used a cloth to dry my chin and neck.

"Okay so far?"

"Y—yes, Sir," I said. My voice shook, and my cock twitched.

"Drink of water?"

"Yes, Sir."

There was a mini-fridge beside the door that we'd examined on our previous visit. It held bottles of water and a tray of ice in the freezer section. Aiden got one of the waters, unscrewed the cap and tipped it to my lips so I could drink. Our gazes met and held.

"Not too much. No bathroom break until later," he said, taking it away. "Now, wait here."

"Yes, Sir."

Aiden bent to undo the latches on the legs of the adjustable bondage bench and drew it upward. When he had it at a height that worked for him, he locked the legs in place and came back to me. The only sounds were our breaths as he untied the rope that held my hands together. He took the silk robe away along with it and told me to stand by the bench.

I padded over in my bare feet, feeling strung out and so aroused already, my brain exploding at the prospect of what awaited me. Aiden came up behind me and fastened a leather collar, with a metal D-ring at the front, around my neck.

"Do you want a collar, Fletcher?"

"Huh?"

"A collar. So everyone will know you're mine?"

"Um, might inspire some uncomfortable questions from my folks."

Daniel laughed. "I don't mean a thick leather one with a D-ring. I mean…something that looks like a necklace. A simple gold or silver chain. Something like that?"

"Oh. Huh. Maybe? Can I think about it? You know I'm yours. Isn't that what matters?"

I remembered feeling bad about deciding against it, in the end. Instead, he'd gotten me a leather wrist bracelet that I'd worn for approximately three months before having to take it off for something and never putting it back on. He hadn't seemed to care, and after he'd passed, I'd looked for it but couldn't find it.

Aiden's hand landing softly on my hip got me out of the memory. He helped me into position.

The bench had platforms for my knees at a lower height, and my chest rested atop the padded surface. I was basically kneeling over with my wrists cuffed behind me. The D-ring of the collar he attached to a ring in the bench, to keep me centered and immobile. But I was able to lay my head on its side, so it wasn't uncomfortable.

"I'm going to bind your thighs, as well," Aiden said.

"Yes, Sir."

He circled leather cuffs around each leg just above where my knees were bent and buckled them, so they were snug. Then he attached them to rings on the bench.

"Now ankle cuffs, so you'll be secure. I don't want you coming off the bench when you're all wiggly and desperate."

I tried to control my breathing as he finished securing me.

"Okay. Wow. Well. You look like you should be in a painting."

What?

I snorted a laugh. "What kind of painting, Sir?"

He slapped my bare behind. "The kind I'd hang in my living room, just to embarrass you."

I sighed, chastened. "Yes, Sir."

"No questions. If you can't be quiet on your own, I'll get the gag."

I didn't say a word, not wanting the gag, mostly because it would add to the discomfort of the position. Right now, it was tolerable. I was supported and able to rest my head. I had no illusions about the ability of a Dom to make their sub *extremely* uncomfortable if they so desired.

I waited. I stared at the wall across from me, which held various implements designed to torment a naked sub. But I had a suspicion that Aiden wasn't going to use any of those. Of course, he could surprise me. I still didn't know him as a Dom that well, but I was getting there—and simply happy to be on the journey with someone who seemed to care as much as Aiden did.

Was it possible that over the course of one life, a person could be lucky enough to find two people who could take care of them, in different ways, but with the same level of attention and compassion? My skeptical side said no. My romantic and hopeful side said *maybe*. But Aiden and I were only at the beginning of something, and I wouldn't ruin it by getting ahead of myself.

Chapter Thirteen

His

"Okay. Let's get started," Aiden said under his breath.

I heard rustling and footsteps, saw some shadows on the wall, then felt gloved fingers delving between my cheeks as liquid dripped onto my skin.

"Oh." I said, startled at the cool temperature.

Aiden's fingers stilled, and I remembered his order to be quiet. I kept my mouth shut as they resumed, spreading lube all along my cleft, down to my balls and over my distended cock as I closed my eyes and tried to be silent.

"You can make noise, Fletcher. Just no talking. I like to hear your reactions to what I'm doing."

In response, I gave a little moan as he traced my hole and spread tons of lube around it. Without warning, he pressed his finger against me and slipped inside, all the way to the knuckle.

I made a noise of surprise and pleasure, my thighs trembling as he probed me, caressing my insides as if he needed to know everything about me. When he brushed his fingertip over my prostate, I made a high-pitched whine.

"Mmm," he said.

Then he did it again.

"Ahhh." My instinct was to curse at how good it felt, but I held back, leaving my mouth open and stuttering breaths as he twisted his wrist and prodded me everywhere.

"Okay. Now for something bigger," he said, sounding like a kid getting ready to grab the most substantial donut off a plate. "We're going to play with some very fun toys, my darling. You'll like them."

"Yes, Sir." My heart swelled at the endearment, surprised at how good it felt.

I concentrated on the heady sense of submission and being under someone else's absolute control, so that I literally couldn't screw anything up if I just lay there and let them do what they wanted. We'd already had the hard and soft limits discussion, and I expected Aiden to respect those boundaries.

Something stiff pushed against my entrance. I tried to relax, and after a moment, it slipped in. Only a bit, so I could get the sense of its girth.

"Nice," Aiden said, twirling it back and forth, sending rockets of bliss along my nerves. "Good job."

After I'd accommodated, he pushed it in a bit farther — a moderately sized rubber dildo, by the feel of it. My body received it easily, and the joy of being penetrated that way made me giddy.

"Oh, Yeah. So hot."

I closed my eyes and concentrated on the sensations of having a hard rubber dong inside me, making my nerve endings sing.

"Your ass was made for this. I'm glad I get to play with it."

I was glad, too.

Aiden slipped the dildo back and forth, stretching me in a lazy and confident way, so that all I felt was a delightful stretch and a pleasant invasion. He chuckled at my gasps and sighs, like a pleased athletic coach.

"Mmm. So sexy."

He withdrew the dildo and put it aside. Aiden might as well have blindfolded me, because I couldn't see anything except the wall of implements opposite where I lay. I kept my eyes closed, the better to not be distracted. My focus was entirely on the sensations in my body — the feel of the ropes around my wrists, the stretch in my shoulder muscles, the pressure of the bands around my thighs and ankles, the feel of the pads under my knees and the shifts in air currents on my skin as Aiden moved around behind me.

More lube dribbled down my crack.

A cold shock against my thigh as Aiden pressed something metal against me.

"This is going inside you," he said, moving the object around and pressing its length and shape against the skin of my leg so I could figure it out.

An anal hook. Jesus Christ. A moderately sized steel ball at the end of a hook of slim metal. *Oh fuck, fuck, fuck.*

I whimpered.

"That's the reaction I'm going for. You know what this is."

I whimpered again, and Aiden laughed.

"Oh yeah, you do."

My sphincter clenched and relaxed, eager for the invasion and the sense of helplessness that would come with the serious bondage implement. Daniel and I had never tried one, and once we had Lucy running around, we didn't feel right about storing lots of kinky accouterments in the house.

I swallowed, compulsively pulled at my wrist bindings, if only to feel that delicious sense of powerlessness. I wanted that hook so bad, and I was free to enjoy it without guilt and shame because someone else was choosing it *for* me.

Aiden chuckled as his gloved fingers stretched me again, then the metal sphere pushed against my opening.

Slowly, very slowly, the width of the metal ball sank into me, as I pushed outward with my muscles to receive it. My sphincter opened wider and wider, and the ball felt bigger than it had looked.

Then, all of a sudden, it sank inside me, and my hole closed on the slim metal hook.

I made a sound of intense pleasure as my body adjusted to the fullness.

"Oh yeah. Jesus," Aiden murmured.

I made soft sounds of pleasure. This was what I lived for, honestly—the sense of fullness, the depravity of having someone put something into me this way. It was exquisite. With the metal hook protruding out of me, adding the sense of being a puppet on a string for my stern, attractive Dom.

I was in heaven.

Aiden swiped more lube around my hole as he poked one gloved finger in alongside the hook. I yelped but relaxed as the feeling of being penetrated by more than one object hit me.

"So pretty, this hole. Prettiest hole I've ever seen, touched, teased," Aiden murmured as he touched and teased it, tickling the edge and slipping his finger in, delighting in my moans and murmurs as I became a mere conduit for his will. The soft tenor of his voice hypnotized me, soothed me and assured me that he was taking all the care that was needed.

I took a breath as Aiden grasped the hook and nudged the ball farther into me. I grunted as Aiden rocked it and twisted it, to make me cry out. Then he settled it again, the ball pushed as deep as it could go, the hook twisting up and over my back.

"My pinioned puppet."

The words. His words broke me and made me his completely.

He rocked the hook so that the muscle stretched and relaxed, completely beyond my control.

Aiden moaned then. "This looks so good. You have no idea."

He pushed his finger carefully in and out again, amplifying every sensation. He played with me for a bit like this, and it was all I could do not to scream with pleasure.

Finally, I felt the pressure of Aiden pulling gently on the hook, and the ball pressing against the muscle from the inside. I relaxed and let it slip out, shuddering at the bursts of bliss that resulted. It felt like a cannonball had exited my body.

I whimpered, drool collecting in the corners of my mouth, even without the gag.

"Fuck." Aiden said, clearly as affected as I was. He pressed the steel sphere, now warm from my body heat, against me again, and this time, I opened for it easily and welcomed it inside me.

I waited, strung out on pleasure, while Aiden attached a length of narrow rope to the handle of the hook and tied it to the D-rings on my wrist cuffs.

"Hoisted by your own petard," he said, spanking my ass. "Naughty slut."

All of a sudden, Aiden was beside the bench at my head, peeling the gloves off and gazing at me with intensity. Was he done with me?

He leaned down and crossed his arms on the spanking bench, so that his face was level with mine.

"Hey. How are you?" He smiled. "You can talk now."

"Good. So good," I breathed. "Are you stopping?" My voice sounded dim and far away.

"Only re-evaluating the situation," Aiden said, staring at my mouth with malicious intent.

Oh fuck. Oh God. Oh yes.

He straightened with a languid ease.

I licked my lips and struggled in my bindings. The ball of the hook filled me, reminding me of my lowly place, as Aiden's fingers went to his belt then the buttons of his fly. He pulled his swollen cock out.

"Do you want this?" he asked, in a seemingly benign and disinterested way, as if he were offering me the last piece of pie.

"Yes, Sir. Please. Please, Sir. Yes." I was mumbling and incoherent with desire, for the need to be used and stuffed at both ends. I wanted it with the deepest fiber of my being.

"Huh," he said. "Open your mouth."

I'd parted my lips before he'd finished talking, sticking my tongue out in eagerness.

He didn't smile, but stepped forward and slapped the wet head of his cock on my chin, my lower lip, my tongue. He lifted it away and smeared my cheek with the fluid that had collected at the tip of his exposed glans, all the while gazing at me with contrived contempt.

"I don't know if you deserve it, really," he stated with a frown.

"No, Sir," I whispered, my eyes closed as I reveled in my debasement, the scent of Aiden all over me. I opened my mouth wide and stuck my tongue out as far as it would go.

"Keep that mouth open."

He laid his cock against my tongue, his own mouth open as he gazed down on it. He cursed and rocked the head back and forth over the flat of my tongue as I tried not to drown in anticipation.

"All right, pretty slut. Take it if you want it," he said, letting go of his dick and sliding it forward. His right hand grabbed my hair to keep me still, even though I couldn't move much because of the collar.

I choked and coughed at the sudden invasion, as he pushed himself roughly in and out of my mouth. He pulled back so I could recover and left just the crown in while I swirled my tongue over it.

Aiden sighed and continued in earnest, fucking my throat as I breathed through my nose, the wet sound of flesh on flesh a tasty soundtrack to my ravishment.

"Oh God," he gasped, fucking my mouth harder. He was close, his movements quick, his cock so hard it felt like solid steel. He stuttered, as I breathed and choked, choked and gasped — and made desperate sounds of encouragement.

I kept my eyes shut to fully enjoy the way it felt to be used like this, fucked like this, but I imagined him looking down with wide, dark eyes as he tipped over the edge with a deep groan, and hot spunk filled my mouth, coated my tongue and slid down my open throat.

"Oh. Oh. *Oh*," was all he said as he came, but his steady thrusts slowed down and stilled as he emptied himself into me.

"Swallow it all, my pretty slut."

I closed my mouth but opened my eyes and did what he'd asked, eager to consume what he'd given me, honored to have been his vessel. I was floating and strung out on a wire of intense desire, waiting, hovering in subspace, incapable of speech or coherence.

"Such a good, good slut," Aiden said, stroking my neck and my chin and dragging a finger across my semen-soaked lips. I parted them, and he pushed his finger into my mouth for me to suck.

"Mmm. I love your sweet mouth so much."

I whimpered, quaking with need, unsure if I'd get any kind of satisfaction.

Aiden withdrew his finger and stood, tucking his cock away and fastening his pants. The smug expression on his face was everything.

He moved behind me again. *God, now what?*

The crop cut the air with a swoosh before it struck my ass, causing my inner muscles to contract around the steel ball that I'd almost forgotten. I groaned, and my cock dripped. Aiden tapped my balls, just enough to alarm me and to mix fear into my arousal.

"I want to milk you," Aiden said, with breathless enthusiasm. "I want to milk the jizz out of you, my sweet slut, like you're an animal come to stud and I need your semen for my breeding program. What do you think about that?"

I whimpered as my brain turned to mush, and Aiden chuckled.

"Jesus. You almost melted on the spot."

He untied the hook from my wrist cuffs and slowly eased it out of me. But at almost the same instant he was pushing it into me again. My body opened with ease as Aiden pressed the hook into me the other way around, with its' arm between my legs and lying alongside my erection.

He'd flipped the hook around. I didn't understand why until he rocked it against my prostate.

I hissed like a leaked balloon, and lots of things happened at once.

Aiden rocked the ball of the hook against my prostate with one hand and wrapped his other around my cock, jerking it in a rough and hasty way as I trembled with tension.

"You can come," he said.

He rocked the steel ball against that sensitive spot, and in a matter of seconds I was spurting and shaking and screaming, my body convulsing out of control—the intensity of it taking me by surprise. In a way it was frightening. But Aiden had me, and he kept up his steady movements until he'd milked me of every ounce, drained me of all my pent-up desire and utterly erased anything that was left of my will.

I was nothing. I was *everything*. I was a tiny speck on the floor of existence. I was *the universe itself.*

It took me a long time to come back to reality.

Aiden must have unbound me from the spanking bench and helped me over to the bed, but I had no memory of it when I opened my eyes.

"How long have I been out?" I asked.

"Not long enough to scare me. But if you hadn't come to just now, I might have started to worry," Aiden said, gazing down on me with relief.

"Does that…happen a lot?" I asked.

"It depends, right? That scene was pretty intense."

"Yeah. Fuck, it was. It was perfect."

He smiled. "I'm so glad you think so! That makes me happy."

"Did *you* like it?" I asked.

"I loved every minute of that." He reached over and brought the open bottle of water to my lips. "Here. Drink."

I swallowed a few gulps of water then Aiden drank some. He put the bottle on the table and spooned me from behind.

"You still have all your clothes on," I murmured.

"Yes, and you're naked…the way I like it."

I huffed and snuggled closer. "Pervert."

Chapter Fourteen

Smashing

When we got back to my place, after letting the dogs out into the yard to pee, I showered and put on some comfortable pajamas. My ass felt weird and bereft after holding on to that steel ball for so long. But there was also a delicious ache that made me remember.

Aiden and I cuddled in front of the TV after I'd checked my phone and made sure there were no texts or calls from either Lucy or her grandparents. But everything seemed fine.

By 'fine', I meant that none of them had tried to contact me while I was otherwise occupied. I was still unnerved by the idea that Daniel's parents might try to take Lucy from me. At least getting thoroughly worked over by Aiden in the Bordello had helped me to relax, even in the face of that.

My bones felt like jelly, and I hadn't yet fully exited my submissive frame of mind — in the sense that I was still deferring to Aiden for everything and enjoying the caretaking he liked doing after a scene.

Daniel had looked after me in similar ways, and I was finally able to remember without too much heartache. Having another man in my life, one who treated me well and didn't make unreasonable demands, meant that I could continue to process Daniel's death. It seemed to be helping, and I didn't question that, beyond realizing that if Aiden and I broke up, it would hit me hard. But I was convinced that the journey that I'd begun with Aiden, no matter where it might lead, was a journey of recovery and growth. I knew the odds were against us ending up together forever, and I'd made peace with that. I was grateful to have someone by my side for now, and I resisted putting any more pressure on our relationship than that.

The odds of finding someone who was willing to engage with me the way that Daniel had, but with his own style of Dominance, had been exceedingly rare.

A pain, like a gut punch, hit me all of a sudden. I looked upward, even though I didn't actually believe in Heaven. But was it possible that Daniel was still looking out for me? Had Daniel sent me Aiden? It was the most comforting idea I'd had concerning Daniel's passing in a very long while—maybe ever. I might not believe in Heaven, but I did believe in energy and the idea that the inner essence of a person—the soul—might disperse into the universe upon death. The energy that had made up Daniel was still floating around out there—in the trees and clouds and ether—somehow. Whether I believed it completely or not, the thought soothed me. I snuggled closer to Aiden and closed my eyes, enjoying his comforting presence and the turn my thoughts had taken.

When I woke, about two hours later, Aiden was still watching television. I blinked up at him in the dim light and yawned.

"Hey."

"How come you're still awake? Aren't you tired?"

"Getting there," he said. "I was wired when we got back. I'm getting drowsy now."

"Wired in a good way?"

"Wired in the best way." He shrugged, finding my hand and clasping it. "I'm excited about the future."

"You mean...us?"

"Yeah." He laughed. "Only because I want to stick so many things up your ass. Not for any other reason at all."

I could tell he was lying, and the fact that he could joke about it and benignly lay his feelings out without expressly saying he wanted a serious relationship, was expert level romancing.

"Let's go to bed."

"Sure."

We headed upstairs. When he got to the top, Aiden turned in the direction of the guest room.

"Hey," I said, touching his elbow. "We're going to sleep in my room tonight," I said.

He turned and looked at me, squinting in the darkness. "Are you sure?"

"Yeah."

Aiden nodded. "All right."

I led him into the main bedroom. We stripped to our boxer briefs and got under the covers. I'd bought all new bedding after Daniel had passed because I couldn't bear to sleep in the sheets he had used, even if they'd been washed. They were scrunched up in a box in the attic, and one day I'd get rid of them.

I snuggled up to Aiden again and rested my head on his chest, like I'd done with Daniel on many a night. And although it felt different, it comforted me in the same way, and I realized that Daniel would want to see me cared for in the way that he could no longer manage.

* * * *

Since we hadn't gone for brunch on Saturday, due to not wanting to overindulge before a complex scene, we decided to go Sunday. But first we lounged around having coffee and enjoying a relaxed morning.

I sent my usual *Good morning* text to Lucy at around nine, and she responded with a happy face, followed by a photo of the cutest little black and white kitten I'd ever seen.

Look what they got me! Kitten emoji, starburst emoji, heart emoji

I sat up and texted back, silently telling myself not to overreact.

A kitten?

My phone rang. I hit Accept.

"They got you a kitten?" I tried to channel surprise more than irritation, as my gaze met Aiden's. "A *kitten?*"

"I know, right? Her name is Lilly, so kind of close to my name. She's so cute! Dad, you've got to see her when you pick me up!"

"Is she…?" I swallowed hard. "Is she going to live at their place?"

"Yeah, so I can play with her when I'm here. That's going to be hard, though, because I'm usually with you and the dogs. But it will be great when I'm visiting! Maybe I can stay with Granny and Grandpa more often..."

My gaze met Aiden's. "Yeah. Sure."

"Are you okay, Dad? You sound weird," Lucy said. "Ow, Lilly get your claws out of my leg."

"I'm fine. Just tired. I was out late," I admitted.

She gasped. "On a date?"

"Yeah."

"With Aiden?"

"Of course, with Aiden."

"Cool! Anyway, I have to go because we're going to Cora's for breakfast. See you later!"

"Yeah. See you later. Love you."

I hit End Call and sat there staring at my phone, trying to process.

Aiden came and sat down beside me. "They're playing dirty."

"Yeah."

"I'm sorry, Fletcher."

"How am I going to compete with that?" I asked. "I should just give up now and let them have her."

Aiden stiffened. He reached out and turned my face to his. "Hey," he said. "Come on, now. You can't just give up."

"Can't I?" I said, not feeling any will to fight. Perhaps submitting to Aiden hadn't been a good idea after all. "Maybe she'd be better off living with them."

Aiden's face fell. "You don't really believe that."

I shrugged. "I don't know anymore. I'm sure I haven't been the perfect father."

Aiden gave me a stern look. "Doesn't exist. There are no perfect parents," he said. "There are parents, and there are grandparents. And parents are supposed to raise the children."

"Not in all circumstances," I said.

"In most. Look… I've been a supply teacher for a few years now, and I can tell you that committed parents are the best thing for a child."

"Parent," I said, feeling lower than I had in a long time. "It's just me, Aiden. And I've been floundering. And I'm so disorganized. And Lucy, and the dogs. It's a lot."

"Listen. Lucy is healthy, and she's come a long way since…since Daniel's death, right? You told me that."

I shrugged. "Yeah. We both have. But I don't think I'm over it."

"Of course, you're not. Neither is Lucy. Neither of you will ever be over it. It's a lifelong process, dealing with that kind of grief. Ask me how I know."

My gaze flashed to his. I didn't want to ask him at that moment, but I could see that he'd suffered a major loss at some point.

"You may be only one guy, but you have the heart of two men. You hold all of Daniel's love for you *and* Lucy inside you. She needs that, more than she needs a new pet or a different place to live."

I blinked rapidly, overcome by emotion. "Think so?"

"Yeah. I do. Come here, you old softie," he muttered, pulling me close and kissing the top of my head like I was the child. "You know you can let go with me…in all kinds of ways."

"Thank you, Aiden. You don't know how much I appreciate having you here while this is going on. If I didn't have you, I'd —"

"You'd be strong, and you'd be fine. But I'm glad to be here to lend my comfort and strength."

* * * *

When Aiden dropped me at home after a delicious brunch, the place seemed super empty, even with the dogs there.

"Well, guys, Lucy will be back after supper. Until then, it's just me."

Cocoa, my old girl, gazed at me with sad eyes and gave a little growl.

"Yeah. I know."

She made a mournful, whiny noise and laid down with her muzzle between her paws, then huffed a long sigh.

"They got Lucy a kitten," I said, talking to Cocoa and Eddie. "A fucking kitten. Can you believe that?"

Eddie yipped and wagged his tail, as if the idea were outrageous.

"Right? Lucy's a sucker for baby animals. They know that."

Cocoa growled low in her throat.

"But we're not going to let that bother us, are we? She loves us. All of us. It's not like she'd abandon us for a new baby, just because it's tiny and adorable," I said, my conviction wavering.

The dogs looked at me. I looked at them.

"Fuck."

* * * *

When I got to Brian and Annie's to get Lucy, she insisted on having me come in to meet the new kitten.

"Okay, sure. But we can't stay long."

"Hello, Fletcher," Annie said, barely able to conceal a smug little smile. "How are you?"

"Just dandy, Annie, thanks for asking," I said, trying to sound better than I felt.

"That's good. Lucy was awfully surprised by our little gift."

"I'm sure she was, Annie. What a lovely thought. Strange that you wouldn't just bring it to our place, though."

Her smile faded. "I think there are more than enough animals at your place," she said, as Lucy passed me the black and white kitten to hold.

"She's only nine weeks old, but she's so good at using her litter box. She's cute, right?"

The little ball of fur made a small mewl. Mostly black, with patches of white here and there, she gazed at me with benign curiosity. I gave her back to Lucy.

"We've got to go. Say goodbye to Granny and Grandpa."

"Awe, man. I don't want to leave her…" Lucy said, reluctantly handing the kitten to Annie.

I didn't look at Annie. I knew she'd be trying not to smile, and I was worried I'd lash out.

"I know. But you've got school tomorrow, and I want to catch up with you. I missed you."

"I missed you too, Dad," Lucy said. "But I was only gone for two days."

"Don't forget about Lilly," Annie said. "You'll have to come visit us more often."

"I will. I promise," Lucy said, in an excited voice that just about broke my heart.

"Bye, Annie." I forced the words out and managed to sound relatively normal. I'm not sure how.

"Bye, Fletcher."

In the car, Lucy looked at me strangely. "Don't you like the kitten?"

"Lilly? Sure. What's not to like?" I said, faking enthusiasm.

"I don't know. You seemed kind of weird at Granny and Grandpa's. Is everything okay? Did you and Aiden have a fight?"

My heart swelled at her concern.

"No, no. We had a wonderful weekend."

"Oh. Good," she said, clearly pleased.

I gave Lucy as reassuring a gaze as I could manage. "I'm fine. Don't worry."

She watched me after I faced forward.

"Okay. I don't believe you, but whatever."

"Lucy…"

"Dad. I know when you're lying to me."

"You do?"

"Most of the time. You're not very good at it."

"Thanks a lot."

She grinned and put her sneakered foot on the dash. "I'm a much better liar than you."

"Oh, really?"

"Obviously."

I laughed, my mood improving. She was such a little shit disturber. I glanced over, and she was still watching me with concern.

"Anyway, Aiden and I had a great time this weekend. He's a very special person," I said.

"I knew it!" she said, taking her foot off the dash and sitting properly. "So what did you guys do?"

Oh fuck. I blinked and drove and tried to think of something to say.

"Oh, well, we went out for lunch on Saturday and for brunch today. Otherwise, we kind of just hung out."

"Uh-huh. Did you smash? You smashed Aiden, didn't you?"

"What? What does that mean? And why would I smash him? It doesn't sound very nice."

Her laughter was so loud I couldn't hear the radio.

"Oh my God! *Dad*!"

"What"

"Smashing is…it's…*you know*!" She looked around, as if the car might have another person in it. "*Sex*!" she said.

Oh!

"Smash means to fu—I mean, have sex, with someone?" Huh. I couldn't keep up with all the lingo.

"Yeah, duh. You're supposed to be smart."

"Very funny."

"So? Did you? Did you and Aiden smash? You can tell me, Dad. It won't gross me out."

"Lucy, I am not having this conversation with you."

"Why not?"

"Because what Aiden and I did together is private."

Her mouth went into a big O, and I realized I'd been tricked.

"Fuck," I said.

"I knew it!"

"Lucy…"

"It's okay, Dad. You shouldn't be embarrassed, just because you're old. Old people can smash."

"What? I'm not *old*!"

She laughed and giggled and smiled all the way home.

* * * *

After Lucy had gone to bed, I went into the master bedroom, got under the covers, and called Aiden. Cocoa hopped up next to me and lay down with her back against my hip.

I was very glad that Lucy's room was on the other side of the house, because that kid had ears like a hawk. Still, I turned on the TV to muffle any conversation.

"Do we really need to have a TV in the bedroom?"

Daniel looked at me like I was from outer space.

"Why wouldn't we?"

"Because a bedroom is for sleeping. And…other things."

"Sure. And now we can watch TV."

"I don't want to watch TV in the bedroom," I said.

"You know," Daniel said, giving me a lustful glance. "It's also a cover for those other things you mentioned, so that Lucy doesn't hear anything when we're…you know."

When Aiden answered my call at the other end, he was laughing and talking to someone. It took me by surprise, and I felt a surge of unexpected jealousy.

"That's not what I meant," he said to whomever was there. "Hey, babe."

"Hi," I said. "Sorry to interrupt." The endearment helped me to push my jealous reaction down a bit.

"No worries. My buddy, Tyler, is here and he's being very annoying."

"Fuck off! You love it," said Tyler from across the room.

"Oh. You've mentioned him. He's another teacher, right? And he's in your band?" I said, eager to place the strange man in my boyfriend's apartment.

"Yeah. He's the drummer. We're having beers and exchanging strategies. Tyler and his wife just had a baby, so he wanted to get out of the house and away from the chaos for a bit."

"Oh! What about his poor wife?"

"Good point. What about Marie? Did you just leave her in the trenches?"

Tyler said something that I didn't hear.

"He says she went out last night. They're taking turns."

"Commendable. I remember those days."

"I...do not. But from everything I hear, I'm glad I've avoided it so far."

So far? "So far?"

There was a pregnant pause. "Really, Fletcher? You want to discuss this on the phone?"

"Discuss what?"

Another pause. "Would you ever have more kids? Or is one enough?"

What...is happening?

I couldn't think of anything to say. I cleared my throat. "Pardon?"

I heard Tyler laughing in the background.

"I haven't absolutely ruled out having kids myself. But it's not something I need."

"Aiden," I said, "are we really at a point in our relationship to discuss this?" I asked, feeling weak in the knees.

"Fletcher, I'm twenty-eight years old. My biological clock is ticking."

Tyler shouted, "You're such a dick, Aiden. He's joking, Fletcher. He's had a couple of beers and now he thinks he's hilarious."

"Nice. Ha-ha," I said.

"Sorry. I'm sorry," Aiden murmured into his phone. "Were you hoping for a private conversation?"

"I mean, kind of. But it's fine. You're allowed to have friends."

Aiden laughed. "Oh good. You, too."

"I don't think I have any."

"Really?"

"Well, there's Patrick. Does he count?"

"Sure," Aiden said.

"Cool." I wanted to tell him about the conversation in the car. "Lucy asked me if we smashed."

"Oh no! What did you say?"

"I asked her what 'smashed' meant."

"No!" Aiden started laughing hysterically. "Oh, Fletcher."

"What?" Tyler asked.

"Fletcher doesn't know what 'smash' means."

More laughter.

"I do now."

"What did you tell her?"

"I *tried* not to tell her anything, but she figured it out."

"Of course, she did. That girl isn't stupid."

"Yeah, well, I wish she wasn't so perceptive. She knew there was something wrong when I picked her up."

"Oh, honey," Aiden murmured, serious now.

"I had to go in and meet the new kitten."

"Of course you did," Aiden said. "Is it cute?"

"Of course, it's cute. It's a fucking kitten."

"Sorry."

"Well, the grandparents were acting all smug, and Lucy was obviously head over heels with the kitten. It was uncomfortable."

"I'm really sorry, Fletcher."

"Thanks," I said, glad to have someone to talk to about it, even if my boyfriend was getting drunk with someone else right now. "I'll let you go. But I wanted to tell you about Lucy's embarrassing question."

"At least you know what 'smash' means."

"Uh-huh. Maybe you can explain it better the next time we're together. I'm still a little...*confused*."

"I'd like nothing better." Aiden purred. "I'd love to go into explicit fucking detail with you."

"I'd like that, too," I said.

"Is Patrick free to watch Lucy on Friday?"

"I can find out."

"Should we book the Bordello?"

"The *what?*" Tyler shouted from across the room.

"Never mind," Aiden said to him. "Do you want me to?" he said into the phone.

"Hell, yes. I'm going to need it."

He laughed softly. "Well, Fletcher. I am dedicated to giving you exactly what you need."

"I love that about you."

"Okay, you love birds," Tyler said in the background. "Wrap it up. Aiden and I have a game of Super Smash Bros to get through before I go back to the ball and chain."

Aiden gave a horrified gasp while I smiled.

"I'm going to tell Marie you called her that," Aiden said to Tyler.

"She refers to me the same way. It's our love language."

"Jesus," Aiden said. "Charming. Bye, Fletcher."

"Bye, Aiden."

We hung up, and I texted Patrick.

Hey. Can you watch Lucy on Friday?

Awe, shit. I'm working.

I thought you said you weren't.

My ringer went off. It was Patrick, calling me.

"Sorry. I said I'd fill in for Cory."

"Yeah, it's just that Aiden wants to book the kink room."

"Oh, really?" Patrick sounded entirely too delighted.

"I guess I'll have to tell him not to," I said, feeling depressed.

"Wait! How about Robin?"

"What?"

"He's looking for extra cash. Lucy would love him."

She probably would love the saucy young man who worked at Molly's with Patrick and had treated us so well the other night. But...

"Do you think he'll want to babysit?"

"It's not really babysitting. Lucy's twelve. I think he'd do it."

"I don't know," I said, trying to imagine the flamboyant server in my home.

"Fletcher, Robin is many things, but he's responsible and conscientious in a strange, sort of irreverent way. I promise. Do you want me to ask him?"

I thought it over for about two seconds. "Sure. Yes. Please."

"Can you give him twenty bucks an hour?"

"Sure." Totally worth it. And that was probably the going rate, anyway. I got away with paying Patrick less since he was family. "Wait. Do you want twenty an hour, too?"

"No, no. It's fine. I'm happy to do it for whatever."

"I don't want to stiff you, though..."

"Fletcher. It's fine. It's just that if I can tell Robin twenty an hour, it will be a done deal."

"Okay. Thanks."

* * * *

I woke up the next morning to a text from Patrick that Robin was on board for Friday. I let Fletcher know I had a sitter for Friday when he called me at lunch.

"Not Patrick?"

"No, he's covering for someone at the club. But he said Robin would do it."

There was a pause. "Wait. *Robin*? The molly boy with the Miss Piggy jokes? The one that showed me his *nipples*?"

"Yeah. Why? Do you think that's a bad idea?"

"No, Fletcher, I think it's amazing. Lucy's going to love him."

"Maybe it's a bad idea."

"I already booked the Bordello. If Patrick vouches for him, I'm sure he'll be great."

Chapter Fifteen

Treasure

On Monday, while I was still finishing up at the office, I called my sister-in-law, Catherine, Patrick's mom. I thought she might have some insight into how to deal with Annie and Brian's plans. I texted her first to make sure she had a moment to talk.

"Hey, long time no speak."

"Fletcher! How are you and Lucy? Eh, I get all the info from Patrick."

"Yeah, not all the info, I'm afraid."

"What do you mean?"

I hesitated. Now that I had her on the phone, I wondered if this was a good idea. What if she already knew? What if she thought they were right?

"Ah…are you aware that Annie and Brian want full custody of Lucy?"

There was a long pause. "No. I didn't know that. What the hell?"

Oh, thank God.

"Are you serious?" she asked.

"Unfortunately, yes."

"Hold on. Let me sit. When did they drop this on you?"

"Last week. You know they won't be able to take her away from me. I've spoken to a lawyer."

"Thank God."

"Yes. But...Catherine...I don't want Lucy to know, and I don't want to get into a ridiculous battle that they're going to lose. It seems so...ridiculous and useless."

"Oh, Fletcher. I'm so sorry."

"I was actually wondering...if maybe you could speak to them? I tried to explain that it was pointless and would just be hurtful to Lucy and me. But Annie is determined..."

"Oh God. Fletcher, I'll do what I can. But I have to tell you...when Mom gets something into her head that she thinks is 'the right thing to do', it's really hard to dissuade her." Catherine explained. "Normally, that's a good thing. But in this case..."

"Thank you. Maybe if you can explain, and it's not just me desperately trying to get them to change their minds."

"I'll do my best."

"Thank you so much. I owe you big time for this."

"You don't owe me anything. I'm sorry my parents are being dicks."

I felt better, now that I knew I had Catherine on my side. But I wondered if it would make any difference.

* * * *

Lucy adored Robin from the moment he stepped into the house.

"Well, hello, there, Daddy," he said, looking me over with a wink. "Where's the little one?"

Lucy, admiring Robin's red and black winter coat, laughed at the 'Daddy' reference then frowned.

"I'm twelve," she stated.

Robin looked at her with the sort of amicable disdain that only he could convey. "And I'm twenty-four. Twice your age and just as bratty. Hello, Lucy."

She couldn't help but be charmed.

"Hi," she said, with a tentative smile.

"Lucy, this is Robin. He works with Patrick."

"At the sex club?"

Robin narrowed his eyes and gazed from Lucy to me.

"What on Earth has your daddy been telling you? Molly's is *not* a sex club. It is a very sophisticated, artistic, bohemian enclave."

"A…what now?" Lucy asked.

"An *enclave*. Google it, child."

Normally, if anyone had had the audacity to call Lucy a 'child', they'd have got an earful. Robin got a giggle and a begrudging, "Fine."

I gave him props for not being intimidated. Then again, this was Robin.

"I'll give you my contact information, in case of an emergency," I said, as Robin took off his fancy coat and held it out.

I stared at it for a second and glanced at Robin. He raised his eyebrows.

I took his coat and hung it up.

Lucy gazed in fascination at Robin's fancy, bejeweled blouse and copious necklaces.

"Whoa," she said. "I love your outfit!"

Robin preened. "Oh, this old stuff? You should see what I hide in my closet."

He winked at me and handed his phone over.

"Don't open my photo gallery."

"I wouldn't dare," I said, blithely, as Lucy put a hand over her mouth, giggling again. What had this man done to my cynical, sharp-witted preteen?

I sent myself a text and was about to put my name in his contacts when Robin held his hand out.

"Hold up. Give it to me."

I gave the phone back.

He tapped on the screen. "What's your last name again?"

I rolled my eyes. "Well, if you'd let me—"

Robin gave me a look of absolute astonishment at the gall I'd had to interrupt him, and I withered inside. Oh yeah. He'd do just fine with Lucy.

"Uh, it's Marin. My first name is Fletcher."

After tapping again, he showed me the screen with a coy smile. Lucy and I looked at where Robin had me listed in his contacts as *Daddy Marin*.

"Oh my God," Lucy whispered, covering her mouth and glancing at me.

I gave Robin a steely look and nodded. "Fine. I suppose you have other"—I did air quotes—"'Daddies' in there?"

"A few. Never you mind."

"Uh-huh."

Robin toed off his black Chelsea boots to reveal white frilly socks with strawberries all over them. His snug black jeans showed off his full figure. The man was a legend already, and he hadn't got past the front hall.

"All right, girl. Show me around," he said, holding out his hand to Lucy, who took it and jovially showed Robin the main floor as I stood there, stunned but happy that I had an evening with Aiden to look forward to, knowing that Lucy would be in good— well, *spectacular*—hands.

I headed upstairs to change.

Aiden was picking me up. We'd decided to take one car this time, since parking near the club could be tricky.

I was still getting dressed when he rang the doorbell.

"Ah, fuck," I said, finishing quick and heading downstairs.

When I got to the living room, the three of them were standing in a semi-circle at the entrance, staring at me. Aiden was smiling, as if he had a secret—which he did, and it was whatever he was going to do to me in the Bordello. Robin looked like he was judging my outfit, and Lucy was grinning like a kid who knew that all the respectable grown-ups were leaving.

"Oh, Fletcher," Robin said, giving my outfit a disappointed look. "*Tsk tsk tsk.*"

"You look great," Aiden said, as if to defend my choice of black slacks and a tan sweater. The weather was getting colder, and I didn't want to be chilly. Besides, it didn't matter what I wore, because I doubted if Aiden would keep me in these clothes once we passed through the doors of the Bordello.

"Dad, you need to go shopping," Lucy stated.

"Girl!" Robin said, holding his hand up and giving me another once-over.

Lucy high-fived Robin, and I realized I'd just ensured a lifelong friendship between them.

"Are you ready?" Aiden asked, with a subtext that, hopefully, only I was aware of.

"Sure."

I turned to Lucy.

"Listen to Robin. And don't get so carried away having fun that you set the house on fire."

I looked pointedly at Robin, who was fondling a soft wool throw that lay on the back of the couch. He put a hand to his chest in shock.

"As if." He turned to Lucy. "Girl, your daddy is super paranoid."

"Yeah, I know," Lucy said, plopping down on the couch and eyeing me with disdain.

"Okay, let's go," I said to Aiden.

"Nice blouse," he said to Robin, who preened and smiled.

"Have *lots* of fun," Robin said, giving us a knowing wave then turning to Lucy and clapping his hands together. "Okay. Where are the matches?"

Lucy snorted and dissolved into hysterical laughter as Aiden hustled me out of the door.

"Never mind. Let's go. It'll be fine."

"Are you sure? Maybe this is a bad idea…"

"Fletcher, it's fine," he said, guiding me to his car. "I need to take you in hand. And something tells me you need that, too."

"Yeah. But…" I gazed back at the house.

"Are you really uncomfortable leaving Lucy with Robin? Or is this just the unease of a dad who thinks he shouldn't have any fun?"

"I don't know."

"Fletcher, get in the car."

I got in the car. Aiden got into the driver's side.

"Now be quiet and repeat after me. I deserve to have a life above and beyond being Lucy's dad."

He started the car as I repeated his words.

"Now look. Robin may be flamboyant and irreverent, but Patrick vouched for him, and I'm sure he's responsible and capable of watching Lucy for a few hours."

"Thank you," I said to Aiden, as we drove away. "Sometimes it's hard to—"

"I know, babe. And that's because you take fatherhood very seriously. But sometimes you need to be just Fletcher."

"Yeah."

He glanced at me, looking me over like I was prime rib.

"And sometimes, you need to be my pretty little slut."

I swallowed, meeting Aiden's sultry glance, my cock swelling in my pants.

* * * *

When we got into the room, Aiden told me to stand by the door with my hands on my head and my eyes closed while he got things ready. I listened to the sounds of him walking around, opening drawers and gathering items, the anticipation building on top of what had already accumulated on the ride here and the short wait in the gaming parlor. The molly boys were getting to know us now and had flirted outrageously, whetting our appetites. What a spectacular place this club was.

"All right," Aiden said finally, after he'd returned to me. "Give me your hand, but don't open your eyes."

"Yes, Sir," I said.

Aiden led me forward. "Such a good slut. My sexy, obedient, naughty little slut."

His words felt like butter melting over my skin.

"Thank you, Sir."

He led me around some of the bondage furniture then stopped, placing my hand against rough wood.

He guided my fingers over a cold metal loop that was attached there with bolts.

"Do you know what this is?" Aiden asked.

"No, Sir," I said, quaking with trepidation and curiosity.

"Hmm. Well, let me ask you another question," he said, as he trailed something slim and leathery against my skin. "Do you know what the Victorians enjoyed, besides getting kinky with each other in back rooms?"

"Um…no, Sir."

"Riding."

Is that another word for fucking?

"Riding, Sir?"

"Yes. Horses, leather boots and bridles…all that jazz." Aiden's lips tickled my ear. "Do you want to be my pretty pony?"

I stiffened as a jolt of unexpected arousal passed through me. Arousal plus interest, fear, fascination, intrigue, curiosity—all at once.

I made a sound.

"Sorry, what?"

"Yes," I said, letting the 'S' sound drag on a precipice of desire.

He chuckled. "Thought so." He traced the leather implement over my backside. "Pet play is fun. It's so…immersive and humiliating."

I shuddered, my cock surging, a bubble of fluid making my glans cold as the air in the room hit it.

"You can open your eyes."

I did. I stood before a rough wooden board that was attached to the wall, with a sign above it that said 'Hitching Post'. Someone had scrawled *'For naughty ponies'* below that in red.

I whimpered.

"Are you a naughty pony, Fletcher?" Aiden said, stroking my hair. "Or a good, obedient one?"

I couldn't make words.

"Can't wait to find out," Aiden said, showing me something he held in his hand.

It was a small harness of some kind, made with slim leather straps and buckles. My gaze fixed on the long ears that were fastened to the sides of a crosspiece between four thin bands. They were made of stiff leather that had been shaped into a horse's ears.

"Now, are you going to stand still and let me put this bridle on you? Or are you going to fight me?"

I gaped at Aiden. He had the most delighted, benign smile on his beautiful face, and it fucking broke me. I'd do whatever this man wanted me to do. How could I fight him?

I closed my eyes, trying to contain my emotions.

"Oh, my good, sweet pony," Aiden murmured.

Something hard pressed against my lips.

"Open."

I opened my mouth, and Aiden pushed the soft leather bit between my teeth, fitting the leather harness over my head and fussing with buckles. I kept my eyes closed. This was such a weird experience.

My breaths came in quick pants. I realized I was still dressed. I didn't know what to do with my hands.

"Let me get this on then I'll help you out of those silly clothes."

When he'd gotten the bridle into place, he took the reins that dangled and looped them through the ring on the hitching post. Not tight, just enough to show me he wanted me to stay where I was.

Then he carefully undressed me. His fingers trembled as if he were as excited as I was to explore this new dynamic. He used wrist cuffs to attach my hands at the small of my back.

The bridle was a mind-fuck for sure. The bit made me feel tamed, and the weight of the ears ensured I didn't forget about them.

Once I was naked and positioned where he wanted me, Aiden pulled the reins tighter through the hitch and knotted the ends, so that I stood directly at the wall, with about an inch or two to spare. I stared wide-eyed at the hitching post in front of me, the words on the sign combining with Aiden's murmured endearments to remind me that I was a lowly animal, subject to my master's wishes.

My mind spun with possibilities. Would he put a saddle on me and make me crawl around on all fours? Would he try to ride me as if I were an actual pony? The idea seemed ludicrous and impractical, and I hadn't seen anything that looked like a saddle in this room.

The hiss of leather slicing through air, and Aiden's soft words, brought me back to reality.

"Hmm, so many riding crops to choose from," he said, and I remembered that ponies didn't always receive gentle care.

I pulled on the reins and shuffled my feet, then attempted to look around, but my chin was immobilized by the hitch. So I stared straight ahead — my eyes wide, my cock hard — and waited.

Aiden dragged the leather tip of the crop over my body, tracing my shoulders and my back, my thighs and calves, my buttocks and hips, making me crazy with the teasing pressure.

"My pretty pony. So, so pretty," he crooned. I thought I might die of embarrassment but floated on bliss and contentment. It was so nice to be praised, when so many of my efforts in the real world went unremarked.

Now and then he would tap the crop against my skin, and occasionally give me a sharp swat, solely to keep my attention.

By the time Aiden began to strike me in earnest, I was aching for it.

"Such a nice ass on my pony!" he said, his words making waves of excitement go through me. "But I need to bring some blood to the surface."

The sting spread over my bottom and sent warmth throughout my body, like a low fire on a winter's day. I closed my eyes and leaned into the discomfort in order to appreciate it.

Finally, Aiden stopped. He came close and kissed the shell of my ear, then laid a hand against my burning skin.

"Did you like that?"

"Yes, Sir," I whispered, words somewhat garbled by the leather bit.

"Good. But something's missing. I noticed it while I was whipping this beautiful ass."

I waited in the same confined position while Aiden left me then returned, trailing something smooth and silky against the sensitive skin of my rear end. It felt like a wig of long hair, and I couldn't parse it, unless it was a horse's mane he planned to add to my costume.

Then a solid, rubbery lump bumped my thigh, and it seemed the hair was attached to that.

Oh, fuck me.

It was a *tail*. It was *my* tail. And Aiden's words confirmed it.

"A pretty pony needs a tail," he said, the excitement in his voice a palpable thing.

"No," I said.

Aiden hesitated.

"No?" he asked.

"Wait," I said instead. I wasn't sure. I needed a moment.

"Fletcher? Talk to me."

"I'm not sure..."

"No?"

I shuffled my bare feet. How to say it without sounding persnickety or embarrassed, even though I was both of those things?

"We didn't...do the...enema. You know..." Talking with the bit in my mouth was difficult and humbling. My words sounded strange.

"Oh," Aiden said. "But you did...*something*."

"Yes, Sir. I used a disposable douche." Yeah, that sounded great with the lisp. "But it might not be enough. I'm sorry."

He came around beside my head.

"Hey, don't apologize. I know we didn't fully prepare, but I'll take the risk. The douche should be enough. And, if not, I'll deal with it."

"You will?" My cheeks were aflame.

He chuckled. "You keep forgetting. I was almost a nurse."

"Oh."

"You're getting out of character. I need to give you a name."

"Yes, Sir."

I waited patiently, feeling conflicted about the butt plug tail. On the one hand, I enjoyed butt plugs in general, so the actual sensation of being filled and of it going in were desirable. I wasn't sure how I felt about being made into a pony that way. The bridle was one thing, the hitching post another. The tail seemed final, as if that would transform me into Aiden's pet once and for all. But did I hate that idea…or love it?

"Treasure," Aiden said. "That's what I'll call you. Because that's what you are. Even without a ponytail and bridle."

My heart swelled with happiness.

"Spread your legs."

The happiness remained in the background as anxiety and shameful desire took over. I did as I was told.

I heard Aiden lube up the plug and my heartbeat quickened. I could only stare straight ahead. He might as well have blindfolded me.

A gloved hand landed on my hip, and Aiden guided me back a couple of steps so I was leaning forward with my legs spread. I was a little unsteady because my wrists were bound.

"Don't worry, Treasure. I've got you," Aiden crooned.

His gloved fingers spread lube between my crack and around my hole, swirling and stroking then pushing into me as I gasped with the pleasure of it.

"Good pony. Open up for me."

I groaned as one finger became two, and Aiden stretched me in a pragmatic way that left me feeling lowly and objectified. I loved every minute of it. Too soon, those fingers were gone, and the slick tip of the plug pressed against my hole.

"Relax, pretty pony. Open up, now. You want your tail, don't you?"

I did want my tail. I wanted it more than I'd admit to anyone but Aiden, and even then, not in words.

I closed my eyes and allowed the plug to sink into my body, as Aiden used a steady pressure to breach me. I couldn't help the soft moan that I made as it slipped in, and my body closed on the narrow end. The wide flange rested against my buttocks, and the soft fall of hair tickled the backs of my knees. Aiden's hand on my hip steadied me as he rocked the horse tail-plug to make sure it was seated, the motion making me groan.

"There we go. You can straighten up now."

He helped me step forward, the plug feeling huge and the horse hair brushing the backs of my legs.

I heard the sound of Aiden peeling off his nitrile glove then he fluffed the hair of the tail, spreading it out. I made a choking sound as the reality of being made into a pony for a whim of Aiden's hit me.

"Are you okay?" he asked, laying his hand against my lower back.

I nodded my head, as much as I could with it hitched to the ring.

"Oh, man. You would not believe how good you look. Fuck. So pretty. So sexy. So fucking perverse."

I shuddered and tried to slow my breathing. I was so turned on at being objectified and humiliated in this way. It was humbling and everything I'd ever secretly wanted.

Aiden spanked one flank, then the other, and the size and hardness of the plug in my ass was made even more apparent when my sphincter clenched in response.

I made an almost inhuman noise of anguish and pleasure both, as my cock bounced in front of me, still hard, still leaking and still a little bitch to anything Aiden devised.

"Oh yes," he murmured. "My beautiful Treasure is a natural. Such a good pony."

He placed his palms on my butt cheeks and pushed them together, then pulled them apart, then pushed them together again, all of it to make me feel the plug and the soft hair more, and thus lean into my debasement.

"I could come just looking at you," Aiden said.

I whimpered and thrust into the air, my ass tightening on the plug that filled me so perfectly.

"How about a grooming session? Isn't that what ponies get? A good brushing to make their coat all shiny and smooth?"

I turned into a puddle of horny goo at Aiden's words, wondering what he meant.

"Shhh," Aiden said, as he brought soft bristles down on my shoulder and dragged them along my arm. "Be a good pony and stay still."

Chapter Sixteen

Ambushed

The soft brush strokes felt good on my sweaty skin, soothing itches that I hadn't even been aware of until the cushiony bristles relieved them. Aiden brushed me all over, taking great care to soothe and tease me everywhere. When he brought the silky brush over the reddened skin of my buttocks, the pain came to the surface again and made me aware of every sore spot.

When he'd finished attending to my entire body, he tickled my balls and cock with the bristles, running them up and over the head of my penis, causing me to gasp and jerk. He must have liked that because he repeated the motion until I whimpered and stomped my foot.

"Oh, you saucy thing. You need to stay still."

I huffed and whined but submitted to being teased and tortured until, thankfully, Aiden put the brush aside.

"All right, now. You've been such a good pony, I suppose I should give you a reward."

Yes, yes, yes.

"Does my sweet Treasure want a reward?"

"Yes, Sir. Please, please, Sir." I sounded ridiculous with the lisp from the gag ruining all my 'S's, but I was getting used to it.

"Fine. But I don't want to hear words from you. You're a pony, so you can neigh or nicker to get my attention."

Oh my fucking God. Is this actually my life?

I hesitated.

"Do you want a reward, Treasure?" Aiden murmured, his fingers stroking the skin along my buttock.

He wasn't going to make me do horse noises, was he?

"Hmm. I guess my pony just wants to be put back in the stable with a leaking cock and blue balls."

I closed my eyes and made an approximation of a horse's whinny, my cheeks flaming with the humiliation of it. But there was no way I was opting out of a reward. '

"You can do better. Try again."

I tried again and sounded more like a horse and less like a confused human. It was so embarrassing. But I *really* needed to come. There were a lot of humiliating things I'd do to get an orgasm at this point. I only hoped that sounding like a horse was all that Aiden would ask of me.

"Oh, much better, Treasure. Much better." He wiggled the plug and thrust it forward a couple of times, making me cry out.

"Mmm. You like that."

He continued to tease me with the plug, and I whinnied in desperation, dying to come and so strung out on this surprisingly intense pet play that I was beginning to feel a bit lightheaded.

Finally, *finally*, I heard the squirt of the lube bottle, and slick fingers wrapped around my aching cock.

I gasped — then remembered, and whinnied. I would be his goddamned pony if it would get me off with a desperately needed hand job.

Aiden chuckled and kissed my ear as he jerked me, while rocking the butt plug horse tail in my rear. I went off like a popped champagne bottle, spurting, making a mess and uttering the most ridiculous sounds. The darkness behind my closed eyes filled with fireworks, stars and colored lights as I came hard, my body jerking, my ass clamping down in spasms on the solid rubber plug. The fall of horse hair swished against my trembling legs.

The only sounds in the room were the loud beating of my frantic heart and my staggered breaths as I came down from the intensity. I tried to calm my breathing as my muscles relaxed and became almost liquid.

Aiden supported me as I staggered.

"Hold on. I'm going to untie you."

His fingers worked quickly on the hitch, and soon I was free.

"Now, on your knees, my Treasure."

I fell to my knees, grateful to be on the ground and at the feet of my noble master. I rested my forehead against Aiden's thigh as he opened his pants and took out his dick.

With deft fingers, Aiden removed the bit, wet with my saliva, from the bridle and tossed it onto the floor.

"Open your mouth. I'm going to fuck it. It's my favorite thing."

I groaned in answer and opened my mouth wide, as Aiden guided his cock into it.

"Oh fuck yes. My pretty pony. Such a pretty pony," he murmured as he thrust roughly into my mouth, one hand gripping the bridle and the other on my chin, his thumb pulling down on my lower lip.

I opened my eyes and watched his face as he tipped over the edge and came, shooting down my throat in hot bursts.

* * * *

I was in a daze as we returned the key to Sebastian. He looked at me strangely then glanced at Aiden with his eyes raised.

"Pony bridle," Aiden whispered, as I almost died of embarrassment. He gazed at me with apology. "You've got some marks from the leather straps."

"Oh my God. Why didn't you tell me?" I said, trying to hide my face while Sebastian smiled.

"I only just noticed," Aiden said. "Sorry."

"Don't worry," Sebastian said. "It's nothing to be ashamed of."

"Easy for you to say."

"Why? Do you think I've never been tied to the hitching post before? Jacob does it every morning."

Aiden and I looked at him in shock.

"Okay, not really. But it has happened a few times. When in Rome and all that."

I felt a bit better knowing that Sebastian, this fine gentleman and co-owner of Maverick Molly's, liked to be a pony, too. But I was tired and sweaty and needed a shower.

While sitting in the passenger seat of Aiden's car, I checked my phone.

"Fuck," I said, scrolling through a bunch of texts and missed calls from Robin. "Fuck, fuck, fuck. Oh my God."

Aiden glanced over. "Are you okay?"

"*No.* Robin's been trying to get in touch with me for an hour!"

I hit the call button, not even reading his texts except to see him mention Annie and Brian. If the grandparents were there, it must be fucking serious.

"Robin!" I said, when he answered.

"Oh hi, Fletcher. I wondered when you'd get back to me. Sorry to bother you." Robin's words held a note of irony.

I heard Annie's muttering in the background.

"Lucy! Is she okay?" I stammered, convinced something terrible had happened.

"What? Oh, she's fine. She beat my ass at Scrabble and went to bed."

"Oh…" My brain swirled. "So…okay. Thank God. But why all the texts?"

"Did you not read them?"

"We just got in the car to come home. I panicked. I thought something was wrong. Why did you try to call me?"

"Oh, well, it's only that Lucy's grandparents decided to drop by. Did you know they were coming?"

Oh fuck.

"No. They didn't tell me they were planning to stop by, or I wouldn't have gone out."

"Mm-hmm. Well, they're here with me. So you might want to come home and explain that I'm a responsible, mature person who is quite capable of looking after their granddaughter for a few hours." Robin sounded sweet and amenable, but I heard the sharp crack of ice beneath the surface. "They told me I could leave, but I refused. You're the one who hired me to watch Lucy."

"Oh fuck."

More muttering.

"They can hear you," Robin said.

"You have me on speaker?"

"No. But my volume is up. I'm half deaf in one ear."

"I didn't know that," I said.

"It's fine. Anyway…"

I glanced at Aiden. "We'll be there in ten minutes."

"Oh good. It's been a fun evening," Robin said, still maintaining a sweet outer demeanor.

"I'm so sorry, Robin."

"Did you have fun?"

"I did. Thank you for watching Lucy."

"Actually, she was great," he said, his voice losing a bit of the edge. "If you can convince Annie and Brian that I'm not a sex worker—"

Gasps from off the phone.

"Then I'll be happy to hang out with her again. Ta-ta."

We disconnected, and I let my head fall back against the seat.

"Everything…okay?" Aiden asked. I wasn't sure how much of that he'd heard.

"Annie and Brian are there."

"Shit. Lucy's okay?"

"She's fine. She's in bed," I said, my voice dull as I processed everything. "They don't approve of Robin."

"Robin is amazing."

"I know."

"Are you...going to be all right?" Aiden asked, glancing at me with concern as he drove. "You're dropping, aren't you?"

"Like a fucking stone."

"Shit," he said. "Should I pull over? You can have a moment to get it together..."

"No," I said, shaking my head and putting a hand to my forehead. "I'm fine. I'm okay."

"Fletcher, you need something to drink and a snack. We should have stayed at Molly's for a bit. I'm so sorry."

"I'm fine," I said. "Jesus, Aiden, you don't need to baby me." My voice sounded sharp.

"I'm not trying to *baby* you. I'm trying to be a good Dom," Aiden explained.

I took a deep breath, closing my eyes, and listened to the engine and the tires and the ambient sounds of the car.

"You are a good Dom. You're a *great* Dom. I loved everything about tonight."

"You don't know how wonderful it is to hear that."

"Except for the past ten minutes."

"Understandable."

We drove in silence until we got to my place. As he turned into the driveway, Aiden asked, "Would you prefer if I just dropped you off?"

"No. You might as well come in." I hadn't meant that to sound as dismissive as it did. "I'm sorry. I mean, *would* you come in? I may need your support."

"Fletcher, of course. You will always have that."

I grinned wryly. "Even if we break up?"

"Yes. As a friend in that case."

"Huh."

Aiden raised his eyebrows. "Are you planning to break up with me? Just so I know?"

"Not a chance."

"Oh, good."

We chuckled then sobered as we exited Aiden's car. I took a few deep breaths and decided that the goal was to get Annie and Brian out of my house as quickly as possible, so that I could finish coming down from that incredible scene with a cup of herbal tea and a bath. In the meantime, I'd somehow retain control of my emotions.

"You're angry," Daniel said. "I know."

"Because you always do this!" I said, throwing the dish towel onto the counter.

"What do you mean?"

"You can't tell me before we do a scene? Why do you have to wait until I'm dropping to pull something like this out of your hat?"

"I'm sorry. I didn't realize you were dropping."

"Daniel. We just had the most intense scene. I'm exhausted and feeling very vulnerable right now. And now you tell me that you're not sure about this parenting thing? Jesus! It's too fucking late!"

"I know. I know it is. I'm just…I'm struggling, and I wanted you to know that."

"I already know."

"Is it that obvious?"

"Kind of. But I'm struggling, too. I think all parents struggle. I think it's a part of the landscape. There's no getting away from it."

"Yeah."

"You just have to deal with it."

"Right."

"And we'll deal with it together. Because we're Lucy's parents and we love her."

I opened the door, and we stepped into an uncomfortable silence.

Robin was sitting on the very end of the sofa in the living room with his hands in his lap and a bored expression on his face. He looked up with relief when we came in.

Annie and Brian looked grim, sitting at the dining table, and regarding me and Aiden with disapproval.

*Ten, nine, eight, seven, six…*I counted down from ten in order not to lose my temper.

How dare they? How dare they come into my home and make Robin feel uncomfortable when he'd done me a solid and taken care of Lucy for the evening? I had no doubt that Lucy would be singing Robin's praises all the next day. Aiden was right. Robin was amazing. And I hated that Annie and Brian had given him reason to believe that his presence was inappropriate.

"Hi, Robin," I said, ignoring them for the time being. We had things to discuss, but the first round of business was to let my sitter go home. "Thank you so much for looking after Lucy."

Annie let out a *humpf* from the table but I ignored her.

Robin stood, keeping his gaze on me.

"You're welcome, Fletcher. She was an absolute angel." I doubted that was true but appreciated the spirit of it. I had no doubt that Lucy had tried to get away with staying up late or watching an R-rated movie but that Robin had been equal to her wiles. I couldn't see Robin letting anyone take advantage of him, even a twelve-year-old expert negotiator like Lucy.

He glanced at Annie and Brian and swallowed his pride. "Nice to meet you both."

They didn't respond, and I felt like shit for him.

"Anyway, I'd better call an Uber," he said.

"I'll pay for it," I said. "Let me know how much. And text me your email address so I can send an e-transfer for tonight."

Robin would be getting a bonus for putting up with all this in such a graceful way, when I knew that he could have easily flattened Lucy's grandparents with a few sharp words and his acerbic wit. It would have been wasted on them, though, and would have only made them angrier.

"Sure. I'll wait outside. By the way, Lucy is pretty fucking smart. I can't believe she beat me at Scrabble. I know a lot of words that she doesn't."

I heard a gasp from Annie as Brian cleared his throat.

"Yes, she is. And I'm sure you do."

Aiden laughed lightly, and I was reminded that there were still reasonable people in the world.

"I'll, uh, wait for my Uber outside," Robin said again.

"Good idea. Thanks again, eh? You're a lifesaver."

"Yeah, thanks. Good luck," he whispered. "And, sorry."

"You didn't do anything wrong. I'll sort it out."

"Okay. Thanks."

Aiden nodded at Robin as he went by.

Ten, nine, eight, seven, six, five…

"Where on Earth were you, Fletcher?" Brian asked. "It's almost midnight."

…four, three, two, one…

"Hello, Brian. Annie. I wasn't expecting you."

"Well, that's obvious," Annie muttered.

I toed off my boots and hung my jacket on a hook, while Aiden did the same.

"You must be Lucy's grandparents," Aiden said, with a charming smile, stepping forward. "I'm Aiden Thompson."

Brian and Annie didn't say anything. They shot me with accusatory glances instead.

"Aiden is my boyfriend. We were out on a date."

"Well, I'm glad that your personal relationships are taking precedence over fatherhood," Annie said.

Ten, nine, eight, seven, six...breathe in, breathe out, smile.

"Robin says Lucy's in bed, which is exactly where she'd be if I'd been home. I'm not sure what you're implying."

Annie stood from her chair and glared at me. "I don't think it's very responsible to have a young man in a blouse and makeup looking after our granddaughter."

I blinked. "I'm sorry. What?"

Brian cleared his throat. "We were very surprised to find that young man here. If it had been Patrick, well, that's one thing."

"But it's not Patrick, is it?" Annie stated. "Where did you meet this Robin character?"

"That's actually none of your business, Annie."

"He works with Patrick," Aiden said. "Robin is very responsible and —"

"I beg your pardon, but I'm speaking to my son-in-law," Annie interrupted.

And that was it. I slammed my hand on the dining room table, making everyone jump. Brian's eyes went wide, and he put a hand on his wife's arm.

"Don't you dare speak to him that way. Don't you dare come into my home, intimidate my babysitter and speak rudely to Aiden."

"We're Lucy's *grandparents*. We have a right to know if she's being looked after."

"She *was* being looked after."

"Not by her father, though," Annie said, waving her hand at the sofa. "By some namby-pamby boy in frilly clothes and makeup!"

"You keep saying that," I said. "Do you have a problem with those particular pieces of clothing? And I believe *you're* wearing makeup, Annie."

Annie glanced at Brian for support, but he stayed quiet.

"Oh, come on. It's not normal for a boy to dress like that."

Aiden cleared his throat. "Actually, un-gendered dressing is becoming very popular. Lots of men and women dress opposite to their assumed gender."

I closed my eyes. I appreciated Aiden trying to help, but honestly, his words were flying against deaf ears.

"It's ridiculous," Annie said. "I don't know why people can't just wear the clothes they're supposed to."

I couldn't even argue with her anymore. It was too ridiculous, and I didn't have the brain cells.

"Now that you know Lucy is safe, is there anything else I can help you with?" I asked.

"Fletcher, we don't think you should be going out with other men until all hours of the evening."

"For fuck's sake, it's Friday night. Wait! What do you mean by 'other' men?" I asked.

Brian tugged on his wife's arm. "Annie, we should go."

But it was too late.

"Other than *Daniel*?" I asked, realization dawning. "Is that what you mean?"

Annie shook her head, as if waking from a dream.

"I don't—" she started to say.

"That can't be what you meant, Annie, because Daniel is *dead*. My husband, *Daniel*, is *dead*."

"Fletcher," Aiden said in low tones.

"What? Daniel is dead, Aiden. And apparently Brian and Annie think that means I can't have another relationship."

"I'm sure they don't think that," Aiden said, putting a hand on my back, trying to contain the imminent explosion.

"I won't stand here and have my son's name—" Annie stuttered.

"What? I can't speak about Daniel, either?" I put my hand on the table and leaned toward her. "What gives you the right to tell me what to do?"

"Lucy is… Lucy is our granddaughter."

"Yes, and she's my daughter. She's my *daughter*!"

"Daniel would have wanted us to—"

"Daniel would have wanted Lucy to stay with me," I said, trying to keep my voice low. I didn't want to wake Lucy.

"You don't know that. If he could see you now with—"

"Oh, my fucking God," I said, then steadied myself. I took two deep breaths and glared at Annie. "Daniel would give me his blessing. Daniel would have wanted me to find"—I almost said 'love' but backed off of that ledge—"someone. And I've found Aiden."

"Well, that's wonderful for you, then. Brian, I think we'd better go."

"Annie," I said, staring in a blood-red rage at the top of the dining room table. "I won't give her up."

She didn't respond. She and Brian left, and Aiden locked the door behind them. I collapsed into a chair, feeling the remnant sting of the crop. I relished it. It gave me a distraction from my anger.

"How dare they?" I said to Aiden when he came and sat down beside me. "How fucking *dare* they?"

"Yeah. Wow. I didn't really know what you were dealing with."

"The frustrating thing is that we all think we know what's best for Lucy."

"Okay, true, but who has more of a right to decide that?"

"I do."

"Exactly. Do they actually think they'd win a custody battle?"

"Maybe. But I don't want Lucy to go through that. So, basically, I have to decide if her mental health is worth me giving in and letting them have her. Maybe we can come to some kind of arrangement."

"Fletcher," Aiden said, "what are you talking about?"

I didn't answer right away, and in the silence we heard the soft pat-pat of bare feet on the hardwood.

We turned around at the same time and watched Lucy, in her panda pajamas, walk to the couch and sit down.

"Oh, hey," Aiden said, glancing at me. "How's it going? Great pajamas!"

"Thanks. What are you guys talking about? Did Granny and Grandpa go home?"

I couldn't deal with this. I was still dropping from our session, and everything had just been too much. I put my face in my hands with a groan.

"Is Daddy okay?"

No. No, Daddy is not okay.

I felt Aiden's hand on my back, rubbing gently.

"He's just got a very bad headache, that's all," Aiden said. "I'm going to make him some tea. Do you want anything?"

"No, I'm gonna go back to bed. I just wanted to make sure everything was okay. I thought I heard angry voices."

Aiden chuckled. "I'm sorry if we were loud. How did you and Robin get along?"

"Oh my God. He's great. I love him! Can he babysit me again?"

I made some unintelligible noises.

"I'm sure he can," Aiden said. "Good night, Lucy."

"Good night. I'm glad you're here to look after my dad."

There was a pause while I'm sure Aiden swallowed his feelings. "I'm glad I am, too."

Lucy's soft footsteps disappeared as she returned to her room.

"That kid—" Aiden started.

"I know. Thank you."

"I'm getting you some toast and tea—then running you a bath."

"Thank you."

"Fletcher. Everything's going to be all right."

Chapter Seventeen

Peacemaking

The tea and toast did wonders for my mood. I hadn't realized how exhausted and emotionally spent I'd been until I felt better.

While Aiden was running the bath, I went to my bedside table and picked up the photo of Daniel.

"Have I showed you this?" I asked.

Aiden looked at the picture and shook his head.

"Well…this is Daniel," I said.

Aiden took the photo frame and looked at the image of my late husband. He was on the ground in a pile of leaves with Cocoa on top of him, grinning like a fool.

"He's…handsome."

"Yeah, he was."

"Gorgeous blue eyes."

I sighed. "Recognize them?"

"Of course. Lucy's are the exact same shade," Aiden said. "She looks like him."

I nodded, then held out my hand. Aiden put the photo frame back in my hand and I placed it back on the bedside table. Then I opened the drawer and got out a piece of folded notepaper.

"I want to show you this letter."

Aiden sat on the edge of the bed. "Is it from Daniel?"

I shook my head. "No. I mostly have emails from Daniel. I have a folder of them."

"That's good."

I passed the letter over. Aiden unfolded it.

"It's from our surrogate, Tamara — the woman who carried Lucy while she was growing."

"Oh!" Aiden said.

"We kept in touch. She sends Lucy a birthday card and Christmas card every year."

"Is she… Did she…?"

"We used a donated egg and Daniel's sperm."

"That's really incredible."

"It really is."

"Why…why Daniel's?"

I smiled, remembering the conversations we'd had.

"We almost flipped a coin, but that didn't feel right. So we looked at family histories. Daniel doesn't have any relatives with cancer. I have two in my lineage. That was basically the reason." I realized I'd used the present tense. "It's hard to remember to use the past tense."

"It must be."

"Tamara has three kids of her own, and it was something she wanted to do for us." I sighed. "She saw the obituary. I wasn't in any state to inform her of Daniel's passing and nobody else thought to. She wrote me this letter."

I watched as Aiden started to read.

I had memorized it, because I'd looked at it so often in the months after Daniel's passing.

Dear Fletcher,

I'm so sorry about Daniel. I can't possibly imagine what you're going through right now, but I wanted to tell you that Lucy is very lucky to have you to look after her in this trying time. It must be very hard for you both, but you have each other to lean on.

I know that none of us expected this to happen and didn't even think of the possibility when we were expecting Lucy. It was a beautiful, wonderful time, only to be topped by the day of Lucy's birth. When the doctor took her and put her into your arms, and Daniel looked over your shoulder, it was such an important moment in my life.

You might not have realized how much I felt honored to be chosen and trusted with such a precious cargo. Thank you for letting me carry your daughter inside my body, and nurture her, and grow her, so that you and Daniel could experience fatherhood.

Lucy is so special, and so are you. And so was Daniel.

Please remember that he is still a part of this universe, watches the two of you and cares for the two of you. I am completely certain of that.

Take good care, and don't be a stranger.

Love Tamara.

P.S. I've enclosed a note for Lucy as well, basically saying the same things. I will leave it up to you if you want to give it to her now or wait for a later time.

"Fletcher, this is so lovely," Aiden murmured.

"It helped a lot. I gave Lucy hers. We talked a lot about Tamara and the process we went through to make Lucy happen, and I think that helped her grieve her father. Finding a surrogate, having a successful pregnancy, the waiting and hoping and planning... It was a crazy, wonderful, terrifying time, which I imagine it is for any couple. It just so happened there were three people involved."

Aiden blinked rapidly and nodded.

I sighed. "There are no guarantees in life. I know that. There were some scary moments during the pregnancy. And we had no idea if the baby would be healthy or not. But we decided we were in it, no matter what," I said. "And we still are. I mean...I am."

"And Lucy is amazing."

"If I didn't have her, I probably wouldn't be standing here right now."

"Are you talking about...?"

"Yes."

"I'm so sorry, Fletcher. I have no idea what to say."

"You don't have to say anything. And I want you to know that with the help of a lot of therapy, and I guess, time, thought and realizing there is so much to enjoy in life, even now, I'm...I'm not anywhere near that place. But I was in it for a while. And it's only because of Lucy that I'm here." I took a deep breath and glanced in the direction of Lucy's bedroom. I shrugged. "Maybe it was the same with her. We kept each other going—for Daniel, for each other. And we're both really solid right now. But...if Annie goes ahead with this custody thing, I don't know... I don't know..."

Aiden put the letter down and came over, wrapping me in his arms.

"Hey. It's going to be all right. Whatever happens, you'll both be okay."

"You can't know that."

"Maybe. But what I do know is that I'm here for you and I'm here for Lucy, and we're going to get through it. I promise."

"I want to believe you."

"Then do it. It's an order."

I sighed.

"And now you need to get into that bath and relax. I don't have a teaching gig tomorrow, so we can get Lucy off to school then figure some of this stuff out."

"Okay."

"But please don't worry about it tonight."

"Okay."

"I think Tamara's right. I think Daniel is up there looking down on you and Lucy, and he'll do what he can to help."

I glanced at Aiden with a twinkle in my eye, starting to feel like myself again. "Do you think he's watching us in the Bordello?"

Aiden threw back his head and laughed. "I mean, how could he not? I'm sure he's enjoying himself."

"I hope so."

I was starting to think the late hour and emotionally draining evening was catching up to me.

"Now, into the bath…then to bed."

"Yes, Dad."

"Sure, we can play it that way," Aiden murmured, taking my hand and leading me into the bathroom.

* * * *

I couldn't bear to wake Aiden when my alarm went off and he didn't stir. So I went downstairs and got some coffee going and made breakfast for Lucy.

She was eating her scrambled eggs and bacon when Aiden wandered into the kitchen. Her eyes got huge, and she looked back and forth between us.

"Oh!" she said. "I mean. Wow. Did you sleep over?"

Aiden blushed. "Well...we got back late from our date, so..."

"Yes, Aiden slept over," I said, "How do you feel about that?"

Aiden pulled out a chair and sat down at the breakfast table, winking at Lucy.

"How do I feel about it?" She shrugged. "I like Aiden, so it's cool." She looked at me with waggly eyes. "How do *you* feel about it?"

Now it was my turn to blush. "Well, obviously I'm okay with it," I said, glancing at the handsome man at the table.

"Oh my God," Lucy said, with a giggle. "You just went all schmoopy-eyed."

"I did not go schmoopy-eyed," I protested, giving her a look. "Robin said you beat him at Scrabble."

"Yeah, I did. I'm still the queen. He made a good effort, but" — she shrugged again, chewing smugly on a piece of toast — "I beat his sorry ass."

Aiden barked a laugh as I put some scrambled eggs onto his plate and offered him some buttered toast.

"Thank you. Wow, this is good service."

"Ha-ha," I said. "Maybe I want you to come back."

We saw Lucy off. I was pleased that she felt okay about Aiden sleeping over. She was twelve years old and not stupid. She knew there was sex involved. Sometimes I still felt weird about having a boyfriend, when I'd promised my heart to Daniel. But the vows were *'until death do us part'* for a reason. I had no doubt that Daniel would have wanted me to find someone else so that I could be happy and also so that Lucy could have another person to look out for her.

For the first time in a long time, I felt that I might actually survive this — except for the whole Annie and Brian factor.

Aiden and I sat down over second cups of coffee to discuss it.

"Have you told your therapist about it?"

"Yes."

"What does she think?"

"She's as concerned as I am. She thinks it would be further traumatizing to Lucy. It's already traumatizing me."

"Would Annie and Brian be willing to sit down with her?"

I shook my head. "No. They're from a generation that doesn't believe in psychological therapy. Fuck, I hadn't thought about that. They'd probably take Lucy out of therapy if she went to live with them."

Aiden made a face.

"So…what can we do about Annie and Brian?"

"I honestly don't have a clue…except try not to lose my temper again because that will only make the situation worse. They already think I'm a bad parent."

"I don't know about that."

"They thought I was pretty irresponsible last night, leaving her with Robin and going out with you."

"I think…they are under the delusion that they could do a better job, if only because there are two of them. Or…"

"Hmm? Or what?"

"Or it's something else. Some way to hold on to Daniel, maybe?"

"Huh. That's what my therapist said…and Catherine."

"Who's Catherine?"

"Daniel's sister. Patrick's mom. I told her what was going on, and she talked to Annie and Brian. But she says they're determined, and she can't stop them. She did try to talk some sense into them."

"You know, people grieve in all kinds of ways. Daniel was their son, and all he's left behind is Lucy."

"And me. Don't forget about me."

"How could I forget that? It's the only reason I've got you."

I reached out to hold Aiden's hand.

He continued. "But, for them, maybe holding tighter to Lucy is how they're trying to process their grief."

I let go of Aiden's hand. "But they can't have her! She's my daughter."

"I know that. But maybe what they're feeling isn't rational."

I frowned. "It sounds like you're on their side."

"I'm not. Fletcher, I'm just trying to look at this from their perspective. I happen to think it's horrible, what they're putting you through."

I nodded. "For Christ's sake they're acting like she's an orphan or that I'm incapable of raising her properly."

He gave me an indignant look. "We both know that's bullshit. And somehow, you have to help them see that they aren't going to win this, and that it's going to hurt Lucy to try to take her away from you."

I nodded. "Right. I suppose we could have them for dinner?"

It was actually a joke, but Aiden didn't laugh or smile.

"I think that's a great idea."

I sobered. "You and me?"

He held up his hands. "I'd only be here to support you, to make sure they weren't bullying you and overriding you."

"I don't know."

Would they even agree to come?

"You invite them for dinner. Get Patrick—or Robin—to take Lucy out for a special treat. Don't even mention me. But I'll be here, helping with the cooking and everything."

I grinned, feeling better to have sneaky Aiden on my side. "Oh. That's diabolical."

"You don't think they'd turn around and leave, do you?" he asked.

"I have no fucking idea. But I feel like we should try. If the three of us can talk about this rationally, maybe there's a chance to avoid hurting Lucy. I'm more than willing to give them more time with her. That would honestly help me out."

"Sure."

I shrugged. "It's worth a try. And if it still goes to court, I can blame Annie and Brian for Lucy's trauma."

"Oh, Fletcher. I'm so sorry."

"I never thought, in a million years, that Daniel's parents would ever want to hurt me like this…or their granddaughter," I said. "And, no offense, but just as I'm starting to recover from the shock and unfairness of Daniel's death, when I finally think I can possibly move on, I find myself wishing once again that he'd never died. And I know it's pointless, because I can't change my circumstances, but it just makes everything so damn confusing, because I feel so lucky to have you in my life, Aiden. You don't understand what you've done for me. What our relationship means to me."

He gave me a look that expressed his own vulnerabilities and emotion.

I continued. "It's not all about the kink, you know."

He smiled and reached out for my hand. I gave it to him.

"I know."

"Even though, a lot of it is about the kink. Can we talk about that last session?"

Aiden groaned. "Yes! I'm glad it went so well. I wasn't sure how you'd react."

"I can honestly say that that isn't something I ever did with Daniel. And that makes it super special and new and...I think that's what I needed. To know that...to know that my submissive, kinky side is alive and well and didn't end up buried with him."

My voice broke on those last words, and Aiden pulled me into his arms.

"It didn't. It definitely didn't."

"No. And apparently, it likes to play horsey," I said, my cheeks burning.

Aiden laughed. "Oh yes. You were fantastic. An equine dream."

I blushed. "What gave you the idea?"

"Huh. Honestly?"

I gave him a look.

"I'd always wanted to try it, and I had a sneaky suspicion that you might like it. My Treasure," he said, cupping my chin and kissing me softly. "I hope we get to play that game again."

"Aiden, it's my new favorite thing."

* * * *

In an email, I told Annie that I wanted to have them over for supper because I regretted the tone of the last conversation we'd had. I apologized for being tired, on my last nerve and raising my voice.

She agreed to come, only stating and I quote, *If this is to try to change our minds about Lucy, it won't work.* At least she'd admitted that they'd been out of line with some of the things they'd said that night.

I restrained myself from throwing my laptop across the room and, even though that was exactly the reason I wanted them to come over, said that I would try to keep that in mind. I also said that I would cook a lasagna from scratch, which I regretted as soon as I'd sent the email.

I was a decent enough cook. I'd made this lasagna a few times already, and it had been Daniel's favorite meal, so I'd figured I could make it again without too much trouble. When I actually began the process, I realized that Daniel had been alive the last time I'd made it.

"Here. Careful. Why don't I chop the carrots?" Daniel asked.

"It's fine. I've got it under control."

"Really?"

"Yes, really. Go sit down. Have a glass of wine."

"Well, if you insist."

Fifteen minutes later, when I was swearing and cussing and trying to be quiet, because Lucy was in the other room watching Beauty and The Beast, *he came into the kitchen again and placed a soft kiss behind my ear.*

"Fletcher, darling. Let me help you. I'm a pretty good sous chef, remember?"

"Okay, fine. But I wanted to do it all myself."

"Why? What are you trying to prove?"

"I don't know. That I can take care of you?"

"You do take care of me. In lots of ways."

"I wanted to feed you. I should be able to do this by myself."

"Who says?"

"I don't know."

"Just shut up and move over. I'm only helping. You're steering the ship."

Aiden had come over to help get the house looking ship shape, so he was vacuuming and tidying up, bless his heart. Lucy had gone out with Patrick *and* Robin to see the new Marvel movie and go for dessert after. And I was in the kitchen remembering the last time I'd made lasagna and crying into my noodles.

"Oh my God, what's wrong?" Aiden said when he noticed.

I shook my head and waved him away. "It's fine. I'm fine."

"You're obviously not."

I grabbed a tea towel and brushed it over my face.

"Is it…not going well?"

At least that made me kind of laugh. I shook my head.

"It's not that," I said, trying to keep control of my emotions. "This was Daniel's favorite recipe."

"Oh, honey," Aiden said. "Come here."

He came into the kitchen, and I practically collapsed into his embrace.

"I'm sorry," I mumbled, sniffling against his shirt.

"You have nothing to be sorry for."

"It's been so long since I've made a special meal for anybody. And I forgot that I hadn't made this since before he died."

Aiden looked at the ingredients and half-done lasagna on the counter.

"Do you want me to take over? I've never made it before, but I can follow a recipe."

"No. No, I can do it. But...could you chop up the carrots and celery?"

"Yeah, of course. Where do you keep your knives?"

"In there," I said, sniffling and trying to remember that Daniel was here with me, though not in physical form. He'd love that I was making this for his parents, even if they had misguided ideas about the raising of his daughter.

"And...can you just, I don't know, talk to me? While we're working? About whatever — the news, your job, the band. Are you playing any gigs in the near future?"

"As a matter of fact..."

So Aiden chopped and talked, and I did the rest. By the time I was sliding the casserole in the oven for its final bake, I had a hold of myself — and that was another thing got through. Hopefully it wouldn't be so hard the next time.

"Okay, what time is it?" I asked, loading the dishes into the dishwasher and turning it on. "Do I have time to change?"

Aiden looked me over. "I mean, I hope so. You've got tomato sauce everywhere.'"

I looked down at myself. Sure enough, I was splattered with little red dots and splotches and smeared cottage cheese.

"Fuck," I said.

The doorbell rang.

I ran past Aiden and up the stairs. "Just answer it, and I'll be down in a minute!"

"But they don't even know I'm here. Fletcher, you look fine, I was only teasing."

"You'll have to wing it."

I felt bad for him. I really did, but as I flew into my bedroom and frantically changed into clean jeans and a blue button-down, I had faith that Daniel's parents wouldn't do anything drastic when Aiden answered the door, like leave immediately or yell at him.

As soon as I'd finished dressing, I checked my hair and face in the bathroom mirror, took a deep breath, and headed downstairs. Miraculously, Aiden was holding his own, and filling glasses for Annie and Brian while regaling them with some crazy work story.

"Oh, there he is," he said, with relief.

"Hi," I said. "I just had to change my clothes. How are you both?"

"Hello, Fletcher," Annie said, gazing at me with a smug smile while Brian shook my hand. He greeted me warmly. It seemed like Brian at least wanted to start things off on the right foot.

"It's so strange to see someone else in your kitchen," Annie said, gesturing to Aiden.

"Aiden offered to help. I haven't made a fancy meal in a long time."

"Smells good," Brian said, taking his glass of wine to a spot on the couch.

"Aiden's a supply teacher," I said, hoping to get him into their good books.

"Oh really? Elementary or high school?" Annie asked him, directly.

"Elementary," he replied.

"Oh. You must have to go through some kind of background check for that job, I suppose?"

I opened my mouth to protest when I felt Aiden's calming hand on my elbow.

"Oh, yes, of course. I must have checked out okay," Aiden said, laughing nervously.

"You're a wonderful teacher," I said.

Annie's eyes widened. "Aiden's not *Lucy's* teacher, is he?"

"Annie," Brian said. Apparently, this was the limit of his interference in his wife's meddling.

I stared at her. "Aiden is working as a supply teacher while he waits for a permanent position. He did teach her class, for a few weeks. We met at the school."

"Really," Annie said, crossing her arms and dripping with disapproval.

"Annie," Brian said, "would you please leave Fletcher alone."

Everyone turned to stare at Brian, who normally didn't say much.

"Pardon?"

"Annie, we're guests here."

Annie looked back and forth between Brian, me and Aiden.

"I didn't mean to cause a problem," she said, subdued.

Annie and I stared at each other for a long moment, neither of us sure how to proceed.

Then Aiden clapped his hands together.

"Anyone up for a game of Jenga?"

Chapter Eighteen

Impasse

"Why Jenga?" I asked. "I don't even have Jenga."

Annie and Brian had gone to sit on the living room sofa.

"Oh, I thought I'd seen the box in the living room..."

"That has LEGO in it," I said.

"Because that makes sense," Aiden smiled. "What *have* you got?"

I looked into the living room. "Uh. Twister?"

His eyes went wide. "Wait! That's perfect!"

"No, come on. We are not playing Twister with Lucy's grandparents! For God's sake, Brian just had a hip replacement."

"Huh. So they want to parent an energetic twelve-year-old, but can't even play fun games with her?"

"Honestly, I'm not sure I could get through a game of Twister at this point. Have you even played it?"

This discussion was serving to amuse me, at the very least. And picturing Brian and Annie trying to play Twister with Lucy was highly entertaining.

"Yes, I have. And I can still play it. And I foresee an enthusiastic game of naked Twister with you at some point."

I raised my eyes, and Aiden grinned.

"Please don't mention that to Annie."

"Oh, I promise I will," he joked. At least, I hoped he was joking.

We went into the living room and sat down together across from Annie and Brian.

"How's the new hip?" I asked Brian.

"He's fine," Annie said. "Fit as a fiddle."

"I've got most of my mobility back," Brian said. "And it throbs a bit at night, but that's easily controlled."

"That's good," I said. "It'll come in handy when you take Lucy hiking."

"Pardon?" Brian looked startled. He gazed at Annie.

"Oh, just that Lucy enjoys hiking in the Gatineau hills, remember? So I figure if she's staying with you and Annie, you'll be taking her hiking and camping and doing all those things with her, right?" If they could play dirty, so could I.

"Well now, we thought you'd still be able to do those things with Lucy."

"Me? You mean you'd trust me with her out in the wilderness, but I'm not capable of looking after her on a daily basis?"

"This isn't a comment on your abilities, Fletcher," Annie stated. "We simply think —"

"Annie, there is nothing simple about this. You'll be taking the only stability Lucy's had since Daniel died."

I glanced at Aiden, who looked wary. I hadn't planned on getting into this until we'd finished dinner.

Annie gave me a tolerant look. "Of course, we know that it will be difficult for you."

I gaped at her. "Difficult for *me*? Lucy will be the one to suffer. I'm going to win this fight, Annie, but Lucy will be the one to suffer."

"So don't fight with us, Fletcher. Why don't you make this easy on us all and admit that you're in over your head parenting a child by yourself? Lucy will be with us, and you can live your life the way you want to."

"This is the way I want to live my life!"

"Is it? Bringing casual sexual partners into the home where your twelve-year-old daughter lives?"

"Aiden isn't my casual sex partner. And he's gay, so I can assure you he's absolutely no threat to my twelve-year-old daughter."

Annie looked skeptical. Aiden and Brian looked horrified at the way the conversation had turned.

"My personal life is none of your business," I said to Annie, careful to control the tenor of my voice. "Wait. Are you actually homophobic? Is that part of what this is about?"

Annie's lips pressed together. "I watched you marry my son. I watched you hold his newborn child in your arms. I never said anything, made any kind of protest or complaint. I figured if you were what Daniel wanted, then I would support him. But...now that he's gone..."

"Now that he's gone, what? You only care about Lucy?" I stared at Annie. "Did you ever actually like me, Annie? Or did you only pretend, for Daniel's sake?"

For the first time, Annie looked embarrassed and caught out.

"Fletcher, I... I only think that Lucy would be better off with us. I think that, in the circumstances, Daniel would feel that way, too."

Brian stepped forward. "Annie, you have no idea what Daniel would think about any of this, and the only reason Fletcher has a new boyfriend is because his husband, our son, *died*."

Well, at least one of them was reasonable.

"Exactly," Annie said, folding her arms over her chest. "Lucy is all we have left of Daniel. Can you blame us for wanting to spend more time with her?"

"No, that's the only part of this I understand. Because Lucy is all I have left of Daniel, too. But I'm pretty sure—no, I'm absolutely positive—that Daniel wouldn't want us to fight over her."

"No, he wouldn't," Annie said.

"Good. I'm glad we agree on that, at least."

"What I want," Annie said softly, "is for you to really think about what you're doing, Fletcher. Starting a new relationship, gallivanting all over the city, leaving your daughter with questionable young men..."

"You mean Robin?" I asked.

"Yes. Robin. The boy in the makeup who was here the other day."

"For one thing, Robin is in his early twenties. For another thing, he's a kind and responsible person. He's also funny and charming, and Lucy loves him."

"Lucy is twelve years old."

"This discussion is going nowhere," Brian said.

"I have a right to my personal time, Annie. If I want to go out with Aiden, or anyone else for that matter, it's none of your business."

"Not when you're a single parent, you don't," Annie said. "Lucy and Lucy's needs should be your absolute priority, Fletcher. Take it from someone who's raised a child once already."

Oh, she was going to use that one on me.

"Lucy's needs *are* my priority. But my needs are important, too," I said. "And I'm perfectly happy to arrange a more frequent schedule if you want to see Lucy more often."

"*Hmph*," Annie muttered.

There was an awkward silence as we sat in disagreement. Then Brian spoke.

"Annie, parenting is different than it was when we had Daniel."

"What?" Annie asked, gazing at Brian with confusion.

I could see that Brian was trying to be diplomatic about all of this, and I appreciated that.

"Parents aren't expected to give up everything for their children anymore," he said. "And...I think that it would have benefited you to have looked after yourself better and not done everything for Daniel for so long."

I bit my tongue, because, yeah, it had taken some time for Daniel to realize that I wasn't going to take over from Annie and look after his every need. We had had some arguments early on about what I expected from another adult in a relationship, and that I wasn't prepared to sacrifice myself for his needs. He'd changed his habits, or there wouldn't have been a long-term partnership between us. When Lucy had come along, it had been a struggle for the both of us, but we'd done our best to share responsibilities equally.

Now it was only me, but I knew the importance of finding some space for my own needs and wants, even if I felt guilty about it sometimes. My therapist had emphasized it, too.

Because what I had with Aiden had helped to fulfill me, and that benefited Lucy, too — not to mention that I had someone to help me out with practical things, as well. He wasn't a co-parent...yet. But he had my back. He was proving that right now.

He'd been quietly watching everything unfold, and now cleared his throat.

"May I say something? As an objective third party and an elementary teacher."

Annie rolled her eyes, but Brian gestured for Aiden to continue.

"Of course," he said, ignoring the look Annie gave him.

"I think," Aiden said, choosing his words with care, "that regardless of who might be a better parent objectively to Lucy — and, so there's no confusion, I think that would be Fletcher — but regardless of that, don't you think that Lucy's had enough upheaval in her life?"

Annie blinked at him, thinking that over. When she started speaking, she seemed calmer, and I had some renewed hope for the evening.

"I don't think it would be an upheaval for Lucy to come and live with us. She already has space in our home. She's used to staying with us for lengthy periods over the summer."

I couldn't let that rest.

"Yes, when she's on vacation. But Lucy has her regular life here," I said, putting my hands in my pockets to keep me from walking over and trying to strangle Daniel's mother. "She has a friend who lives down the street. We have school bus pick-up arranged, right out of the front door. I don't think she'd qualify for school bus transportation from your zone. Have you thought about that?"

Annie grunted. "Brian will drive Lucy to school."

"I didn't really think about that," Brian said, shrugging. "But, yes, I can drive her."

"Great," I said, giving them a fake smile. "But did you know she enjoys riding the bus with her friends? It's not a long ride, and it's a way for her to destress after a long day."

Annie glanced at Brian.

"Actually, I was looking at a couple of the schools in our zone. I think one of those might be better suited to Lucy and would provide a much better learning environment."

Wait, what?

"You want her to switch schools? Are you kidding me?"

"Saint Bartholomew is supposed to be a very good school. I've heard that the Catholic board is better all-around than the public one."

Well, this was getting better and better.

"You want to put Lucy in the Catholic Board." I couldn't even believe they were proposing something so offensive.

"Well, I just think it's a better —"

"Wow." It was Aiden.

We looked over at him. He was staring at Annie with a stunned expression.

"Do you...do you know what the kids in the Ontario Catholic Board learn about gay and trans rights?"

"I don't think that's relevant," Annie said.

"Absolutely nothing," Aiden stated. "They don't get proper sex education, either."

My head was spinning.

"Lucy is *not* going to attend a Catholic school," I stated. "Daniel wouldn't want that. And I certainly don't. And neither does Lucy."

"But if it's what's best for her —" Annie tried.

But I couldn't even discuss it anymore.

"I'm sorry. I cannot continue this conversation."

I stood and went into the kitchen. I checked the timer on the lasagna. It still had another twenty minutes of cooking time. I didn't think I was going to make it.

I heard subdued conversation and sounds of movement from the living area. Then Aiden came into the kitchen.

"They're leaving."

I looked at him, wondering how on earth we'd gotten to this place.

"But...but we haven't had the lasagna." All that work and hope that somehow this could fix the situation.

"I'm so sorry, Fletcher. I tried to get them to stay."

I nodded, wiping tears of frustration from the corners of my eyes with the heel of my hand.

"God, Aiden. I'd give anything to be in the Bordello with you right now. I want to be Treasure for a little while — not Daniel's grieving husband, not Lucy's dad, not Annie and Brian's fucking son-in-law." I lifted my gaze to his. "I just want to be me."

He stared at me for a long moment. "When are Robin and Patrick bringing Lucy home?"

"We've probably got a few hours."

Aiden looked sober. He walked past where I was standing and turned the oven off.

"Follow me," he said.

What was happening? Was this what I thought it was? My brain began to swim but I focused on Aiden's words. All I had to do was what he told me.

I followed.

He led me upstairs. "Guest room or main room?"

It didn't take me long to decide. "Main room."

"Take off your clothes, fold them and put them here," Aiden said, pulling the straight chair out from my desk. "And I want you to count your breaths while you do that. Ten on the inhale and ten on the exhale."

"Thank you," I said, my trembling fingers working on the buttons of my shirt.

Aiden went to my bedside table and gently turned the framed photo of Daniel on its face.

"When you're done, come over here and kneel at my feet." He sat on the bed and placed his hands on his thighs.

I obeyed, concentrating on my breathing like he'd instructed. When I was completely naked, I kneeled at Aiden's feet.

"I'm sorry," I said.

"What are you sorry for?" he asked.

I inhaled—*one, two, three, four, five, six, seven, eight, nine, ten*. "For fucking up dinner. For chasing them away. For not being able to—to fix this." I exhaled—*one, two, three, four, five, six, seven, eight, nine, ten*.

"Fletcher," Aiden said, stroking my hair in a way that made me feel cherished. "None of that is your fault."

I nodded. I couldn't speak. I continued to count my breaths, feeling a sense of calm return.

"And you're only a horse, my Treasure, so you can't possibly figure this out right now. And I need you here, your mind and your body, at my feet and under my command. Can you be Treasure for me?"

"Yes, Sir," I whispered.

"Good pony. Stand up." Aiden stood.

I did as he'd instructed.

"Cross your wrists behind your back. Where do you keep your ties?"

"Oh," I said, crossing my wrists behind me. "In the top drawer on the right."

"I won't use any that look expensive, but I need a couple of them."

He returned to me and used one tie to bind my wrists together and another over my eyes.

"You know, when horses are anxious and scared, a blindfold can calm them down."

"Yes, Sir," I said, my voice quiet and subdued.

"It forces them to place their focus inward, be in the moment and not to worry about their surroundings," he said, in a calm, steady voice. "I want you to pay attention to your body and what I'm going to do with it—and on the things you can hear and smell around you. I want you to know that you are in a safe space with me. You believe that, don't you?"

"Yes."

"What's your safeword, Fletcher?"

"It's 'lamp'."

"That's right. Use it if you need to. I won't be mad."

"Yes, Sir."

"I'm going to keep talking to you, but I want you to be silent, unless there's something you need to say. Ponies don't talk, of course, and I want you to be my Treasure right now and nothing more."

I gave him a nod, already feeling the stress of the evening beginning to dissipate.

"Hold on. I'll be right back."

And he was gone.

I focused on the ambient sounds of the room around me and the rest of the house. The HVAC fan hummed and the clock on my wall made a soft, steady ticking. I'd never been more grateful for it than in this moment. It was the rhythm of a heartbeat, the memory of an in-the-womb sense of security, and it imbued me with calm.

Aiden rustled around in the ensuite, opening drawers and closing them. Finally, I heard him return to the bedroom. He laid a palm on my flank as he leaned into my ear.

"Is the black brush with the soft bristles yours?"

I nodded.

"All right. I'm going to use it to groom you."

I nodded again and licked my lips.

When Aiden began to draw the brush along my skin, I focused on the soothing sensation and on the strength behind Aiden's gentle care. He could have used the back of the brush on my ass—I wouldn't have complained and a part of me wanted to ask for it. Instead, he gently caressed my skin with it, stroking me everywhere, in intimate and not-so-intimate places, while I felt my muscles unclench and relax.

Soon, a different kind of tension built, and I turned some of my focus to that.

Aiden noticed.

"You're feeling better, my pretty pony."

He stroked his fingers along my erection. I groaned and shifted my bare feet.

"Oh, my Treasure is a very sweet, very obedient pony," he murmured, playing his fingers over my length, cupping my balls, and otherwise making me desperate, "I'm going to take care of this for you."

I didn't fully comprehend what he meant until air currents suggested he'd moved, right before his warm mouth engulfed my cock.

I gasped as he grabbed my ass and pulled me closer. "Oh fuck," I grunted.

With my hands bound at my back and the blindfold on, every sensation was amplified, and the feeling of not being in control was heightened. Every coherent thought left me, and I dissolved into the bliss of getting sucked off by someone so enthusiastic and dear to me.

He slobbered over me, letting his saliva get things oh, so messy. It dripped down to my balls. The sounds of sucking, wet flesh and Aiden's soft grunts filled the room. My desire rose, along with my desperation, and the volume of my groans.

The tension built and threatened to break apart the tentative hold I had on myself.

Aiden must have realized. He tightened his grip on my ass and moved his head rapidly back and forth as he worked my cock. I staggered with the force of his pulls, and when he took a hand off my ass to squeeze my balls and finger my hole, I exploded.

I let out a shout that became a groan then a whine as Aiden worked to keep up. He moaned as he swallowed it all and brought me down from the pinnacle, then laughed when his attentions became too much for my super-sensitive glans and I pulled away.

I heard shuffling as he got up and the creak of the mattress as he sat.

"Mmm. Spent and panting and utterly wrecked. That's how I like you."

I concentrated on slowing my breathing and subduing the tremble in my muscles. Aiden stood and lifted the blindfold from my face, gazing at me with a satisfied smile.

"Feel better?"

"Aiden. Thank you."

He wrapped his arms around me and undid the tie holding my wrists together. Once I was free, I embraced him and held him close, enjoying the way his clothed body contrasted with my nakedness.

"I'm glad I could help."

"I think I might be able to sleep later."

"I'm so sorry the evening didn't turn out like we'd hoped."

"I just don't know what to do. I can't let them disrupt Lucy's life, but I also won't put her through a court battle."

"Yeah, it's a shitty situation to be in," he conceded. "But, you don't have to do anything right away. Even if" — Aiden held up his hands — "worst-case scenario, they file legal papers tomorrow, Lucy won't know about it and you'd still have time to negotiate."

I nodded, feeling hopeless and sad.

"Maybe something will come to you if you don't get all wrapped up in figuring out a way to stop them. You can't control their actions, only your own," he said, kissing me softly. "Now, you'd better get dressed, because the boys and Lucy will be back any time."

"Good idea," I said, disengaging from Aiden's embrace. I glanced at his crotch. "Do you want me to...?" I asked.

"I don't think we have time. But I will definitely take a rain check."

Chapter Nineteen

Breaking Point

We turned the oven back on and finished cooking the lasagna. I'd put it into the fridge, and Lucy and I could have it tomorrow. Maybe Aiden could come for supper.

We made peanut butter and jelly sandwiches and ate them with Pringles chips, standing at the kitchen island. When the lasagna was done, I put it on the stove to cool.

Robin, Patrick and Lucy returned soon after, and came in laughing and yelling. Lucy regaled us about the movie and Robin's wild antics, and Patrick watched with a grin. I noticed the way he was looking at Robin, and I started to wonder if something might be going on there.

"I guess you had fun," I said, smiling. At least my mood had improved.

"How did it go with the grandparents?" Patrick asked, while Lucy and Robin played rock-paper-scissors to see who got the bag of leftover popcorn that Robin was holding.

"Not so good," I admitted. "We didn't even make it to dinner."

"Oh man," Patrick said with a frown. "I'm sorry. My mom tried to talk to them, but she didn't get anywhere."

"Yeah, she told me. I'm glad for the support from both of you."

"Dad! Robin's not playing fair!" Lucy said, running over to us with Robin at her heels.

He put a hand to his chest.

"Excuse me! I always play fair, missy. Ask your dad."

"How the hell would I know?" I said, giving him a look.

"Please," Robin scoffed, as if it weren't even in question. "Anyway, here." He handed the bag of popcorn to Lucy. "You can have it. I need to worry about my girlish figure."

She gave him a skeptical look. "Um, your girlish figure is fine. But I'll take it."

"Huh," Robin said, leaning seductively on the breakfast bar and gazing at me and Aiden. "So, looks like nobody's here but you two. What *have* you been up to?"

"Not a whole lot. Our guests left in a huff. The lasagna's going in the fridge. But, on the positive side"—a glance at Aiden showed he was worried I would say too much about how we'd gotten past it—"I'd forgotten how good peanut butter sandwiches were."

Robin cocked his head. "Is that some kind of euphemism?"

"No!" I said.

"Why wouldn't you have just eaten the lasagna?" Patrick asked.

"Unless," Robin said, smiling, "Aiden was too busy making Fletcher feel better…"

"Ew," Lucy said. "Dad."

"We weren't that hungry," I said, between clenched teeth, glaring at Robin and Patrick.

"Not for food, anyway," Robin said.

"Oh my God, good one!" She held her hand up for a high five, and Robin obliged, giving me a triumphant look.

* * * *

Over the next few weeks, despite Aiden's suggestion to stop, I wracked my brain for a way to dissuade Annie and Brian from fighting me for custody of Lucy, while expecting to be served legal documents at any moment.

It wasn't an ideal way to live.

If not for weekly sessions in the Bordello with Aiden, I'm pretty sure I'd have had some kind of nervous breakdown.

I went to see Aiden's band play again, and it was fun to be the lead singer's boyfriend. Again, I admired the easy way Aiden seemed to exist in his body, especially when he was living his best life as lead singer of The Tardy Boys. I teased him that they should have named the band 'The Tarty Boys', because they all wore T-shirts that were too small and very tight jeans. Not that I was complaining.

Tuesday dawned with buckets of rain coming down, and I decided to work at home instead of going into the office. I texted Patrick that I didn't need him to watch Lucy.

From nine to eleven I worked hard on a couple of different projects, then took a break to make a cup of tea and relax before lunch. While I waited for my tea to steep, my phone went off. Annie Marin's name came up on the lock screen.

My first thought was, *Jesus, this is it*. She was going to tell me that they were serving legal papers. I almost didn't answer, but I couldn't ignore a phone call from Daniel's mom.

I tapped my phone with dread swirling in my gut and a cold sweat spreading on my forehead.

"Hello?"

There was nothing but breathing for a second and I wondered what the hell was going on. Then Annie sniffled and said, "It's Lilly. Something's wrong!"

"Pardon?" I said. It took me a minute to catch up. "Annie, what's wrong?"

"The kitten," she blurted. "She's collapsed... I don't know what to do!" Her voice wobbled, and I remembered that she was a sixty-eight-year-old woman who'd lost her only son a few years earlier.

"Oh no," I said. "You should probably take her to the vet."

Annie started crying. "I don't— I can't— She's not moving... Oh, God!"

"Shit. Is Brian there?"

"No. No. He went out. I don't know what..."

"I'll be there as soon as I can."

I grabbed my car fob and jacket and headed out of the door, skidding on the step that I'd forgotten to salt and almost falling. The dogs didn't even have time to notice I was leaving.

I pulled into Annie and Brian's drive a short time later. I was in such a rush that I snagged my jacket on the door of the car and cursed my clumsiness. The panic in Annie's voice had me very concerned.

I knocked twice and tried the handle. It wasn't locked, so I pushed it open and went inside.

"Annie?" I yelled. "It's Fletcher."

I heard a cry and then, "The bathroom. The bathroom."

When I got there, I was hit by the smell of cat piss and shit, and the sight of Annie sitting on the closed toilet, staring at a tiny strip of fur on the wet floor. She raised her gaze to mine, and it was full of so much sorrow and so much dread that I felt my heart ache for her. The animosity that I'd had for her and Brian somehow vanished in this one desperate moment, and I put everything else aside.

The kitten lay in a puddle of fluid — urine, feces and even a bit of blood.

"Can I use one of these towels?" I asked, pulling a soft-looking blue towel out of the cabinet.

Annie nodded, her eyes wide, her hands over her mouth and nose.

I stepped forward and bent down, trying to scoop up the kitten without getting the towel wet with everything else. The poor creature didn't weigh anything and didn't make any sign of life, limp and floppy in my grasp. I held her to my chest, crooning words to soothe her if she were able to hear me, the way I did to Lucy when she was upset or ill.

I glanced at Annie, who was in the same position, her gaze still on the floor. I wondered if she'd gone into shock. "We need to take her to a vet, Annie. Where's the nearest animal hospital?"

Annie didn't respond. She took her hand from her face and opened her mouth, but nothing came out.

"Annie?"

I stuck a finger into the towel against Lilly's tiny throat. I felt a very faint pulse and she made a tiny mewl, then her chest inflated and collapsed, and I stood there as the life left her tiny body. I wondered if I should try CPR, but she was so little and I'd probably break her tiny ribs. She'd already suffered enough.

"Shit," I said. I lowered her into my lap and unwrapped her. "She's gone."

Annie stared at me with a blank expression.

"What?"

"I'm sorry. But she's dead."

Annie shook her head. "No. No. I can't..." She covered her ears and squeezed her eyes shut. She started to rock back and forth, her head going side to side, and her mouth moving.

"No. No. No. *No*."

I saw the reflection of my own grief in Annie's crazed, sorrowful eyes. I put the kitten down and moved toward Annie.

"It's okay, Annie. It's going to be all right."

This wasn't about the kitten anymore.

"*No. No. No. No.*"

Annie's breathing was ragged, and I was worried she might go into cardiac arrest or have a stroke. I had to calm her down.

"Annie," I said, putting an arm around her, "I know. I know...how it feels..." I said, my own voice breaking.

"*No. No. No. No.*"

She clutched at my arm and gazed into my eyes with such desperation, I felt it to my bones.

I spoke in a whisper, my mouth close to her ear. "I know how it feels. Trust me. You lost a son. I lost a—a husband, and the—father of my daughter." I took a breath that felt like a razor to my chest. "But it wasn't anybody's fault. Nobody could help Daniel. Not you. Not me. Not Lucy. Not Brian."

As if I'd given her permission, Annie took a deep, shuddering breath and collapsed against me, sobbing and shaking, the withheld grief of the last three years finally taking hold.

"I'm so sorry," I whispered, and I meant for Daniel's untimely death, but also for the hateful feelings I'd had for Annie and Brian, and the way we'd been fighting each other, when we should be standing strong together.

I held her while she let out all of her sadness and pain, and the body of the dead kitten lay, forgotten, on the floor.

After a long time, Annie's breathing evened out, and I thought she might have fallen asleep. Then I started to worry she'd had a medical incident. And the smell in that room was becoming too difficult to bear.

I shook her gently.

"Annie. Hey, Annie."

She jerked—maybe she *had* dozed off. She stared at me with her wet, grief- stricken face. She looked so old.

"Oh, Fletcher," she said, and I was worried she'd start crying again. "I'm so sorry. I'm so sorry for…everything." Her voice was a whisper. "You're a good father. Lucy is better off with you looking after her," she said, choking on emotion. '

I nodded, unable to say anything as I pulled her close again. My heart broke for the pain Annie must have been feeling and swelled with relief at having the threat of a court battle for Lucy taken away. I blinked back tears and wondered at the way the world worked.

When Annie was able to get up, I wrapped the kitten's body in a clean towel then drove us to a nearby veterinary hospital. I explained what had happened, and the person at reception got one of the vets to come and get the kitten, asking us to wait while they did some tests and checked things out.

I was pretty sure it was too late for any chance at reviving the wee thing, but I wasn't a vet, so I'd let the professionals take over and they could break the news officially to Annie.

We sat side by side. Annie's hair was in disarray, and she was wearing track pants and a T-shirt under her jacket. I was so used to seeing her all put together and made up that it was sobering to see her this way, raw and unkempt.

We both smelled like cat piss.

I held Annie's hand. We didn't speak, but we seemed, for the first time, united in our grief. The vet had come out and asked Annie all the pertinent questions. She'd answered them in faltering sentences:

Yes, the kitten had been eating and drinking...all the time.

No, it hadn't gotten into anything to Annie's knowledge.

Yes, it had been sleeping a lot but wasn't that normal? It had been active, chasing toys and trying to climb the curtains.

Had she noticed any blood in the kitten's stools? She hadn't.

Finally, Dr. Ortiz invited us into an examination room. She closed the door and offered Annie a seat in one of the chairs.

"I'm so sorry, but I'm afraid Lilly has passed."

I tightened my grip on Annie's hand as she nodded. She seemed more herself now and at least had had some time to adjust to this probability.

The vet glanced at me.

"Are you Mrs. Marin's son?"

I opened my mouth to explain but before I had a chance, Annie spoke up.

"Yes," she said, reaching for my hand again. I had to blink a few times to keep control.

"Well," Dr. Ortiz said, her gaze moving back and forth between us, "we can do an autopsy to determine the exact cause of death, but that's going to be expensive. I can tell you what we think it was, if you'd like?"

"Yes, please." Annie's voice was a whisper.

Dr. Ortiz gave Annie a kind look. "It was most likely hypoproteinemia — or protein-losing enteropathy."

We gave her blank looks.

"We call it PLE for short. It's when an animal's body isn't absorbing the protein from food properly."

"Oh," Annie said. "She was eating a lot. I gave her what she wanted."

"Yes, that's why you wouldn't have noticed that anything was wrong. But I'm afraid her body wasn't getting the nutrients — specifically, the proteins — it needed, and there would have been fluid build-up, which is very hard on kittens as young as this. I'm so sorry."

"So, it wasn't anything we did or didn't do?" I wanted that made clear, so Annie wouldn't feel bad that she'd missed the signs.

"No. This is, unfortunately, quite common in young cats, and most people don't notice anything until it's too late...as in this case."

Annie nodded and did seem reassured. But then her face fell and she looked up at me.

"Oh, Fletcher. What are we going to tell Lucy?"

* * * *

I had texted Aiden from the waiting room.

Long story. Annie's kitten collapsed and died. We are at the vet.

He had replied with a shocked face emoji.

Keep me updated.

I texted him while Annie finished up at the counter. I'd offered to help pay for the disposal and the fees, which added up to more than two hundred dollars, but Annie had refused, thanking me but indicating that she could pay it.

I'm driving Annie home. I told her we'd break the news to Lucy.

Horrified face emoji. Then sobbing face emoji. Then three hearts.

At least I wouldn't have to break Lucy's heart by myself.

Btw, she's not going to try to get custody anymore.

A whole line of confetti emojis.

I smiled in response and finally took in everything that had happened over the past few hours. Maybe a kitten's life was a high price to pay for the clarity of a crisis, but I was so fucking relieved.
Lucy, however, would be devastated.

* * * *

Aiden came over to be emotional support for both me and Lucy.

She was very upset when I told her, but she seemed more worried about Annie than anything.

"God, poor Granny! Is she okay?"

"Yes. She's going to be fine. She was very upset, and she cried a lot. But she's a tough cookie."

"I'm glad you were there, Dad. You always know what to say."

I glanced at Aiden, who was looking at me with so much affection I almost couldn't take it.

"Well…I hope I was some comfort to her."

Aiden came close and put his arm around me. "I'm sure you were a huge help and comfort."

"Yeah, Dad," Lucy said, smiling as she looked at Aiden and I all cozy together. "Give yourself some credit. You're pretty good in a crisis."

"Am I?" I asked, pleased to be told so.

"Yeah." Lucy sighed. "Anyway, a craptastic end to a craptastic day. I did my drama presentation. I don't think it was very good."

"Oh, honey," I said.

"All right. You know what this means?" Aiden said, clapping his hands together.

Lucy and I looked at him.

"I'm ordering pizza, and we're going to sit around here and feel sad about Lilly, but happy that she's not suffering. Then, if we feel up to it, we can watch a movie."

Lucy glanced at Aiden with excitement but then turned to me with skepticism.

"But I have school tomorrow."

"You can stay home. Bereavement leave," I said.

"Oh yeah," she said. "You mean, it works for animals, too?"

"Sure." Maybe not officially. But in my books it did.

She had stayed home for a couple of weeks after Daniel's death, and we'd done things together, cried together and ordered takeout a lot and eaten casseroles that friends and family had dropped off.

"Just one day this time," I said. "But you need a chance to process."

"Thanks, Dad," Lucy said, hugging me again.

"What do you want on your pizza?" Aiden asked as I threw him a grateful glance.

"Mushroom and pineapple," Lucy said.

Aiden paled. "Really?"

"Yeah. It's delicious."

He glanced at me. "Do you want—?"

"Never. Pepperoni and olives."

"Oh, thank God," Aiden said, putting a hand to his heart.

* * * *

We had a picnic on the living room floor and talked and laughed and teased each other. Lucy wanted to watch *Moana*. Aiden had never seen it.

"You've never seen *Moana*?" I asked, scandalized.

He laughed. "No. Hey, I don't have kids."

"But you're a teacher," Lucy pointed out. "You must have heard about it. It's literally the best movie Disney has ever made. Well, *Tangled* is close, but *Moana* is the best."

My phone rang while they were talking, and I excused myself and went into the kitchen. It was Brian Marin, and I hoped he wasn't calling to say that the custody battle was back on.

"Hi, Brian," I said.

"Fletcher."

"How is Annie?" I asked.

Brian sighed. "I think she'll be okay. She's crying a lot. I don't think it's only about the kitten. We've been talking about Daniel."

"Yeah? She did mention him earlier."

"Good. She needs to talk about him more. It's been...too painful, you know?"

"I know. Trust me."

"That's just it, Fletcher. We do trust you, especially after what you did for Annie today."

"I'm glad she called me."

"Did she tell you that we're not going to go ahead with the...other thing?"

"Yes. And you don't know how relieved I am."

"I'd already told her I wasn't sure we were doing the right thing." He cleared his throat. "It was a way to hold on to Daniel. I'm sure of it."

"Yes. I'm sorry it led to so much animosity."

"You know, seeing you fight for her? That was something. We can see how important Lucy is to you."

"Yeah," I said, blinking back emotion.

"Anyway, we'll have to come over for that lasagna we never had."

I couldn't help smiling. "Aiden and I would love that."

"And, Fletcher?"

"Yes?"

"I'm...I'm very glad you've found someone—and a way to enjoy life again."

"Thank you, Brian. Aiden was a turn of fate. And I've had a lot of therapy."

Brian chuckled. "Yeah, maybe that would be a good idea for us. It's been three years now, and it hurts just as bad."

"I can give you the name of my counselor, if you like. She's fantastic."

"I'd appreciate that. Thank you." There was a pause. "When you're my age, you think you can deal with anything. But there's no shame in asking for help." Brian's voice broke, and I realized that we were all still recovering from Daniel's death.

"No, there isn't."

I went back to the living room just as the movie started. Aiden beckoned me over to sit with him on the sofa. Lucy was in the armchair with Eddie on her lap. I cozied up to Aiden and nuzzled his cheek.

"Absolutely no kissing," Lucy said, holding her hand up. "Got it?"

Aiden snorted, and I smiled. For the first time in ages, I thought perhaps I had a good future to look forward to.

* * * *

After Lucy went to bed, Aiden helped me tidy up. We were gathering the empty pizza boxes when I was hit with a wave of sorrow so strong it took me by surprise.

I put my empty box down on the kitchen counter and turned to Aiden, and I just started choking on sobs. I kind of fell into his waiting arms while he dropped the pizza box he was carrying onto the kitchen floor in order to hold me.

"Hey, hey. It's okay. It's all right now."

The intense events from the day had caught up to me, and I felt a resurgence of my grief — at the death of the kitten, at the close call with Daniel's parents wanting custody of Lucy and at the unfairness of his early demise. I knew this would happen every now and then, and by now I knew it wouldn't destroy me and that the best thing to do was to ride it out until I could breathe again.

"I'm sorry," I said, pressing my face into his shoulder.

"Don't be. I'm not afraid. I can handle it."

"Thank God. Because it's probably going to happen again."

"Your grief is a part of you. And, do you know what it tells me?"

"What?"

"That you're capable of so much love. That you're not scared to love."

I sniffled into Aiden's shoulder.

"But what if... What if I can't do it again? What if I'm scared to... to love someone, again?"

Aiden pulled back and cupped my face, gazing hard into my eyes.

"Are you scared to love me?" he whispered.

"Terrified," I said. "I'm fucking terrified."

He smiled, and kissed my forehead, then my nose, then my mouth.

"I kind of think this is a done deal, the thing between us."

"Yeah?"

"Yeah. I think it's too late."

I smiled, trying not to start crying again.

"I can't help loving you, Fletcher Marin. I love you when you're Lucy's Dad, I love you when you're Daniel's grieving spouse and I love you when you're on your knees for me. And I can't see that ever changing."

Chapter Twenty

Pearls Before Swine

"Oh my goodness, look who's back!" Robin squealed as Aiden and I walked into the gaming parlor at Maverick Molly's a couple of weeks later.

Somehow it was the beginning of December, and now there was a small artificial Christmas tree in the corner by the piano, decorated with strings of popcorn and dried orange slices, as well as a handful of pretty ornaments — and lit with soft white fairy lights. There were more fairy lights strung in random places, giving the cozy room a festive vibe.

"Hello, Robin," I said, admiring him in his Victorian finery. "You look lovely."

"Don't I always?" he asked.

"Absolutely," Aiden said, taking a seat at an empty table and gesturing for me to join him.

"Lucy talks about you constantly," I told Robin. "I think she has a crush on you."

Robin grinned. "Her and half the men in this city. Please. That's not news. I hope she knows it's pointless."

"Because you're gay or because she's twelve?" I asked.

Robin grinned. "Let me tell you what *I* was doing when I was twelve…"

I covered my ears. "Nope. Nope. I don't want to know."

He rolled his eyes. "Oh, nothing like that…only lusting after all the guys on the football team. I didn't get any action until I was *fourteen*."

"Oh my God," I said.

"*Fourteen*?" Aiden said.

"What? I was old enough to know better but young enough not to care." He waved his hand in the air. "It wasn't anything major. Just a couple of blowies behind the bleachers. Those football players weren't as straight as they pretended."

"They never are," Aiden said, laughing.

We had some time to spare before our booking in the Bordello. Maverick Molly's was one of a kind, and we enjoyed the ambience of the gaming parlor. The seductively clad molly boys and occasional ribald performances primed our appetites for later.

I'd noticed a glint in Aiden's eye ever since we'd gotten in the car to come to Molly's for a much-needed visit to the Bordello. He was planning something, but he hadn't told me what. I wondered if it would be more pony play, or a simple—it was *never* simple—session on the St. Andrew's cross or the spanking bench. We'd talked about formal kinds of medical play but for now stuck with practical applications at his place.

Now that things in my life had stabilized, I wasn't feeling so stressed, and I didn't need the distraction of a session in the same way as I had before—but boy did I want it.

I had arranged with Annie and Brian to let them have Lucy for two weekends a month instead of one, and for an extra couple of weeks in the summer. I expected another kitten to appear at some point, but I think Annie was still dealing with the trauma of Lilly's death and the resurgence of her grief over the death of their son.

In fact, Lucy was there this weekend, so I had the freedom to enjoy Aiden's company without the worry of any interruptions.

Annie had written a very nice note in which she had apologized to Robin for her behavior the night they'd found him looking after Lucy, and she'd even wrapped up a pretty blue and pink scarf that she thought he might like. He'd looked skeptical when I'd passed him the parcel and the note, but after reading it, he blinked rapidly then ripped open the present, exclaiming at Annie's generosity and immediately wrapping the gauzy scarf around his slim neck.

"Tell her she's forgiven," he said, flouncing off to show the other molly boys his gift and letting the note flutter to the floor. I picked it up and put it in my pocket, giving Aiden a wry look.

"At least we know how to get on his good side if we ever screw up," I said.

"Come on," Aiden said. "Let's get the key."

As we approached the bar, Sebastian smiled.

"Good evening, Fletcher," he said in a rather smug way, and I looked at Aiden, who also had a secret smile on his face.

"Oh no. Something's going on," I said, gazing back and forth between the two of them.

"Oh no," Sebastian said, leaning forward on his elbows, seemingly innocent. *Too innocent.* "Nothing's going on."

"Nothing at all," Aiden echoed.

They looked at me like they had a secret, but they weren't going to tell me anything.

"Uh-huh. Gaslighting at its finest," I muttered. "Whatever. It had better be good."

"What had?" Aiden asked blithely.

"Whatever you two are plotting. If it's not something spectacularly depraved, I'm going to be sorely disappointed."

Sebastian smiled wider and he straightened. "Well then. I don't think we have anything to worry about. Do you?" he asked Aiden.

Aiden only shook his head slowly back and forth and held out his hand. Sebastian gave him the key.

* * * *

"Why is there a…plastic sheet under the spanking bench?" I asked. "And what the fuck is that?"

"It's a pig mask," Aiden said, lifting the pink rubber hood off the bench and showing it to me from all angles. "I had Sebastian prepare a few things for us."

"You're not gonna murder me, are you? I've seen *American Psycho.*"

"I'm not going to murder you, Fletcher. Don't forget, there are security cameras."

"Oh, shit." I had forgotten. Jesus, what if they looked at them all the time? What if they'd lied about only looking if there was a problem?

"Fletcher."

I stared at the pig mask. "I said I liked *pet* play. I meant I liked being your pony and maybe I'd enjoy being a puppy or a kitten. I didn't mean...*that*!"

"Fletcher. I think you're forgetting how you're supposed to act in this room."

I looked at the pig mask and the plastic sheet and tried to reconcile it. My brain was screaming *no,* but every other part of me was shouting *yes.*

"No, Sir," I said, swallowing thickly.

"You can always safeword."

"Yes, Sir."

I flashed back to an earlier conversation:

"Humiliation and objectification. Those are big with you," Aiden said.

We were sitting at the kitchen table in his apartment, and he was writing stuff down in a little blue notebook.

"Yeah. I don't know why. And I...I'm not sure how much humiliation I can take. Or how much would still be...you know...arousing."

"Hmm. Might be fun to find out." He scribbled something down.

"Well, I did like the pony play...a lot."

"Yeah, there's humiliation in that, for sure. And objectification, too."

"Oh yeah."

He gazed at me, contemplating. "Also caretaking."

"Yeah."

"Would you be interested in exploring all that a bit more?" he asked, with seemingly benign curiosity. It was anything but.

"Sure."

Now I wasn't so sure. What had I gotten myself into?

"Take off your clothes. You don't have to fold them. Just toss them beside the bed."

Normally he had me fold them neatly, so that was the first strange thing. But I did what I was told, feeling that sense of freedom that came with submission. Even though I was unsure, I was still happy to give control to Aiden.

I stood there, trying not to let the nerves take over and watched Aiden pick up the rubber pig hood. It looked soft and flexible, and I wondered how it would feel going over my head. It was a half-mask, with piggy ears and a snub nose with breathing holes, as well as eye holes for me to see through. The mask was kind of cute in one way, terrifying in another.

He held it out to me.

"Put it on, little piggy," he said, and warmth suffused my whole body—a mix of shame, embarrassment and sudden, massive arousal that took me by surprise. My hands shook as I pulled it over my head. The rubber smelled plasticky but not terribly unpleasant. The inside of the half-mask was soft and smooth against my skin.

I waited for Aiden to tell me how wonderful I looked in my piggy hood, but he wasn't even looking at me. Instead, he was throwing things onto the bed:

Pink leather cuffs. A black spreader bar. A black butt plug corkscrew tail.

My beating heart filled my ears, and the heat from the blood rising all over my body made me dizzy.

"Get up here, piggy," he said, slapping the surface of the bed. "All fours. *Now.*"

Oooh, this was a new Aiden, not the soft, benevolent Dom I'd gotten used to. This was something else. And this new Aiden excited me, at the same time that my heart was in my throat, wondering what was about to happen.

Aiden slapped my ass.

I made a sound that was half gasp, half moan.

"Squeal. You're a pig, not a person."

Oh my God.

I tried to wrap my head around it. I wanted to do it, but I couldn't make my throat work.

"Hmm. Maybe you need direct motivation."

He wrapped the soft leather cuffs around my ankles and buckled me into the spreader bar. The clang of metal on metal made everything so real.

"Such a bad piggy. Can't even squeal for me," Aiden sighed.

I thought again about letting out a little piggy squeal, but I didn't think I could do it well enough and it would only sound ridiculous. I wanted to please Aiden, but this was so hard. I was filled with conflicting emotions and frustration at not being able to do what he wanted of me.

Cold lube dripped down my ass crack, and I had an inkling what was coming. The black corkscrew tail flashed into my brain, and I made a strange sound as my cock surged and jerked. But it wasn't quite a squeal.

"Piggy needs a tail, doesn't he?" Aiden murmured.

Yes, yes, he does. Piggy needs something to get him to squeal, because Fletcher is having a really hard time with that request.

The rubber of the tail-plug pressed against my hole as Aiden made clicking noises with his tongue.

"Here, piggy, piggy. Open up for your swirly, curly tail," he said, pushing the lubed plug into me.

I stuttered my breath and tried to relax as the plug spread me apart.

"Squeal, piggy!" Aiden barked as he pressed the plug relentlessly forward.

And I did it. I let out an actual, honest-to-goodness, sounds-like-a-scared-little-piggy squeal as Aiden pressed the tail-plug home.

"There you go," he said, lodging it in place as my whole body blushed with shame. "Do it again."

I made the same noise, a little louder this time, a feeling of euphoria filling me. I wasn't embarrassed. I was actually quite proud of the noise I'd made. And it felt so liberating. Aiden's satisfaction was all that mattered.

"That's my good little piggy," Aiden murmured, making my heart melt and my cock twitch as he rocked my piggy plug to seat it properly. "Such a good piggy."

He slapped my ass again, and I felt my squiggly tail wobble, which created a reverberation through my body. I squealed again, and Aiden laughed.

"Oh, such a happy, happy piggy," he crooned, and I went to heaven.

He unbuckled me from the spreader and told me to get on the floor.

Oh God. When I got off the bed, the piggy tail swayed, and the sensation added to the sense of fullness the plug gave me. My cock was like rock and made it difficult for me to move around.

I went onto my hands and knees. On an impulse, I moved forward and pressed a kiss against Aiden's foot, then snorted, just like a pig rooting for apples. It killed me a little how much I was into this, but in the moment, fully inside my piggy brain, I didn't care how silly that made me. I was allowed to be silly here, because Aiden liked it, Aiden demanded it, and fuck, it felt amazing.

"Good piggy," Aiden said, slapping my buttock with the end of the crop he was holding. "Now crawl around and find all the treats I've left for you."

Treats? I looked through my piggy hood and caught sight of a baby carrot on the wood floor. Sure enough, there were baby carrots scattered around the room, mostly in this section, but I still had to crawl to get them. When I got to the first one, I reached for it with my hand.

"Uh-uh. You don't have hands, only hooves. You're a pig, for fuck's sake. Also, I want you to pretend to snuffle for it. I want to see verifiable piggy antics here — or no reward when we're done."

He was playing hardball today. *And speaking of hard balls…*

I closed my eyes and bent my rubber snout to the floor, making snuffling noises and 'searching' for the carrot. When I 'found' it, I used my teeth to grab it then chewed it carefully as Aiden watched, idly tapping the crop against his thigh.

"Another," he said, when I'd finished eating. He pointed toward another baby carrot. "Gotta find them all."

In reality, there were only five, but time and distance were skewed, and it seemed like I crawled around for hours eating carrots like a good little piggy. My universe shrank to just this room, and this task and this person. It felt so good and right.

"Okay, piggy, that's enough," Aiden said finally, calling me over. When I got there, he told me to sit up and hold out my 'hooves'.

I reared up in a begging position and snorted. I was right in character now. He buckled the pink cuffs around my wrists, and I saw him fighting a smile. "Look at you…all pale and flushed and horny. That cock is gonna poke me in the eye if it gets any bigger."

I snorted. Aiden grinned.

"Over to the bench, piggy-wiggy," he said, and I went where he led me. The hood and tail felt like a part of me now, and I fully embraced my debasement.

Aiden fastened me onto the spanking bench, with my ass and its little curly tail in the air, my cock jutting underneath. I settled into position, wondering what was in store.

"I think this little piggy is ready for milking," Aiden said, and my vision might have blanked out. Suddenly, there was a hand on my neck, and Aiden was at my ear.

"Did you know that naughty little piggies who eat all the carrots get their cocks milked?"

Shame and embarrassment flushed me with heady heat. My cock pulsed, and bliss sparked from my stuffed innards.

I gave a little squeal of protest, but there wasn't much force behind it.

"Quiet, now," Aiden said.

He took hold of my squiggly tail and pulled gently. I felt the pressure from the plug inside me as it began to exit my body, stretching me wide as I squealed and moaned.

It squelched out of me with satisfying ease.

Aiden wrapped a cord around my cock and balls, and snapped it tight, giving my erection a slap in the meantime. I groaned as Aiden eased some kind of rubber prostate wand into my ass.

I stuttered a gasp when the hard ball at the end made contact.

"There," Aiden said. "All right. Let's get this piggy milked."

The prostate wand began a gentle vibration that sent waves of soft delight through me. I made a very un-pig-like moan as the wand began to do its work. Aiden pressed the bulbous tip against my prostate to make sure I felt the vibration, stroking my cock and aiming it at the plastic sheet.

The sensation was indescribable. The psychological effect of being treated this way, like an animal in a milking pen, merged with the intense physical sensations. I closed my eyes, whimpering and moaning, as I leaked like a broken radiator under Aiden's expert manipulations.

"That's my good piggy. Enjoy your milking. Maybe I'll let you come. We'll see. But right now I'm getting plenty of semen from this procedure."

Aiden milked my cock like it was a cow's teat, and every now and then he'd shake it so that drops of seminal fluid landed on the plastic sheet, making little splats.

Fuck, fuck, fuck.

I wanted to come, but I also didn't want this agonizing pleasure to stop. I was strung out on a wire of bliss as Aiden milked me until I didn't think I had anything left, his hand on my cock, squeezing the juice out of me in tiny, trickling batches.

This was enough. This was everything.

Aiden shook my cock to get the last drips off.

"Good job, little piggy. Look at all that jizz. I'm a fucking artist."

I craned my head and gazed at the plastic sheet, which had a Pollock design of milky splotches all over it.

I made a little squeal, and Aiden laughed. "Oh yes, my sweet little piggy. Now for your reward." His voice was rough with desire and harsh with need.

Metal clanged softly, and I heard a zip as Aiden moved behind me. He eased the prostate wand out and settled the head of his lubed dick at my hole.

I wiggled with anticipation and desperate desire. My cock had softened from the milking, but as Aiden sank his into me, pleasure bloomed from inside.

I snorted, and Aiden cursed.

"I'm going to give you something to hold on to, my dirty little piggy," he grunted, and I knew what was happening here. He wasn't going to let me come, at least not yet.

"Such a lucky little piggy, to get what I'm going to give you..." he panted out, fucking me with pragmatic and steady motions, with only one aim, to get himself off so he could dump a quart of semen inside me — *my reward*.

The sense of objectification and debasement quadrupled, and I squealed my appreciation.

Use me and abuse me! Dump your spunk in me and let me wallow in my shame and accept my lowly place. I ask for nothing but scraps of irrelevant pleasure from the process.

I squealed and snorted as he thrust into me, acting like I hated every minute, when the opposite was true. I doubled down on what he'd asked of me, figuring he'd enjoy it.

"Squeal, little piggy, squeal. I'll give you what you need."

He went faster, his breaths quick and bracketed by soft moans. Deep thrusts now — one, two, three and he stilled, snugging against me and unloading with a drawn-out groan, bending over me so far that I felt his hot breath on the skin of my back.

I squealed, quieter now, the knowledge that he'd buried his hot spunk in me making me dizzy. He sighed and finished up with slow, seductive thrusts of his still-hard cock, to demonstrate how pleased he was.

"Oh yeah. Such a good little piggy. Such a dirty little piggy." He was tired after all that.

I whimpered, desperate for more.

"Mmm. Now I'm going to keep you dirty," Aiden murmured, sliding out and no-doubt watching as a tiny dribble of his spunk escaped. He pushed the piggy tail into me again, as I swooned with happiness.

"Now I've fed your greedy little piggy hole and stopped it up. How do you like that?"

I listened as he cleaned himself and zipped up, then came around and very methodically and impersonally, jerked my cock until I exploded all over the floor in an ecstasy of sublime objectification.

Chapter Twenty-One

Not a Proposal

Afterward, as he unbound me and cleaned me up, removing the tail and having me sit on a towel for a few minutes so I wouldn't soil my underwear, I couldn't meet his gaze. Now that we were out of the scene and I was becoming *Fletcher the single parent* again, I couldn't quite believe where Aiden had taken me and how much I'd fucking loved it.

He seemed to understand and didn't press me to engage. But when he'd finished tidying up, he came over and tipped my chin with a finger to force me to look at him.

"Hey. Are you okay?"

"More than," I said, offering him a smile.

"You loved that."

I frowned. "What the fuck is wrong with me? What have you done to me?"

"Nothing is wrong with you. You're fucking perfect. And I haven't done anything but helped you access some of your most forbidden fantasies. But...I know that can be a bit of a mind-fuck."

"Yeah," I said.

"But, Fletcher."

"Yeah?"

"You are the most perfect, sweetest, dirtiest, little piggy that I could ever hope for, and I love that you let me see it. Thank you."

"You're...welcome?" *What a strange conversation.*

"I'm going to help you get dressed, then I'm going to take you back to your place and shower you with luxury and pampering, all right?"

"That sounds perfect."

But first, we had to face the public.

"Oh, holy shit," Robin said as we walked into the gaming parlor to return the key to Jacob.

For a panicked second, I thought I'd forgotten to take the mask off. I put my hand to my face and felt my own skin. *Phew.*

"You look blissed out," Robin said. He glanced at Aiden, who simply smiled.

Robin grinned and shook his head.

"Wow. You've dommed him so good he can't even talk. Well done."

He offered his fist to Aiden, who gave him a bump.

"Leave him alone, Robin. He's tired," Aiden said.

"I bet he's fucking tired. My mind is spinning, wondering what could possibly reduce this fine specimen to such a useless state."

Aiden laughed. "Come on, Fletcher."

It wasn't until I'd soaked in the tub for half an hour and was lying in bed with Aiden that I was able to vocalize my reaction to what had been a mind-blowing couple of hours.

"I never knew I had such base desires," I said. "But...holy fuck, that was hot."

"Fletcher, that was more than hot, at least for me. Taking you to that place...letting you explore your submission in such a raw, profane way? That was more than I'd ever hoped for."

"I'm glad you had fun," I said, giving him a little smirk.

"I definitely did. You were so fucking hot, my sexy little piggy."

"I still want to be Treasure, though...sometimes."

"I know. I'm hoping we can uncover many more sides to your animal nature in the future."

I kissed him, with the security of a man who knew he was seen and valued and cared for, in the most intimate of ways.

* * * *

We finally had Annie and Brian over for the lasagna that they'd missed.

Aiden helped me again, and this time, I was able to enjoy the reminiscences while we worked, knowing that Daniel would be happy that his parents were coming over and that everything between us was okay again.

This time, Lucy was here, and she set the table and played with the dogs in the backyard so they'd be tired and not too much of a handful.

When Brian and Annie showed up, Annie passed me a pie that she'd made and promised to bring for dessert.

"It's peach. Your favorite."

"Thank you! That's amazing." I leaned in and gave her a kiss on her cheek, and she cupped my chin, gazing into my eyes with real affection. We enjoyed a moment, then Annie cleared her throat and bent to her boots.

I took the pie to the kitchen, blinking back emotion. I wasn't going to cry.

"What's that?" Lucy asked.

"Peach pie," I said.

"Ew. *Peach* pie?"

"I bought brownies," I said. "Go say hello to your grandparents."

"Oh, *phew*," she said, heading into the living room.

Aiden came over to give me a kiss. "I happen to love peach pie.'"

"*Oh my God*!" Lucy screamed from the other room.

Aiden gave me a curious look. I shrugged.

"It's fine. They already cleared it with me."

"Cleared what?" Aiden asked as Lucy came running into the kitchen holding a gray tabby kitten to her chest. The dogs had followed and were sniffing the poor cat, who was looking rather unnerved and confused.

"They got me another *kitten*!" Lucy said, her eyes glistening.

"Wow," Aiden murmured, glancing doubtfully my way.

"It's okay. It's staying here."

"It's living *here*?" Lucy shouted. The dogs started barking.

"Yes, but you have to clean the litter box. I'm not touching that," I said, pointing the knife I was using to spread garlic butter at her.

"I will. I will! Oh my God, thank you Granny and Grandpa!" Lucy yelled, holding the kitten up. "Isn't he gorgeous? I'm going to name him Mando! Or should I call you Grogu?" she said, turning the cat so she could see its face.

"I like Mando," Aidan said, grinning now, as Annie came into the kitchen.

"Hello, Aiden," Annie said.

"Annie," Aiden said with a smile. "How are you?"

She shrugged, returning Aiden's friendly smile. "I can't complain."

"That's not true." Brian's voice sounded from the other room. "You complain all the time."

I smiled, and Aiden laughed.

"So, a new kitten, huh?" Aiden said.

"This one's a bit older," Annie said. "And Fletcher is a fantastic dad and dog owner. I'm sure little...Mando?...will fit right in."

The kitten tried to squiggle free, but Lucy held on to him.

"You'd better put him in the spare room and shut the door. There's already a litter box and water bowl up there," I said. "We can introduce him to the dogs properly tomorrow, after he's had a chance to smell them.

"Okay!" Lucy said, disappearing with the dogs. Annie followed her out, as Brian could be heard greeting the dogs in the other room.

"It's gonna be hard getting Lucy down here for supper," Aiden said.

"Yeah. But worth it."

"And worth all the hassle of cat ownership?"

"Please," I said. "Compared to dogs, cats are easy."

Aiden grinned. "Tell me that again in a couple of months."

"Huh?"

"Never mind. I suppose now is not the best time to tell you I'm allergic?"

My face fell, and I slapped a hand over my mouth.

"No, you're not!" I mumbled, internally freaking out. "Really?"

Aiden held his sober expression for another two seconds, then broke, grinning with glee at having rattled me.

"You bastard."

"What does it matter? I don't *live* here."

We held each other's gazes for a long moment.

"Aiden, do you want to live here?" I asked, before I'd thought too much about it. Before I got too scared to ask him, when it was something I really wanted to know.

He stared at me for a long time, then gave me a soft smile.

"You're asking me if I want to move in with you, your two dogs, your argumentative twelve-year-old and a new kitten?"

"Yes," I said. "I want to sleep with you every night."

"Well, when you put it that way, of course I will. But what do we do with my apartment?"

"Better keep it. You might want to escape after you find out what it's like living here."

"Not a chance."

Dinner went well.

After her grandparents had left, I took Lucy aside and asked her if it was okay for Aiden to move in. I should have asked her before I'd asked Aiden, but it had been a spontaneous invitation.

Lucy was over the moon with excitement about it.

"Yes! That's awesome, Dad."

"Are you sure? You don't think it's too soon?"

She gave me a strange look. "Dad, come on. Does he know he has to help with the animals?"

"I'm sure he does, and I'm sure he will."

"Honestly, am I the best matchmaker or what? I knew you two were perfect for each other. Cool how that worked out, huh?"

"Very cool."

"I know you miss Papa. But I think he'd be glad about Aiden."

I grinned and pulled her in close. "What would I do without you?"

"Probably be way less cool, honestly."

I looked forward to being a family of three again. It wouldn't be the same, but it would be just as wonderful.

* * * *

Aiden and Lucy were planning something.

Christmas was two weeks away, and Aiden had officially moved in the week before. Now he and Lucy kept whispering and giving me smug looks.

"What the fuck is happening?" I asked.

"Nothing," Lucy said.

"Not a thing," Aiden said.

They looked at each other with barely contained excitement.

"Come on. I didn't realize the two of you were going to gang up on me. I don't think it's very nice to keep secrets."

"Oh, relax, Dad. All will become clear. Just you wait."

"For what, though? What am I waiting *for*?"

"Patience, Fletcher. Patience," Aiden soothed.

He must have known by then that patience wasn't one of my strong suits.

When I dropped Lucy off at Annie and Brian's the weekend before Christmas, she waved bye with a very smug look on her face.

In the car, I said to Aiden, "You'd better not be planning anything in the Bordello, because if that's what Lucy's been helping you with, I think it would be a teensy bit inapprops, you know?"

"It's nothing like that. I'm not in this just for the sex, you know."

We drove along the canal, enjoying the view of the city all lit up in the darkness. Colored lights were strung in places and became more plentiful as we reached the downtown area. I was so mesmerized by the pretty lights that I didn't realize Aiden was steering into the Chateau Laurier driveway until he stopped the car in front of the massive doors.

"Come on," Aiden said, putting the car in park and getting out.

"I — What?" I said, but I got out of the passenger seat as Aiden passed his keys to the valet.

"Very good, Sir."

Aiden grinned at me as he opened the trunk, revealing two suitcases and two garment bags with hangers.

"Ta-da!" he said, a jovial smile on his handsome face.

"Are we staying here?" I asked.

"Yes."

"For the night?"

"For two nights."

"Holy shit," I said, blinking with astonishment, staring around me at the lights bouncing off the stone of the historic hotel.

"And one very fancy dinner that we have a reservation for." He glanced at his watch. "So we'd better get to our room."

"Aiden, this is... This is perfect," I said, following him inside.

A massive Christmas tree, decorated with giant ornaments, rose past the second story balcony and shone its festive cheer over the lobby.

Once we'd gotten our room keys, the attendant ushered us away and said someone would bring our bags up.

"I could get used to this," I said, glancing at Aiden as we waited for the elevator.

"I want you to. I like to treat you well. You know you deserve it, right?"

"Why does everyone keep telling me that?"

Aiden contemplated me for a long moment. "Maybe because it's good to see you happy, Fletcher. And they want you to be happy."

I reached for Aiden's hand.

The room on the fourth floor was spacious and clean and had a view of the parliament buildings — but only one window.

"Huh. I thought the windows would be bigger," I said, gazing out at the seat of the Canadian government.

"I can have us moved to a room with a better view..." Aiden said, looking uncomfortable.

Fuck, I was ruining his surprise.

"No, no, it's lovely. It's an old hotel. It's got some quirks, but I like that."

"Okay. Good. We need to get changed."

Suddenly, my eyes went wide. "You're not going to *propose* are you? Oh my God, are you going to *propose*?" I stared at Aiden in horror.

Aiden looked so fucking frustrated with me it was kind of hilarious. But then he smiled blithely.

"Yes, Fletcher. You found me out. That's all I wanted to do, so I brought you up to the fourth floor, and in a moment, the entire staff is going to come in with champagne and chocolate and bugles, celebrating our engagement."

"You're being sarcastic," I said, then wondered if he was. "Are you being sarcastic?"

Part of me danced at the thought of a proposal, but the bigger part was terrified of making that kind of commitment.

There was a knock on the door, and my eyes went wide. Aiden answered it to let the valet in with our luggage.

"Thank you so much," Aiden said, giving the young woman a tip before closing the door.

"Would you calm down and just get dressed?"

When we were ready, I followed Aiden down to Wilfrid's. We were immediately taken to a secluded table for two that had been decorated with candles and had a bottle of champagne in the center.

I looked at Aiden, who only smiled.

"Aiden," I said.

"There's a note on the bottle."

"Do *not* propose to me, Aiden," I said, my voice trembling.

Aiden pulled out his chair and sat down, steepling his hands under his chin and waiting.

"Aiden, please don't propose to me," I said in a whisper, feeling hot then cold, then hot again.

"Read the fucking note, Fletcher." Now he was annoyed.

I reached for the card attached to the bottle.

"Sit down and read it," Aiden said. His Dom voice did its work.

I sat down and read the note.

Dear Fletcher,

You are the best thing that's ever come into my life. I want you to know that. I want you to understand how much I love you, how much I enjoy doing the things we do together. And that means all the boring, regular things, like walking the dogs, watching TV with Lucy and cleaning the kitchen. But it also means the other things, the intimate things, the kinky things – things that have brought us closer and given us both what we needed and wanted.

I'm not going to ask for a commitment right now, but I want you to think about the fact that marriage is something I want to talk about. Maybe after Christmas, or in the spring, when things are a little more settled, and we've proven to each other that we're in it for the long haul.

I love you so much, Fletcher Marin, and I only the see the best for our future.

Yours,
Aiden

I blinked back tears as I came to the end of it. I nodded my head, unable to speak.

"Is that a yes?" Aiden asked, his grin a mile wide and his eyes sparkling.

"Yes. Yes, yes, yes."

* * * *

Later, up in the room, after a lovely meal and a rich dessert, we lounged in our PJs on the King bed. I was replying to a text from Lucy.

Yes, I was very surprised! You two are amazing. Thank you for helping Aiden plan this.

Is your hotel room swanky?

Very. I feel so pampered.

Yay! See you Sunday.

See you Sunday.

I put my phone down on the bedside table.

"Did you pack my toothbrush?" I asked, getting up and walking over to where we'd put the suitcases. They sat open on the luggage bench. I saw something pink poking out from under a couple of pairs of Aiden's boxer briefs in his suitcase.

I looked closer.

"Aiden."

"Yeah?"

I reached into his suitcase and pulled out the pink piggy mask that I'd worn in the Bordello, holding it out on the end of one finger.

"Why do you have this pig mask in your suitcase?"

"Oh!" he said, getting off the bed and walking over to me. He wrapped his arms around me and peered at the hood over my shoulder.

"Well, I was hoping you'd be my dirty little piggy for a bit."

"Um. We're in the fanciest hotel in Ottawa, and you want me to play piggy?" Honestly, my cock was already hard thinking about it.

Aiden grinned and kissed my shoulder. He slid his hand under mine—the one that wasn't holding the mask—and took my thumb between his fingers.

"This little piggy went to market," he murmured, pressing his cloth-covered hard-on against me. "This little piggy stayed home," he said, taking my pointer finger.

My breathing got quicker, and I started to smile.

He took my middle finger, rubbing it with his fingertips in a very sexy way.

"This little piggy ate roast beef."

He licked a trail from my jaw to my earlobe and bit it as I gasped. He took the next finger between his.

"And this little piggy had none."

I sighed and tilted my head back — *his*, always.

"And *this* little piggy," he whispered, taking my smallest finger and leading my hand down to cover my swelling cock in my pajama pants. "Went *wee, wee, wee*...all the way *home*."

He stroked me with aggressive motions until I turned and launched myself at him, kissing him with everything I had as he laughed against my mouth.

Want to see more from this author? Here's a taster for you to enjoy!

Parlor Games: The Laughing Game
AE Lister

Excerpt

The sex had settled my nerves and excess horniness. Vihaal and Gideon were interesting and amusing men. And it was entirely possible that since I'd been so pent up, my horniness had leaked out and now I was fixated on them. But now I had good memories of Rebecca and making her come on my fingers and my cock. I was feeling pretty good when I climbed the steps to Maverick Molly's for my meeting with Jacob and Sebastian.

"Oh, please, keep the cold out!" someone shouted as I stepped inside. I recognized the voice of Robin Webb, Maverick Molly's most flamboyant server-slash-performer.

"Sorry," I said, shutting the door and stomping my boots.

"Jacob!" Robin yelled down the hall. "Mr. Barnett is here!"

He turned back and looked me up and down. I might have imagined the saucy lilt to his expression, except that Robin flirted with anyone and everyone who stepped through these doors. I didn't think it mattered that everyone supposed I was straight.

"Mr. Barnett," Robin said.

"Mr. Webb," I said, grinning at the curvy man in vintage underclothes that contrasted beautifully with his dark skin. The 'molly boys' at the club wore white cotton bloomers, corsets in a variety of shades over cotton chemises, black stockings and little leather booties from another time.

"Oh, now, you don't have to be so formal. I'm not supposed to use your first name, but you can use mine, you know," he said with a wink.

"How are you, Robin?" I said, moving past him to the full coat rack.

"Oh, I'm just dandy, Mr. Barnett. How are you?"

I shrugged and luckily found an empty hangar. "Pretty good. I like that shade of eyeshadow. Is there glitter in it?"

Robin batted his lashes. "Of course! And thank you so much, Ange—" He put a hand to his lips. "Mr. Barnett."

"Do Sebastian and Jacob *really* make you use men's last names? Is that a hard rule?"

"Oh, Mr. Barnett. It's a very *hard* rule." Robin winked again, then rolled his eyes and touched his velvet choker. "They say it helps with the historical ambience. People were so bleeding polite back then, you know? Except when they were stabbing you in back alleys." He scrunched up his face in thought. "Or maybe even then. Who knows?" He shook his head, the lamplight bouncing off his tight brown curls. "Anyway, I just like your name so much. And I wonder if…"

"What?"

"Well, I just wonder if—"

Jacob Moriarty strode up the hall toward us. "Robin, would you leave poor Mr. Barnett alone? He doesn't need any of your tomfoolery."

Robin gave Jacob an amused look. "Tomfoolery? Really? You know we're not actually living in the Victorian age, right?"

Jacob pointed to the gaming parlour to his right.

"Aren't you supposed to be in there?"

"Yes, but—"

"Uh uh. I'll have none of your nonsense tonight, Robin Webb. Get your cheeky British arse in there and serve customers," Jacob said. His skin was darker than Robin's, and he loomed over the younger man who was a little shorter than I was, although he had the attitude of someone taller.

Robin put a hand to his chest. "Well!" He stepped forward and gave Jacob a quick kiss on the cheek. "I honestly love it when you're strict with me."

Jacob narrowed his eyes but his face softened. "Robin. That's inappropriate. You're my employee."

"Mr. Barnett can vouch that it was my idea. How can I resist? You're so strong and..." He looked Jacob Moriarty up and down. "Fit." He turned back to me while Jacob watched with benign tolerance.

"Lovely to see you, Mr. Barnett. Be sure to pop in for a drink when you're done with these killjoys." He threw me a stunning smile and strolled back into the parlor with a sway of his saucy backside.

I couldn't help uttering a laugh.

Jacob rolled his eyes, but he grinned.

"Angel. Glad you're here." He shook my hand and ushered me down the hall to the office in the back. "Sebastian's manning the bar, but he helped me get everything together for the taxes."

"Super," I said, following Jacob's imposing form as he led me to the office.

"Brandy?"

"Hell, yeah."

Jacob and Sebastian had commissioned a spacious room beside the kitchen as an office. They'd decorated it with dark paint and antique pieces of furniture, including three wood armchairs with padded leather seats. There was even a Victrola in the corner, but I'd never asked if it worked.

"Have a seat," Jacob said.

I did, placing my briefcase on the floor, while Jacob went to the rolling bar cart and poured brandy from a decanter into two cut tumblers. He placed one before me then went to sit in the large rolling leather chair opposite, on the other side of the desk.

He held up his glass. "These are real crystal. The ones we use in the gaming parlour are glass."

"Very fancy," I said, lifting mine and examining the way the colors of the liquid danced in the light.

"Long time no see! What have you been up to?"

I took a sip of the brandy, and swallowed. "Oh, that's nice." I shrugged. "Nothing that exciting. Work. The gym sometimes. Same old, same old."

"Any, uh, hope on the romantic side?" he asked, gazing at me in a peculiarly intense way.

"Uh...no. Not really. Why?"

Jacob shrugged. "I hate to see you alone. Surely there's someone out there who can intrigue the great Angel Barnett."

"I haven't met any intriguing women lately. But I did hook up with someone nice last night, as a matter of fact. I met her at the bar near my place. Rebecca."

"Hmm. And she was...nice?"

"Yeah. Nothing special," I said. "God, why do I sound like a dick when I say that? It was okay. The sex, I mean. And why am I telling you this? Jesus."

"Because I'm your friend. You don't sound like a dick, Angel," he said. "But you do sound a bit confused. And definitely lacklustre." He rubbed the side of his glass. "You know there have been rumors…"

I sat forward and put down my glass. "What rumours?"

He held up his hand. "Sorry, not rumours, exactly. Speculation."

"About…about me?"

"Maybe."

I blinked. "Why would there be rumors about me?"

Jacob looked at me like I was the only one not in on an obvious joke.

"Angel. Darling. You're talking about a club filled with kinky gay men."

"Okay…"

"You also profess to be straight."

"So?" I said. "Wait a second, *profess* to be…?"

Sure, maybe I was questioning my sexual orientation in private, but I hadn't realized it was publicly up for debate.

"Sorry, sorry. I shouldn't undermine your sexual orientation. If you say you're straight, you're straight."

I looked at him. He looked at me.

"I don't think I ever *said* I was straight."

"Uh…I'm pretty sure you did. But what does that mean? You might *not* be straight?" He grinned and leaned forward. "Angel Barnett, are you questioning your sexuality?"

I hesitated. "I don't know. Maybe?"

"This is turning into a very interesting conversation."

"Well, I know I'm not gay. I had sex with a woman last night. I've never had sex with a guy."

"Mmm. The question is, have you thought about it? Which of course, doesn't mean you're bisexual. But it might."

I narrowed my eyes. "Is this a come-on? Because unless Sebastian knows about it—"

The man in question appeared, carrying a sheaf of papers.

"I heard my name. What do I not know?"

"It's not a come-on." Jacob groaned, leaning back in his chair. "I'm only curious if you've ever thought about other men in that way."

"That's kind of personal, Jacob."

"Yeah, that is really personal, Jacob." Sebastian remarked, putting the pile of papers down on the desk and sitting on the corner. "So, Angel, we all want to know."

He grabbed a handful of peanuts from a bowl on the desk and popped one in his mouth.

I rolled my eyes.

Jacob laughed. "Yes, well, telling a bunch of kinky gay men that the hot accountant who comes to the club every month or so is straight is like putting a honey-covered beehive in front of a bear's den. I've had questions."

"From who?" I asked. I wondered which of the Maverick Molly's regulars were speculating about my sexuality, and why.

"Well…let's see, now. I think the molly boys have a bet going."

I opened my mouth, then closed it again. Of all the—

Sebastian pointed at me. "They do. They totally do. Most of them think you're at least a *bit* bi." He chewed and swallowed. "Come on. You're not *completely* straight, Angel. The universe isn't that cruel."

Jacob stared at his husband. "What do you care? You can't have him anyway."

"Oh, wow, hold on now." I held up my hand.

"How do I know *you're* not trying to land him?" Sebastian shrugged. "Anyway, I'm the hot one in the relationship."

"Wait. No one's going to land me. I had sex with a woman *last night!*"

"Doesn't mean you're not bisexual."

"Okay, fine. I'll admit that I might be a *little bit* bi. I'll put that on the census form next time it comes around. Happy?"

"Yes, actually. And I know someone else who will be," Sebastian said.

Both Jacob and I said, "Who?"

Sebastian only smiled.

"Who?" I repeated.

He regarded me more seriously. "Do you really want to know?"

I thought about that for a split second.

"Yes. Yes, I do."

"Gideon Foster."

A strange white-hot flash went through me from head to toes. I pretended that that name had had no effect.

"Gideon Foster," I said. His name felt good in my mouth. *Holy shit. I'm probably at least a bit bi.*

"Yes," Sebastian said. "I believe he and Vihaal have a bet also."

My breathing picked up. I uncrossed my leg, then crossed the other one. *Be cool, be cool.*

"Look at him," Jacob said to Sebastian. "It's as if you just handed him a surprise Christmas gift."

"Or a grenade."

I laughed but it sounded totally fake, even to my ears. "Don't be ridiculous. I don't even care. Why would I care?"

"Oh fuck, you're *totally into them!*" Sebastian said. He turned to Jacob. "You owe me fifty bucks."

"Seriously?" I said, standing. I couldn't keep still. It was like a bomb had been dropped, but I couldn't tell if I wanted to run or if I wanted to let it shatter me into a million horny pieces. "*You two* have a bet?"

"So, Gideon thinks you're bi, and he thinks you're *into* him and Vihaal. At least a little teensy bit," Sebastian said with glee, holding his thumb and forefinger a few millimetres apart. "I think you're into them about this much," he said, moving them apart. Quite far apart.

"Come on," I said, my voice barely there.

Jacob leaned forward. "Angel. Are you into Vihaal and Gideon? We'd understand if you were. They're really quite something."

"Um," I murmured, squirming and trying to hide the fact that my cock was swelling at the mere thought of them, even though I hadn't been a horny mess when I'd walked into the club. At least not tonight. "Ah...maybe a little bit?"

"I knew it!" Sebastian shouted, abandoning his chair. He turned to Jacob. "I told you."

Jacob slowly smiled as he stared at me with a strange kind of satisfaction. "Won't Gideon and Vihaal be delighted."

"You can't tell them. Please, don't tell them," I muttered. "God. This is so embarrassing."

"Why is it embarrassing? It would be embarrassing if we'd found out you had a crush on Justin Trudeau or something like that." He narrowed his eyes. "*Do* you have a crush on Justin Trudeau?"

"No, I don't have a fucking crush on Justin Trudeau! I don't have a crush on anyone!"

"Well, maybe Vihaal and Gideon. A little one," Sebastian said.

I seemed to be panting. Why was I panting?

"Is it hot in here? Did you turn the heat up? I can't breathe."

"Oh my God, I think he might be having a panic attack," Jacob said. "Have some more brandy."

Oh yes, brandy. There was brandy in a glass on the table. For me.

I grabbed the glass and lifted it to my lips. My fingers were shaking. I took a sip. Then another. I put the glass down and leaned back in the chair, counting to ten and back until I'd calmed down.

Jacob and Sebastian had gone quiet. I opened my eyes and stared at the ceiling.

"What am I going to do now?"

"Here, let's talk about the paperwork," Jacob said. "I'm so sorry we upset you."

"Yes, that's a good idea," I admitted. "Can we keep the…other stuff…under wraps for now?"

"Angel, we'd never out you without your permission."

"Oh, thank God."

"But aren't you curious as to *why* Gideon and Vihaal have a bet going?"

I lifted my head and stared at Sebastian. "Should I be?"

Sebastian looked at Jacob. Jacob looked at Sebastian.

"We probably shouldn't be telling you this, but Vihaal and Gideon have a bit of a crush on you."a

"*Both* of them?" No, that couldn't be true. How could that be true? They thought I was straight...oh... Oh! "Do gay men really find straight guys *that* alluring?"

"Frankly, yes. Especially intelligent straight guys who look like they should be on the cover of Men's Health."

I snorted. "Oh, please."

"Angel. You're a hot guy."

"I'm *maybe* average. I've got a belly, you know."

Jacob laughed. "Do you think that matters to them?"

"Doesn't it?"

Sebastian rolled his eyes. "You're still thinking like a straight guy."

"Up until a few months ago, I thought I was one."

"Wait. You've been questioning your sexual orientation for *months?*" Sebastian said.

"Ever since..." I put my head in my hands. "Since I started hanging out with them."

Sebastian and Jacob gaped at each other.

"Since when have you been hanging out with them?"

"Oh, it was nothing, really. Coffee here and there. We went to lunch once. Maybe we had dinner?"

We had definitely had dinner. It had been the best time. I thought, now that I was looking back on things, that dinner had been what turned the tables. Had they been...dating me? Had that been a date?

"Hold on. They invited you to *dinner?*"

I nodded. "I. Yeah. I thought it was a business-owner-slash-client thing."

"Did it feel like a business-owner-slash-client thing?"

"Oh fuck," I whispered. "Have they been seducing me?"

"I'm sure they've been trying," Sebastian said, barely keeping a straight face. He seemed delighted.

"Sounds like they succeeded," Jacob muttered.

"But...but they're *married*. Why would they be trying to... I don't get it."

"Angel, Angel. Sweet summer child. Vihaal and Gideon are married, yes. But their marriage is far from traditional, in any sense of the word."

"Oh my god."

My brain was exploding, my belly was swirling at the thought of getting together with them for more than a coffee or a meal, and my palms were definitely sweating. I gazed at Sebastian with desperation.

"So...what do I do now? Now that I know?"

"That you've been denying a part of yourself your whole life? That you have a crush on them? That they've been *trying to get you into bed?*"

I whimpered. "Help."

About the Author

Alison Lister is a Canadian non-binary author.
They write graphic erotic romance (contemporary/historical/paranormal) as AE Lister, and sweet Young Adult LGBTQ+ romance as Alison Lister.
She/he/they

AE Lister loves to hear from readers. You can find their contact information, website details and author profile page at https://www.firstforromance.com/

PUBLISHING

Sign up for our newsletter and find out about all our
romance book releases, eBook sales and promotions,
sneak peeks and FREE romance books!